NUNEAU

Or
Viola's Tale of Derring Do

By Maria Aragon

OTHER BOOKS IN THIS SERIES,
IN THE ORDER THAT THEY OCCUR:

FERNARE ARALDO, PTS. 1 & 2
NUNEAU
A GOOD VILLAIN
THE WANDERING PRINCES
ROCKWELL AND SPURLOCK: TWO VERY ODD BIRDS
GATHLON
CAERMON
MARLORAT

A RELENTLESS ENDEAVOR COURTESY OF LULU.COM

COPYRIGHT 2008 - MARIA ARAGON
REVISED EDITION 2013

ISBN – 978-0-9789507-8-1 (paperback edition only)

1.

Once upon a time... there was a place that was lost to legend, a wondrous great land where the most bewitching and terrifying beings lived. Only the boldest and most curious of everyday people on the continent to the south dared venture into this mysterious northern land. Most who went north in search of adventure or Faerie gold never returned. Indeed, enough people had disappeared over the centuries that it discouraged any sort of organized intrusion.

Long before the written word, these mysterious beings had thrived in the east beyond a great ocean. Then wave upon wave of peoples, mundane mortals, migrated into their territories. They grew in such numbers and were so particular in their own ways that the enchanted ones could no longer live alongside them. Nation by nation, they fled across the ocean to that great virgin land not only to preserve their cultures, but their very existences.

The last of the remarkable ones to sail west were the Wolf Trolls, who in former days of might and glory, once ruled over the entire eastern north. Toward the end, their domain dwindled down to only one mountainous northern realm that they called Bortialande, but which new, determined human immigrants called Bortlande. The new, mortal Bortlanders and their fierce female allies - Fernarian mercenaries - drove the Wolf Trolls from their kingdom, forcing them to migrate to their colonies in the northernmost wilderness tracts of the west. In their new homelands, they flourished. Meanwhile over the generations, their persecutors eventually forgot that the ancient peoples they had driven off were real once and consigned them to myths and to magical tall tales.

Only one of the immigrant peoples failed to survive. The Elven peoples, a graceful, powerful people vanished completely from their burgeoning new kingdom hidden somewhere on the Southern Continent: the Land of Many Kingdoms. Only an infant boy survived. Sorcerer Macy's dragon Andreev Eliathan found the child and brought him back to Shadow Mountain. A beautiful witch named Elspeth the Brave adopted him and named him Sullivan Trooper. When he grew to manhood, he went to live among the independent Faerie peoples who belonged to the Islands Federation east and southeast of the mainland Faerie kingdom of Nuneau. Sullivan Trooper became famous throughout the land, for his mysterious heritage, for his friendship with the princely Heir to the Federations leadership, and for their daring adventures together.

On the western border of the Nuneau Faerielands, there existed a rather small, odd, but revered little province situated on and around the Shadow

Mountain range. This was where the charming Elspeth the Brave lived in a community of fellow scholars and magical adepts, special people culled as children from tribes and nations the world over. There on the central peak called Shadow Mount, they learned how to use their natural born talents and attained a level of enlightenment that would have been nearly impossible anywhere else. On a clear day, any Faerie farmer tending his crops on the meadowlands below the foothills could see the numerous isolated cottages, villas, and little castles where these adepts lived. They could see also the noble, multi-hued dragons that flew and frolicked in the skies above their masters' homes, that is, when they weren't sunning themselves on the rocks or rooftops.

Only one road led up to the central mountain. It wound around through a series of castle gates to the main gate on the west side. Across the central mountain's high stone cliffs the wizards had built an enormous complex that burrowed deep inside the mountain. There the road ended. Its tall, impassable turquoise and golden gate seldom opened and then only on special occasions. Few outsiders were permitted in, and generally those they did let in came to study with the masters within. When they graduated, if they so chose, they left through those same gates, rarely ever to return.

On a peak overlooking a lush green valley descending on both sides of Shadow Mountain sat a modest little castle with an elegant, vine-laced tower. Grape vines and terraced gardens surrounded this castle and often the Faerie farmers could see, if they squinted, the little old sorcerer who tended these crops. He was the oldest of the wizards and renowned everywhere for his gentle, wise, and kindly nature. He was Sorcerer Saire the Ancient.

Sorcerer Saire lived almost completely alone. He had no servants to tend to his needs, but over the countless years he had enjoyed the companionship of various advanced apprentices, called Nobles, sent to him for their education. They helped him about the castle and on the terraces, and he taught them history and how to appreciate it.

His only truly constant companion was a winged dragon - his pet Lindo, who was all velvety light gray and ivory with curving horns like a steer. Saire had endowed Lindo with the ability to change his size at whim. Normally, Lindo was a great as an elephant or a woolly mammoth, but whenever it suited Lindo, he could shrink himself down to the size of a greyhound or a great dane. When the cold weather came, Lindo liked to trot indoors to nap in one of the comfortable chairs in Saire's study.

For the past twenty years though, Saire had enjoyed also the companionship of his ward Viola Marpessa. Master Sorcerer Macy brought her to him when she was an infant and laid her in her swaddling clothes in his arms and bade him raise her well.

"She has much potential for her people," he said, "so we must take great pains."

Although Viola Marpessa was a Faerie, Saire treated her like his own daughter, for that she became. As soon as she could walk, Lindo played with her and taught her how to throw his ball in the air so he could catch it. When Lindo was not insisting on a game of catch, Saire was teaching her everything he knew and afterwards she would go out into the gardens to help him.

As she grew older, Saire caught her many times gazing off to the east over

Nuneau's fertile plain.

"What is that place?" she would ask.

"Nuneau."

"What is Nuneau?"

"That is where the Faerie folk live."

"People like me?"

"People like you."

"Then why don't I live there too?"

"Because once in awhile, a child is born who is different from other children. Those children we seek out and bring here to grow up. Someday, when you are full grown, you will go out there, but for now you must stay here and study and be my little helper." Saire smiled at her as he handed her an empty basket and pointed at the nearest grape vine.

Viola accepted the basket and gave the diminished Lindo a pat on his sleek head as she turned to the vine. They had a good crop that year. There would be plenty for the wine and for Saire's coveted jam.

As she grew up, she came under the intense tutelage of various other associates of Saire's. She had grown up healthy and strong and her tutors had seen to it that they had prepared her mind for the inexplicable world beyond their quiet community, or at least had done the best that was possible. She had full possession of her natural Faerie blood abilities. She could fly when necessity required it, but otherwise she was discouraged from summoning her wings into being. Saire had not wanted her to lose appreciation for real solid earth. She was in full mastery of her more unique talents, but again was told only to use them when the situation merited it. For her own protection, she was discouraged from speaking of her abilities in the outside world should she ever venture out into it.

When she was in her teens and inclined to rebel, Master Sorcerer Macy had Viola come to dinner at his solemn chambers and talked with her long into the night. When he sent her home to Saire, her rebellious spirit had become a sober one and she bent herself even more devotedly to her studies. She never told anyone what Macy had said to her, what fortunes he had portended, but Saire knew Macy had had Sorcerer Walton the Watcher come to dinner that night as well. Whenever Walton was summoned in that manner, it generally meant he brought important advice from the spirit that inhabited the Flame of Prophecy.

She matured. She came of age and yet another two years passed before the day Saire came down from the great temple fortress cresting the mountain's summit with an expression brimming with sadness. Ever since Saire went up to the fortress, she had been sitting alone on the window seat overlooking his gate. As soon as she saw Lindo soar back into view, she abandoned her seat and hurried down to the courtyard. As she rushed through the front door, Lindo and Saire walked through the gate.

"Well, what did Master Macy have to say?" she said as cheerfully as she could.

Saire raised his face and unclasped his hands from behind his back. "Valeria the Grand is coming to see us tonight."

"That's wonderful. I so seldom get to see her," said Viola.

"She is bringing two visitors with her," said Saire.

Viola could hardly contain her excitement. "Visitors! Are they outlanders?"

"They are. We have much work to do in the kitchen." Saire smiled distantly as he put an arm about her shoulder and walked with her back inside.

For the next two hours, Saire kept her busy helping him to prepare a special feast. Bread had to be baked. Pasta made and spicy tomato sauce to go over it. Vegetables had to be picked and washed before they too were sauteed. Lindo was put in charge of a scrumptious fruit salad and getting milk and cream from the prize singing cows belonging to Witch Ingrid the Regal.

Viola was setting up the trestle table on the summer terrace, when she saw an ivory white dragon lift off from the gatekeeper's fortress at the bottom of the slope and swoop up toward them. "Valeria is coming!"

Saire hurried out onto the terrace, wiping his hands on his apron. "Do we have everything ready?"

"Everything, except for the food waiting on the table, and that we're going to do when they arrive."

"Lanterns. Prepare the lanterns. The sun will be setting behind the mountain before long and we'll want the light."

"Can I use the honeysuckle candles?" Viola said.

"Of course. Lindo, I seem to have a knot in my apron. Untie me, will you?"

Lindo bent his brow and applied his long clawed paws to the task. When Saire was hurrying to answer the gate bell, Lindo hobbled behind him trying to extricate his claws from the hopeless knot.

"Oh, here. I'll do it!" groused Saire at last. He snapped his fingers and the apron undid the knot itself and flapped back into the house to its favorite peg on the wall.

Lindo glared after it and flexed his claws a moment when the apron peeked out at him.

"Up now, Lindo," muttered Saire. "Dust yourself off. I'm about to open the gate." He drew back the bolt. "Greetings, Valeria. I'll have the gate open momentarily."

The wide gate swung back easily and there stood a handsome woman with her silver veined chestnut hair tied in a matronly knot. She tossed her smoke-colored riding cloak back over her shoulder and removed the matching riding gloves, while a mountain breeze made her tunic and gown waft and bellow gently about her. She always wore the colors of cornflowers and violets when she was at home. These colors brought out her shining blue eyes - her one token nod to vanity.

"What a lovely afternoon," Valeria said, as she and Saire bowed to each other.

Then she stepped within his courtyard and looked beyond him at Viola. The young Faerie woman leaned against the door arch and twisted her long golden hued brown hair around and around her finger. Usually, Viola would come out to greet her as Saire did, but this time she hung back and watched.

Valeria's two guests shadowed her. Viola's eyes had locked on them immediately.

Valeria turned to Saire. "You know Gualtero Bainbridge."

A tall Faerie man bowed to Saire. He wore his shoulder-length brunette hair in a courtly queue tied with a black ribbon, but instead of fine, courtly clothes, he wore plain riding clothes in shades of green and brown. Even his boots were scuffed and in dire need of a polishing.

"The Prince of the Islands Federation," said Saire. "I have heard of your engagement to Anna Marpessa. Congratulations are in order."

"Thank you, Sir," Gualtero said in an easy-going voice. He stepped aside to make room for his companion.

"Sullivan!" Saire gave the tall chap with the wild fawn brown hair a hearty slap on the shoulders.

"Hello, Saire." Sullivan laughed and tugged on his pointed ear, of which he had a matching pair. "It has been too long. I see Lindo still capers along behind you everywhere you go." The Elf leaned over and scratched Lindo about his ears, while Lindo's foot kicked helplessly. Like Gualtero, he wore traveling clothes, hard-used ones, in frayed forest tones.

"I've been keeping track of you. You've been quite the rascal since you took up sailing in the islands," said Saire. "The both of you ought to be ashamed of yourselves."

"Well," Valeria said," this one is getting married, so that leaves only one rascal. I think he'll be quieter when he can't carouse with his best friend anymore."

An ivory white dragon slipped in behind them. Lindo sprung up to his full-size immediately and accompanied the ivory dragon to the fountain.

"Mind you don't eat too many grapes," Valeria called after her dragon mount. "Lindo, don't let my Bianca stuff herself in the groves."

Lindo chirruped. Bianca walked as though she hadn't heard a word and that she needed nothing more than a guzzle of cool fountain water.

"Come along, everyone," Saire said. "Supper is ready and you haven't met Viola yet." He turned and gestured toward the doorway.

Gualtero and Sullivan turned to look at the silent young Faerie woman in the doorway. She waited for them to reach the doorway, and then she stood upright.

Saire did the honors. "Viola, this is Gualtero Bainbridge, a Prince from the Islands Federation." She bowed her head to him, even as he bowed to her. "This one you have heard of: Sullivan Trooper."

"The last known Elf," Viola said with sudden respect. "I've heard so much about you."

"I wish I knew more about you, Miss Viola," Sullivan said with a quiet smile. "I'm quite at a disadvantage otherwise."

"Come inside and have dinner," Viola said, " before it gets cold."

They had settled down to the table to enjoy the last of the fine afternoon and to wait for the fireflies to come out. The meal had begun in earnest and Saire and Viola and even Lindo came in for much praise for their skills. Saire and Valeria exchanged some small talk about the latest batch of apprentices that had been enrolled in their community. Sullivan and Gualtero were trying to guess what spices had been used in the sauce and then idly counted fireflies. Viola said nothing, but ate and listened to them.

Valeria took a long drink of her wine and set the goblet down. "I suppose we should get on with this."

Everyone fell silent. Sullivan and Gualtero looked at her and waited as attentively as Viola did. Saire shifted in his chair and tried to suppress the look of discomfort in his face.

"The reason we have come here this evening is that it is time for you to go live with your family," Valeria said to Viola.

"Family?" Viola looked at Saire and put her fork down.

"Yes, family," Saire said. "You do have a family besides me and Lindo."

Viola sat in stunned silence staring ahead beyond her plate without seeing, oblivious to the uncomfortable glances of the two strangers, or the compassionate frowns of Saire and Valeria.

"Family," she said again at last, trying to conjure something clear and concise where nothing had been before. "Why wasn't I allowed to see them?"

"Because you had to be prepared. You had to grow up," Valeria said in her no-nonsense manner.

"Prepared for what?" Viola said.

Gualtero and Sullivan exchanged puzzled looks.

"To help your sister and to be of use to your people," Valeria said.

"Sister? I have a sister?"

"Three actually." Saire eyed his ward closely.

Gualtero and Sullivan's puzzled looks gave way to suspicious frowns.

"What are you trying to tell her?" Gualtero said.

"Pull my teeth with a tweezer! Enough mystery!" Valeria smacked her palm on the table. "This is VIOLA MARPESSA, Anna's first sister."

Gualtero's jaw dropped.

"You look nothing like her," Sullivan said, but he was smiling pleasantly. "I don't?"

"No. Anna is blond with blue eyes, willowy, and supremely beautiful," Sullivan said. "Gualt here was in peril the moment she set eyes on him and lost as soon as he got better acquainted with her."

"He's right," Gualtero said at last. "You don't look like her at all. She's taller than you and fairer. You look more like your sister Carissa. She has brown hair like you, with the same shining highlights, but her eyes are blue. Now, your youngest sister Olwen has the prettiest blue eyes of them all."

"So my sisters' names are Anna, Carissa, and Olwen?" Viola sat back in her chair and fell deeply silent. After a long, squirming silence for the others, she spoke up again. "Why wasn't I told?"

"I told you why," Valeria said. "You had to concentrate on your life here and what you needed to learn."

"Did they ever ask about me?"

"Anna did. Every year on your birthday. 'Asked to visit you each time too," said Valeria.

"Your sister Anna is now Queen of Nuneau," Saire said.

"She was most persistent concerning you," Valeria said, " and now that you have attained your majority, she is insisting upon a visit."

"That's why I had to go see Macy," Saire said. "He wanted to know if you were ready to leave home and go live with your sisters. I said you were ready."

"So that must be why we are here," Gualtero said. "Anna said she had a special task for me that I had to undertake before she would marry me. She wouldn't tell either Sullivan or me what it was, but sent us to see Valeria."

"Indeed, your mission is to take Viola home to her sisters," Valeria said with a nod, "and to prepare her for her new life on the journey back."

"I see, that explains why we **had** to ride here on horseback and return in the same fashion. The time would be necessary, if we are to educate Miss Viola here about the court," Sullivan said.

"Yes," Saire said, "and you can tell her what her sisters are like and tell her things about the outer world that we could not. You see, Viola, it has all worked out marvelously well. Your sister is so determined to see you that she entrusted her best man to bring you to her."

Viola nodded. She said nothing else throughout dinner.

There was no lingering after dinner. As soon as the table had cleared itself and the dishrags and scrub brushes set to work, Saire went with Viola to pack her things for the journey.

"Take only practical things. Plain clothes that can bear the fickle weather, a hat to ward off rain and sunshine, your comb, and I suggest you keep your hair tied in a knot as much as possible while you are journeying." Saire opened her chamber door and let her go in first. "Your tramping boots will be more suitable than your garden boots. They're taller and more durable. Let's see, what else?" Saire stood in the middle of the room and scratched his chin while his eyes surveyed the room's contents, the sturdy dark furniture, the many little cherished mementoes and treasures she kept on her high shelves among her books. "Take only what is necessary, Viola. Your all purpose camp knife, for instance."

Viola selected these necessities in stony silence, while he spoke to her. She scarcely looked at him, but intentionally concentrated on what she would be tightly and neatly folding inside her brown canvas rucksack.

Saire observed not only her silence, but also her downcast gaze. "Once you are settled, send word to me, and Lindo and I will bring the rest of your things to your new home. That way you'll feel entirely at home in Nuneau."

Viola opened her mouth to speak, but closed it instead and continued packing.

Saire nodded to himself. "I know this is sudden. We withheld so much from you, but that was a decision made by both Macy and your parents."

Viola turned suddenly. "What of my parents? Who were they?"

"They were King and Queen of Nuneau, until they tired of life in this domain and spread their spirits upon the winds. First went your father. He was so very weary, you see. He was nearly 1,000 years old. Your mother found that she could not bear life without him and two years later followed him. She was 905. That was when your sister Anna Marpessa became Queen. Anna will tell you all about them when you are reunited."

Viola nodded and hung her head. "I think I'm finished."

"No, not quite," Saire said with a kind smile. He took down from a high and very special shelf a thick little book. "Your Omnipedia. This must accompany you everywhere, remember?"

He flicked the pages and the candlelight reflected off of blank pages, until Viola laid her hands upon the book. Then the pages revealed a dense, archaic print. She closed the solid little book and closed the latch upon its embossed cover.

"I almost forgot it," Viola said.

"It's understandable. You're being torn from the life you knew into a whole other one with no warning given and no decent apologies either, except for mine. I wish I could take you there myself, but this is what Macy recommended. Blame no one. Think of it as an opportunity for exploration and adventure. There! I knew your eyes would spark at that word." Saire patted her hand. "Come along then, Viola. Tonight, you'll spend at Valeria's and in the morning, you set off with Gualtero and Sullivan."

Viola tucked her Omnipedia inside her sack and fastened it shut. She gave her cozy chamber one last look and followed Saire.

2.

Valeria the Grand kicked her guests out of bed at sunrise for a hearty breakfast of fruit, omelettes, oatmeal, and muffins. Accustomed to the rigid hours kept by Saire and his comrades, Viola was already dressed when Valeria knocked on her door. She headed directly downstairs.

Meanwhile, the worthy sorceress roused the Faerie prince and the light Elf from their luxurious slumbers with the aid of a cooking skillet and a wooden spoon that gleefully sailed over their pillowed heads banging away. Her resident Invisible Hands tumbled the men from their beds and tossed their freshly cleaned clothes at them. Barely had they fastened their last buttons and tucked in their shirttails when the Invisible Hands shoved them out into the corridor with their saddlebags.

Gualtero and Sullivan exchanged bleary looks across the corridor and wobbled a little in the drafts.

"'Morning," Sullivan said.

"'Morning," Gualtero said through his yawn.

"I'd forgotten about the schedules around here." Sullivan squinted up at the rose-tinted lavender dawn peeking through the ceiling panes. " 'Must be breakfast time."

"Breakfast. Good. Yum," Gualtero muttered as he stumbled down the stairs with his boots and his saddlebags clutched to his chest.

Sullivan trailed erratically behind him.

"Sullivan?" Gualtero said.

"What, Gualt?" Sullivan said.

"I think we're lost."

"Already?"

They wandered about a little while, pausing briefly to pull on their boots. Then Sullivan remembered the particularly useful qualities belonging to the corridor chandeliers, which were shaped like hands holding dainty candelabrums. He asked them to show the way and the chandeliers did just that.

"Thank you," chirped Sullivan, as they set off for the dining hall.

"It's about time you two showed up," Valeria said from the table. Both men bowed.

"Our apologies, your Grace. We got lost," Sullivan said.

"Sit down then. Breakfast is getting cold," Valeria said.

Both men hurried to the table, wearing mere facades of dignity. When Sullivan met Viola's look, he grinned sheepishly and tucked into the food with gusto. Gualtero seemed determined to make up for their unintentional rudeness by amusing Valeria with the latest quack philosophies he had read in Nuneau.

As before, Viola kept silent, watched and listened.

Valeria saw them off through her gates with a smile, a wave, and the usual admonition, "Have a safe journey."

Viola looked back, sadly, as she walked down the steep path behind the Prince and the Elf.

Halfway down the steep slope, Viola saw a little settlement nestled in the woodlands below. "Are we walking all the way to Nuneau?" she asked, as she watched the settlers begin their daily chores in their fields.

"Heavens, no," Sullivan said. "Our horses are waiting in the village. The path to Shadow Mountain's gates is too steep for horses, and besides, they aren't allowed up there."

"Which reminds me," Gualtero said in the front, "we'll have to buy another horse for Viola. Do you suppose one of the farmers will sell one to us?"

"It's plowing season," Sullivan said. "It'll cost us dear."

Gualtero grumbled and kept going. When they neared the village, he drew out a few coins from the pouch he kept hidden beneath his tough old riding coat and counted them out discreetly. "Why don't the two of you wait here by the well, while I go see about buying a horse?" He disappeared around the side of a cottage.

"'Sounds fine to me." Sullivan made a beeline for the bench beside the sheltered well, so he could set his saddlebags down.

Viola followed him more slowly. She kept looking up the lush slopes toward Shadow Mountain and its scattered, eclectic collection of dwellings.

"Homesick?" Sullivan pulled off his boots and dumped out a few pebbles.

"Yes." Viola did not sit down though, but stood watching him pull his boots back on. "Weren't you when you left?"

"There are still times when I wake up in the morning and think I'm in my little room waiting for Elspeth to ring the breakfast bell. I miss the discussions I used to have with Elspeth and Chauncey the Romantic and Olivia the Gracious. When I was very little and sad, Olivia would rock me in her arms and sing me the songs of her homeland, while Elspeth played the lute. I still send Chauncey the latest works of poetry and prose. I see him when he comes down for the bardic festivals every summer. I keep in touch with them all, so any longing I feel for the past is certainly appeased. Now, having waxed eloquent about all that, I must say," he smiled hugely, "it's a big world out there and I'm free to go anywhere. I wouldn't give that up for anything."

"Why didn't they tell me about my family?" Viola said.

"Because once you enter that world up there, the rest of the world rather ceases to exist. It's not that they don't care about what goes on out here. They appear to the outworlders in moments of crisis to offer wisdom and help. They are also dreaded figures of retribution, so they are not to be crossed either. The ones like you and I, who come there so young, are the exceptions. Let me put it this way, we were selected for an upbringing up there, so they had to keep us focused. No distractions. No attachments to anything outside that could divide us from our better selves. It's strict, but it works. They themselves are the products of such an education. I know of so many families out here who are so proud that their children have been summoned to Shadow Mountain. They scarcely see them until they are grown, but they know that their children are being polished in a way that will benefit not just themselves, but everyone around them once they return to the world. They become teachers, artists, healers, and, in desperate times, leaders."

"So, what did they plan for you?" Viola said.

"They never said that they had a plan for me. I was the last of my kind, so it was thought best that I lived up there for my protection and my future well-being."

"Perhaps they meant for you to find out what became of your people."

"Naw, no one will ever find out the truth of that."

"Aren't you curious? I would be."

Sullivan grew very serious. "I think about it every day, but I can't spend my entire life chasing ghosts. My people are gone and there's no bringing them back, but that doesn't mean I don't keep my ear to the ground for clues. Perhaps the truth will find me on my travels." He winked and stood up. "Here comes Gualt."

Gualtero rounded the corner leading the horses - his palomino stallion, Sullivan's buckskin mare, and a third horse, a roan mare with a creamy blond mane and tail. "You were right, Sully," he said. "The barber charged me enough to dower two of his daughters. I think they saw me coming." He handed over the roan mare's reins to Viola. "I suppose it was worth it though. She's a fine horse."

Sullivan took his buckskin mare's reins and ran a fond hand over the animal's forehead as he eyed the roan. "'Beautiful animal. 'Looks like she's got good running legs."

Gualtero nodded and mounted up on his stallion. "We have a great distance to cover."

Sullivan flung his saddlebags over the back of his saddle and climbed on.

Viola lingered though, staring into the mare's eyes. "Does she have a name?"

"Arcadia, I think," Gualtero said.

"Easy, Biscuit," Sullivan said. His buckskin pivoted this way and that. "She's restless to go, I think."

"So's Navis," Gualtero said as he soothed his palomino. "Come along then. We're wasting daylight."

"Right," Viola said. She struggled into the saddle. Once she'd got her feet into the stirrups, she said, "Ready."

"You haven't ridden a horse before, have you?" Gualtero said.

"No. I'm sorry," Viola said.

"We'll go easy then, so you can get used to it," Gualtero said. "Sully, you'd better ride behind her."

"Ladies first," Sullivan said.

Viola gently urged Arcadia forward and was relieved at how mildly the mare complied. They were off.

Sullivan kept a close watch on Viola, watching how she bounced about in the saddle until he could bear it no longer. He rode up alongside her and began instructing her on how to sit in a saddle and how to manage the devilishly clever Faerie horses. He worked with her all morning.

The lessons stopped only when they stopped for luncheon in the next village surrounding the coach station.

"I'm famished," Gualtero said as he reined in Navis beside the water trough. He looked back at Sullivan and Viola. "Hungry?"

"I am," she said. The sunshine was bright and her face was a little pink. She rubbed her brow on her white shirtsleeve. She had long since tied her long coat around her waist and rolled up her shirtsleeves.

"I'd start wearing my hat, if I were you," Gualtero said. "You look a little sun burnt."

"My face is so warm," she said.

Sullivan nodded. "It'll be sore later."

Gualtero dismounted and tied Navis to the rail where it could drink water in the shade of the old trees. Sullivan fairly leapt from his saddle and did the same with Biscuit, but Viola lurched and slid toward the dusty ground with a groan and a grimace. Arcadia pricked her ears toward the water trough and walked toward it eagerly. Viola clung to the stirrups and staggered alongside. She was glad when the roan mare finally stopped moving.

Gualtero restrained himself from laughing. "Saddle sore, eh?"

"Excruciatingly obvious, eh?" Viola groaned.

"Painfully so." Gualtero came up alongside her and put her arm over his right shoulder. "Prop yourself on me and we'll go inside and get something to eat."

"Lovely," replied Viola. "Ooh. Ahh-ah!"

Sullivan sailed inside the tavern ahead of them. They heard his cheerful voice coming from within as he hailed the proprietor of the establishment. "Good sir, have you a table for three travelers?"

"Indeed, I do," replied the Faerie man within.

Gualtero and Viola arrived at the threshold of the tavern in time to see a stout little set of table and chairs scoot themselves out into the center of the room and settle down.

"Thank you," Sullivan said.

"You're welcome," replied both the proprietor and his compliant furnishings.

"What's on special today?" Sullivan glanced at the soup a couple of local farm hands were enjoying.

Gualtero and Viola eased toward the table and chairs. The chairs immediately held themselves out for the visitors. Viola bent tediously into her seat and the carved face in her chair's high back pursed its lips a moment, then called out, "Bring a pillow for this young damsel's backside. She's fairly warm with pain."

Viola nearly jumped out of her seat, but the carved visage in the center of the tabletop smiled at her. "Easy, dearie. A pillow will feel good on you."

Viola watched as a pillow sailed forth from a back room, as though it had been flung. Her chair caught it with its left arm and set it down on its seat.

"Now, sit yourself down," the chair said.

"Oh," said Viola with a confused look at Gualtero's grinning face, "thank you." She sat down. The sigh that escaped her confirmed her gratitude.

"Onion, garlic and mushroom soup," the proprietor was saying, "we sprinkle freshly ground cheese over the top of it. We also serve a fresh loaf of bread to each table."

"And to drink?" Gualtero said.

"Spring water that we keep cool in our cellar. Wine. Apple cider. Lemonade, the perfect refreshment for such a warm day."

"Lemonade," Viola said quickly, "please. I would love some lemonade."

The proprietor smiled at the young Faerie woman with the hair falling down to her waist. Despite her plain clothes, she radiated a ladylike politeness and civility. He bowed to her. "At once, Miss." He clapped his hands and a boy of twelve scurried from behind the tavern counter toward the back room. They heard his light footsteps tearing down a staircase and in due time racing back up.

"And you, gentlemen, what will you have?" the proprietor said.

Gualtero watched the boy re-emerge from the back room with a pitcher and a large cup in his hands. The boy poured out for Viola with hasty assurance. Viola drank down half of it on the spot, so the boy refilled her cup and then left the pitcher on the table for her.

"Apple cider's too heavy for a warm day like this," Sullivan said, as he met Gualtero's equally searching gaze. Both squinted at each other, then Sullivan said, "Do you brew your own beer?"

"Not this week. All of my barley has had to go for other things. We do offer our own particular vintage of wine. We've won prizes at the county fair for our wines," the proprietor said. "I recommend it highly. Good for the blood, you know."

"Wine then," Gualtero said, "and a pitcher of your cooled spring water."

"And we'll have the special too," said Sullivan as he and Gualtero took out some coins for the proprietor.

Gualtero took out an extra gold coin and set it on the counter. "And this is for someone to tend to our horses while we're here."

"Right," said the proprietor. He collected all the money and took it to the back room where he and his wife kept the cash box hidden.

Shortly afterwards, they saw the twelve year old and an older boy of sixteen march outside to the water trough.

The proprietor returned with two goblets and a large bottle of wine, which he uncorked. "I'll have your luncheon shortly."

Sullivan and Gualtero settled to the table under the smiling watch of the table's centerpiece and sipped slowly on their wine, while the muscles and nerves in their bodies unwound. They looked at the other Faerie customers, a nice collection of rural sorts, field hands, a couple of old men playing card games in the corner, two young women in goodly clothes gossiping beneath their fine bonnets over a pot of tea and a dish of baked sweets.

Two other fellows, the wandering sort if one judged by their gypsy attire, sat hunched over their table in the corner closest to the big picture window looking out onto the dirt highway. Gualtero watched them the longest, but neither man betrayed any interest in any of their neighbors. When their meal arrived, he forgot about them and did not notice the furtive glances the two reclusive men cast their way, although he glanced idly at them when they left the tavern.

Sullivan dipped a slice of his bread in his soup and said, "So, Viola, how do you like the countryside so far?"

Viola shifted atop her pillowed seat and grimaced. "Sunny and warm, isn't it? I could get used to it, once my backside feels better."

Gualtero grunted. His mouth was too full for speech.

Viola stirred her soup and looked at Gualtero for a long distant moment.

Gualtero put his spoon down and wiped his mouth on the napkin. "I can tell by the way you're looking at me. You have something to say."

She remained silent instead and looked into her soup bowl.

"You can talk to me. I won't bite you."

Viola took another drink of her lemonade. "What are my sisters like?"

"Where to begin?" Gualtero mused aloud.

"The Lady Olwen?" Sullivan said.

Gualtero shrugged. "I might as well start with the youngest. All right, let's see if I can't summarize the Lady Olwen for you. She's only about five years younger than you. As a teenager, she's ripening quite nicely, but then your mother's daughters all seemed to take after her in that aspect." Sullivan smirked a little, until Gualtero kicked him under the table. "She's shorter and altogether more petite than you are."

Sullivan frowned and rubbed his calf. "She's rather like an exquisite porcelain sculpture -very pale and delicate."

"She's rather quiet and fond of music and reading about the world outside her cloistered existence." Viola's abrupt pointed stare provoked the further explanation. "She hasn't come of age yet, so Olwen must keep to the family's private wing and continue her schooling and polishing, as Anna terms it. What else? Oh! She's good with her hands. She embroiders clothes, makes tapestries, and weaves. She has been taking special instruction from a renowned master of the arts who lives in the Forbidden Realm, a reverent matriarch named Mother Gertrude Horton. The woman comes four times a year and spends two weeks with her for intensive lessons."

"Olwen has the longest hair I've ever seen." Sullivan gestured. "Her hair is like spun gold that falls all the way down to her feet. She tends to wear it in elaborate braids and a bun, but once in a while she ties it back with a ribbon and lets gravity have its way with it."

"She has soft lavender blue eyes," Gualtero said. "Actually, you could owe my good fortune with Anna Marpessa to the benign influence of Olwen. Now, this is the true story of how I met and came to your sister's notice. I had come to pay an official diplomatic call on your sister's Prime Minister. I was asked to wait in the conservatory that connects to the greenhouse. Well, they didn't know she was there or they would have had me wait in the corridor. Underage remember?"

Viola nodded.

Gualtero went on. "Olwen was there studying some patterns in a book when I was shown in. As soon as the footman left, she introduced herself to me and we had ourselves a fine chat. She admired the formal coat I was wearing and asked about its design. By the time the Prime Minister had arrived with Anna Marpessa, I had promised to send design books to Olwen and any concern Anna had about my being shut in alone with her sister pretty rapidly gave way to a genuine sense of appreciation for my courtesy. Olwen and I were friends long before Anna expressed her interest in me."

"Olwen was the instigator," Sullivan said. "She invited him into her work room in the family wing with the full knowledge that Anna would have to come and chaperone the visit. She made sure that Anna was thrown into Gualt's company on a daily basis."

"And we all know the consequences of that," Gualtero said as he rotated the engagement knot around his left wrist.

"Olwen was setting your new rooms in order for your arrival when we left," Sullivan said.

"I'll be sure to thank her for her efforts," Viola said.

"Next is Carissa," Sullivan said.

"Carissa is only two years younger than you, I think," Gualtero said. "She's a little harder to get to know, but she's decent. Her hair is darker than yours, but her eye color is like Anna's. She prefers the company of thinkers, philosophers, artists, and that sort. She wears a lot of dark, flowing clothes, velvets most of the year and only pale lavender blue or dove gray in the height of summer."

"She wears her hair in an intricate collection of braids encircling a bun. However, when she has it in a serpentine coil hanging over her shoulder," Sullivan said, "we know that there is some paramour she is about to meet or someone she wishes to turn into a paramour. She has a stunning smile. Fortunately, she has only used it so far on her thinkers. If she ever looked at me like that..." Sullivan sighed and rolled his eyes toward the sky.

"She won't," Gualtero said. "Neither of us think enough for her liking. Don't get me wrong. She respects and likes Sully and myself, but we're too rough-edged for her."

Sullivan took on a mien of mock gloom. "Ah, the lost opportunities. To be caught in that mahogany coil's silken embrace." He snapped out of it at once. "Now, tell her about your Lady."

"Anna Marpessa," Gualtero said and took a deep breath. "She is the be-all and end-all as far as I can tell. She has a consummate face for every person she encounters and a deft hand for situations. Frankly, I'm in awe of her, but then they say Valeria was her tutor, so that might explain part of it. They packed her head so full of education that she seems and behaves like someone twice her age and with twice the common sense. She can hold forth with the best of them in Carissa's circle, but she has no interest in plying needles, like Olwen does. She likes to putter about with clay though and make bowls and terra cotta statuettes during the warm months. She likes skating in the winter and riding year round. I've been trying to get her accustomed to sailing. I gave her a sleek little craft and have been trying to teach her how to sail." Gualtero shrugged then.

"She doesn't take much to water though, does she?" Viola said.

"Not yet," Gualtero said, "but she's determined to master it, since the water is my second home."

"I blame Thetis Megara," Sullivan said.

"Thetis Megara?" Viola said.

"Queen of the Sea Nymphs and quite a temptress in her own right. The ocean is her vast domain and she is possessive of it and jealous of Gualt and Anna."

"She'll get over it," Gualtero said, "but to be on the safe side, we'll make sure we parade the cream of Faerie manhood before her. One of them is bound to catch the Sea Queen's eye."

Sullivan nodded earnestly. He looked into his bowl and set his wide spoon down inside its now empty depths. "I've done my damage. I'm full. Can we take a siesta?"

Gualtero set his spoon down too and consulted his pocket watch. "Not today."

"Ahhh," groaned Sullivan.

"We'll camp early tonight, so that Viola can have some proper rest," Gualtero said with a friendly smile at her.

Sullivan leaned toward Viola. "Are you ready?"

"I can bear a few more hours of riding, I think," Viola replied, but without much conviction and a slow shift of her backside in her seat. With a sigh, she pushed herself up and away from the table. Without further encouragement, she shuffled out the door.

"She's dogged. 'Got to like her for that," Sullivan said.

"Do you have that balm with you?" Gualtero said as he got up from the table too.

"In my saddle bags," Sullivan said.

"Give it to Viola. She'll need it by the time we camp tonight," Gualtero said.

Then he and Sullivan sauntered outside, leaving the table and chairs to sort themselves out and clear the crockery back to the kitchen.

Viola was already clambering stiffly aboard Arcadia's saddle when they rejoined her. Gualtero helped her get her foot over and then took up Navis' reins.

"Come along, Sully," Gualtero said. "Don't dawdle."

Sullivan stood staring at a colorful gypsy wagon lumbering down a side lane out of sight. "You don't see the Gypsy Faeries around these parts too often."

"Gypsies are gypsies," Gualtero said. "They go where they will." He met Viola's curious glance and added, "Give them a wide and respectful berth, if you can. They are full of mischief."

Viola nodded and made a mental note of it.

Sullivan mounted up on Biscuit and they set off.

The two hooded men from the tavern came out from beneath the farmers' market awning, where they had stood pretending to be interested in the copper pots and pans on sale there. They watched the Prince and the Elf riding eastward across the meadow with the young Faerie woman in mountain clothes, but only for a moment. Then they darted after the gypsy wagon with tight, sharp smiles on their down-turned faces.

3

"Lombard!"

"What is it, Russell?" Lombard said.

"You won't believe who we just saw." The young Faerie man scrambled across the irrigation canal ahead of the gypsy wagon their comrade drove. He shook off his boots a couple of times and resumed running.

A tall Faerie countryman lay sprawled out at his ease beneath a spreading tree. "The Imperial Sorcerer Master Macy himself, right?" Lombard said without enthusiasm.

Twelve other men basked in the shade of neighboring trees with their hats pulled down over their faces. Their horses grazed on the tall wild grass behind the grove.

Lombard sat up and pushed his wide hat back from over his face.

"Naw, Prince Gualtero Bainbridge and Sullivan Trooper."

They all sat up at that and looked toward their leader Lombard.

Lombard climbed to his feet and dusted off his backside with his hat. "Are you sure?"

"Very sure. There's only one Sullivan Trooper in the whole world and everyone knows Gualtero's face from the betrothal announcements. They've got a young Faerie lady with them named Viola, if I heard them correctly."

"Frosting for the cake." Lombard put his hat on, but stopped a moment. "Is she pretty?"

"Her hair is dark, but it gleams where the sun kisses it and hangs all the way to her waist. She is fair and kindly featured. If Pop had brought her to me and said, 'Here, boy, this'll be your wife', I wouldn't have been so eager to leave home."

"At least not until after the honeymoon," Warwick said, as he caught up with Russell and shook the canal water off of his boots.

Russell hit him in the arm. "You don't know that."

"Pop said not to pound me, Russ."

"I'm your elder," Russell said, "so I can do as I like when you smart-mouth me, and Pop said to box you one whenever you got fresh."

"Ma said not to pound me either, Russ," Warwick said.

"Enough," Lombard said. The two brothers shut up and gave each other resentful looks instead. "Warwick, can you follow the Prince and the Elf without being discovered?"

"Like a shadow."

"Then off with you." Lombard turned to Russell. "They were following the eastern road?"

"They were."

"Then it'll be easy to set a trap." Lombard gazed off into the distance. "You realize what this means?"

"I think so," said Russell.

"All my wishes are within my grasp at long last." Lombard turned toward the rest. "Everyone mount up. The hunt is on."

The bandits rallied to their infamous lord's command. They did not see the two farm boys who wandered nearby. They saw the bandits and recognized their leader, the tall, blond Faerie man renowned for his cunning and speed, the infamous Lord of the Bandits. The two boys hid and did not run for home until the bandits were well away with their gypsy wagon across the fields.

Lombard was King of the Bandits in all but official title, but the honor was commonly given and that was enough for him. The plain folk of the land of Nuneau, as well as the lands immediately north and south of the Faerie lands, dreaded and respected him. His name carried both terror and fascination—the wealthy wrung their hands at his mention, but the young folks' eyes lit up in anticipation of any tale involving the Seelie bandit.

Legend had it that he was the offspring of a union between a Faerie damsel who fell into the hands of a knight on the Southern Continent, a forbidden place called the Land of Many Kingdoms. He never denied it, but in pensive moments, would ever so tellingly fondle a locket chained to a badge that he wore inside his tunic. Those few who got a good look at the badge said that it bore the coat of arms of a foreign place and the name of an unknown knight. There were only forty knights at any one time in Nuneau and they were well known, so the badge confirmed his patrimony. The locket was another matter. It was of the brightest Faerie silver and within was said to rest the exquisite portrait of his Seelie mother and a tiny, intricate braid of her golden hair.

What became of her was the fodder of many a troubadour's song both in the Faerielands and the Land of Many Kingdoms. The story went that the Faerie damsel subcumbed to temptation in the person of a handsome prince and broke her fierce knight's heart. She was found dead under suspicious circumstances when she was supposed to be waiting for her new paramour. Her princely lover accused the knight and challenged him to a combat of arms to prove his innocence or guilt. The prince, rightfully, some said, since he had seduced the damsel away from her true companion, was killed in the joust. The knight sold all of his worldly possessions and rode off with only his squire and his young son for company, never to be seen within polite society again. Courtesy of the late prince, Lombard's mother was said to lie in a state of perfect preservation in an abbey vault, beside her unfortunate seducer's tomb, and was the subject of an annual festival in which young hopeful lovers came to her gravesite to pray for better fortune than she had suffered. Lombard's father was said to be buried beneath the flagstones beside his brethren in the castle belonging to his Order.

Lombard neither confirmed nor denied the legend, but then even his comrades did not know him to be very talkative about his sad, brave father and beautiful, foolish mother. He disappeared every winter though and the consensus among his cronies was that he journeyed south to the forbidden southern continent on a personal pilgrimage to his father's Order and his mother's garlanded effigy. Their suspicions were confirmed every spring when he showed up with a wide array of useful goods for their families and for his men - saddles, unusually marked swords and daggers, and sturdy fabric with foreign designs woven or embroidered onto them. Lombard's own sword bore the symbol of his father's Order and so did the signet ring he wore.

Because of his parentage, Lombard stood apart from the common Faerie throng. He lacked the Faerie folks' wings, but he was swift and could climb and leap as surely as any mountain goat. He had tremendous strength and endurance and courtesy of his father, the disciplined training to use it to his advantage. He was tall, well-formed, sturdy, but not stocky. His unruly shoulder length hair was not as pure and golden a blonde as his mother's, but it gleamed well enough after a summer in the sun. He was striking and rugged, with a quick glance and ready smile, but his father's sternness resided in his well-defined face as well. His good-nature glossed over a very serious and determined nature. The only fools he suffered were the ones that made him laugh. His Faerie comrades had nothing but respect for him and would follow him anywhere.

Lombard possessed one book, a small directory and guide of sorts with maps. He kept it in his hip pouch at all times and permitted no one else to read it, although his apprentice-wards Russell and Warwick tried to sneak looks at it whenever he was perusing the well-thumbed volume. As they paused to water their horses in a stream, he brought it out again, looked at a few pages and muttered off calculations as he squinted out across the midday's bright sunlit fields. He knew the region better than the locals. They would be well ahead of their prey by sunset.

Clustered near him, his men grouped their horses on both sides of the stream. Every odd moment or so, Lombard saw the sunlight glance off of their folded and largely invisible Faerie wings, attachments that the Faerie folk could summon into full shape and view on a whim, but neglected more often than not. Only the humblest used their wings as regularly as the birds did, he had noticed. The more well-off they were the more inclined they were to save their wings for show and use on special occasions. He thanked his good fortune that he had been blessed with a plain man's body and the Faerie's mortal-immortal longevity, but not their wings. He had seen often enough when a sudden gust caught his men by surprise and blew them high into the sky and several miles away. His men would flutter back looking chagrined and find him laughing out loud.

There were fifteen bandits under his leadership. They had come from different backgrounds; two of them had come from mighty families, but had been disinherited by older siblings. Most were plain folk, artisans and farmers or the sons of such Faerie folk, who found living at home very difficult.

Russell and Warwick Masham were the most recent recruits and the youngest, being in their teens. Their family was scraping a living out of their vineyards in the south and had jumped at the opportunity of having two fewer mouths to feed, along with the added hopes of the boys making their fortunes with Lombard. They were dutiful boys. They had been told to make their family's fortune, so that they might improve the farm and provide dowries for their sisters. Lombard found them a handful, but they learned quickly, so he tolerated them. He also had the good sense to keep them busy at odd chores.

Montargis and Hawtrey were well-born, but were disinherited by elder siblings. Finding their options both few and confining, they broke free of familial constraints and turned outlaw for Lombard. Hawtrey was the older of the two and his ambitions were greatly diminished by time and dissolution. Lombard frequently had to pry the drinks from his hands whenever they stopped in any town possessing a tavern or two. He still managed to carry himself with some semblance of dignity however when the occasion or strategy required it. Montargis bristled with ambition. He was determined to return home someday a wealthier man than his older brothers and had already a respectable stash of wealth tucked away toward that golden day. Lombard relied on him to steel Hawtrey's ebbing spirit and to be the dashing decoy whenever they infiltrated fetes or balls.

Parslow had belonged to a strict contemplative order along the eastern seacoast, but had proved too fond of worldly things to stay. He enjoyed the life of banditry under Lombard's leadership and lived from hand to mouth, except when his luck with the cards held firm. He was game for any risk and Lombard appreciated that.

Kelyng, Biagio, and Gripwell were farmers until their fields gave out and their families began to starve. They were decent men and Lombard relied on their decency more than they realized. He teamed them up with his more impulsive men to rein them in. For serving him so, he made certain their families did not want while their fathers were away.

Acton had been a starveling when Lombard had found him during one of his rare excursions to the royal city Nuneau beside the ocean. His parents had gone missing some years before and were not missed by their neighbors, who contributed what they could to keep the Faerie boy alive. Acton went willingly with Lombard and his first two partners, Scudamore and Quinzano, and had never gone to sleep hungry again. He regarded Lombard like a big brother and was the only one allowed to journey with Lombard in the winter. If anyone knew Lombard's true background, it was Acton.

Scudamore and Quinzano were Lombard's first partners in infamy and his confidants in all plots. Scudamore had been a warden in the district containing the Enchanted Woodlands. He had been a drifter when he met up with Lombard. His path was less aimless after that. Quinzano had been apprenticed to a counting house, but when some funds turned up missing, he was accused and sent to jail. He was young then, as young as Warwick, and his innocence was not believed. He left jail covered with disgrace and with his wings clipped to mark him for life. His father booted him from the house, but Quinzano soon met Lombard, had him cut off his wings entirely and started a new life, where conformity didn't matter.

Trapnel was a common thief, for no reason other than he despised working. For that reason, Lombard assigned him the toughest chores available and set big, burly Gripwell to watch him. Trapnel liked Lombard nonetheless and liked nothing more than to collect stories to amuse him with over their campfires.

On account of his paramours and his constant quest for new ones, Suedama was always out of funds. He was good-looking and very charming. If company was desired, bandits could always count on Suedama to round up some fair faces to while away the hours. For the sake of their good wives at home, Gripwell, Biagio, and Kelyng always made it a point to politely refuse any companionship he offered to find for them. Lombard never entrusted Suedama with guarding any heiresses that they took for ransom. He assigned that duty to Biagio, a good father, who prized the safety and virtue of his daughters and anyone else's, especially where Suedama was concerned. Still, the countryside was dotted with the fair, fluttering offspring of that elusive, handsome rogue.

Calderon was a resourceful and innovative bloke. Lombard frequently sent Acton and Kelyng with him to salvage things and to make them usable again. He was entrusted with their gypsy wagon and the objects they sold from it whenever they stopped in any populated place. He came from the gypsy Faerie tribes and knew where to find his people at any time of the year in case Lombard and his men needed a place to hide. He was the most unremarkable looking one of the band, so he was Lombard's most useful spy and the one who took letters for Biagio, Kelyng and Gripwell to the postmasters.

De Vere was fearless and enigmatic. He would do whatever Lombard required and more, if desperate circumstances arose. Only Lombard and Quinzano, who brought him into the band, knew his past. A farmer's son, he had murdered to protect his two sisters from the sons of a powerful family. He fled with a bounty on his head and his sisters were abducted anyway. There would be no going back for him. When he joined the band, he had Quinzano and Lombard cut off his wings too. He survived the ensuing fever to become a determined student of the martial arts Lombard had from his father. In a secret place, he was collecting the enchanted black Faerie armor he would wear in the southern land that Lombard promised to take him to one day.

These were Lombard's men, his loyal band. They watered their horses and watched him think. To his right waited Scudamore and to his left was Acton. Quinzano and De Vere faced him across the water.

"Well," Quinzano said, "we have found our prey. What is the plan?"

"To set a trap to capture the Prince Gualtero Bainbridge and Sullivan Trooper."

"Ransom, eh?" Scudamore said.

"And such a ransom," Montargis said. "The Queen's own betrothed."

"And the chief heir to the Islands Federation," Trapnel said. "That's two ransoms right there."

"Queen Anna Marpessa will fork over a vast fortune as well to gain Sullivan Trooper's freedom," Calderon said. "He's the only one of his kind left. No one will want to see him hurt."

"When have we ever hurt a hostage?" Lombard said.

"But he was raised by the Shadow Mountain folks," Biagio said. "Won't they be concerned?"

"They don't interfere in private lives," Lombard said, "only when the fate of nations is involved."

"But Sullivan IS his own nation," Kelyng said.

"Then we'll have to cross our fingers," Scudamore said. "If all we want is money and no harm is done, then they won't have cause to come after us."

"And that's all we want - money, right?" Gripwell said.

Lombard was silent for a moment.

Scudamore and Quinzano exchanged looks.

"That is what it is about, isn't it?" De Vere said, when he saw Quinzano bite on his own lip, not a good sign. "Money, right?"

"Gentlemen," Lombard said, "these two men could be the means to a fabulous end. I have more in mind than mere ransoms, as extravagant as theirs will be."

They all exchanged looks, some uneasy, some growing in eager curiosity.

"Might we know what you have in mind?" Hawtrey said.

"We will ransom them, of course," Lombard said. "We'll do that as soon as we have them, but these are brave men, as brave as ourselves. Prince Gualtero has captained his own ship and Sullivan Trooper has been his right hand in both battles and enterprise. I expect they're more like us than they would care to admit. They've both done some privateering for the Federation."

"They were pirates, you mean," Acton said.

"And good ones too. The Federation's treasury owes its bounty to their command of the privateering fleet. We'll ransom them, but in the meantime, I intend to offer them their freedom unconditionally if they perform a few tasks for us. If they are successful, we can all retire as wealthy men and re-enter society, if it suits us."

"You can't though, Lombard," Suedama said. "You're too well known."

Lombard smiled. "I have several schemes in mind, you'll see."

With a gentle tap of his heels, he urged his horse across the stream and gradually let it break into a canter across the field. The rest of his men followed in single file with their wide hats pulled low over their faces.

4

They rode in no great haste. Viola focused on sightseeing to take her mind off of her miserable backside. The open grasslands and farm lands with their boundary lines of trees and calmly coursing streams gave way to rolling and deeply forested territory. They stuck to the main road where the sunlight shone, but on all sides of them breathed a deep, primeval forest with all of its wild and furtive sounds.

"Where are we?" Viola said.

"In the woods," Sullivan said.

"I mean, where exactly?"

"This is the Enchanted Forest or the Forbidden one," Sullivan said.

"Depending on your point of view," Gualtero said with a grin at the leafy canopy above the trail.

"Or your experience," Sullivan said. "Nuneau is rife with spooky old forests."

"You've been through it before?" Viola said.

"On the way to meet you," Gualtero said.

"And did anything happen to you?" she said.

"Nope," Sullivan said. "'Lovely in here, isn't it?"

"Yes, it is. I've never seen such tall trees." She tilted her head back.

"This forest has been like this since anyone can remember," Sullivan said, "and no one is allowed to disturb it, except as we do now - passing through."

"No trees may be cut down," Gualtero said. "The only wood that can be used here is what is already lying on the ground."

"That's prudent," she said.

"Very prudent," Sullivan said. "You see, legend insists that there are spirits in these trees. It wouldn't do to annoy them."

"I'll be very respectful," she said.

They rode in silence again, idly following the road past enormous trees and watching the occasional blue jay or shy cardinal flutter across their path. Here and there, they heard a woodpecker, but those were harder to spot. They saw a bull elk near a stream and paused themselves to water their horses. The elk shook its antlered head at some gnats and eyed them.

"Good day," Sullivan said, as he dismounted.

"For some," the elk replied with a glance at the sunshine.

Gualtero and Sullivan exchanged looks. Viola was fascinated.

"Why shouldn't it be a good day?" Gualtero said.

The elk shook his head again. "There are too many strangers in the forest."

"Strangers?" Gualtero said. "You mean us."

"And the other skulking folk." The elk turned away from the sunshine toward the deeper forest recesses. "They're up to no good, believe me." He walked softly into the forest and disappeared like a ghost.

"Take care," Sullivan called after the elk. "The animals will be safe, I hope."

"Hunting is forbidden here." Gualtero gazed into the forest depths. "What do you suppose a bunch of people would be doing lurking in the Enchanted Forest? I wouldn't lurk here."

"Me either." Sullivan checked Biscuit's hooves and pried a stone from one of them.

"Is it that dangerous here?" Viola said.

"'Can be," Gualtero said with a sigh, "but then I've never been here before this mission. I've just heard the stories."

"Why is it enchanted then?" she said.

"Wizard Chauncey the Romantic told me a legend one midsummer night. He said that long, long ago before the Faeries built their great kingdom by the sea, there was a great wizard king. No one remembers his name, but he was a lonely man, and he left his kingdom when he could bear the loneliness no longer. His two most prized possessions were a winged horse the color of milk and a small chest containing all of his magic. When he left forever, he took them with him. He was searching for a new home, a place where he'd be welcome for all time. He searched from one end of the continent to the other and found no place as inviting as this forest. It was wild and it was beautiful. He emptied his magic chest over the entire forest so that it was saturated with his special kind of magic. You've seen proof of it already: a talking Elk. Animals **can** talk amongst themselves, but it isn't normal for us to be able to converse so readily with them."

"The magic made that possible," Viola said.

Sullivan nodded.

"What happened to the wizard king?"

"He lived his last days in the forest, in some abode that the forest protects in his memory. He is gone, but his magic lives on. Chauncey the Romantic believes that his spirit lingers here still in the only place where he found peace and contentment. He told me that, although it was an isolated and wild place, he never felt alone when he visited here. In fact, he actually preferred to come here when he needed inspiration for his poetry or to work out the kinks in the courtships he was helping along."

"That's an interesting story," Viola said.

"I wonder if it's true," Gualtero said.

Sullivan shrugged.

Viola grinned suddenly and dug in her saddlebags. "I know where I can find out."

"Where?" Gualtero let go of Navis' reins and joined Viola.

Viola slid a sturdy stout little book out of a saddlebag and turned toward them. It was decidedly plain looking.

"What's that?" Sullivan said.

"It's a secret." She stroked the book's cover. "Promise not to tell anyone what it truly is?"

Gualtero raised his right hand. "Promise."

Sullivan did the same. "Me, too. What is it?"

Viola opened the book and flipped the pages.

"It's blank," Gualtero said.

"It looks blank," she said, "but it isn't for those who know how to use it." She closed the book and held it out flat in front of herself.

"What is it?" Gualtero said.

"It's called an Omnipedia. All the people on Shadow Mountain have one."

"Do they? I never saw Chauncey or Agnetha's or even Elspeth's, and she let me have the run of her library," Sullivan said.

"An Omnipedia wouldn't have been kept with regular books. It's the book of all books. That's why its pages are blank. They stay blank until you need to find out something, then the print or manuscript appears."

"What I wouldn't have given to have one of these tucked in my coat pocket during my exams," Gualtero said.

"They're usually kept locked up and only taken out when needed," she said.

"How is it that you have one?" Gualtero said.

"Because Saire and the rest trust me. They prepared me well." Viola could see the curiosity in their faces. She addressed the book in a plain voice. "What the truth is about this Enchanted Forest?"

The Omnipedia flipped open. Gualtero and Sullivan jumped despite themselves. The pages began to flick across as though pushed by a strong breeze and several pages of ancient, illuminated manuscript appeared, followed further back by plain pages of print. The pages flicked back to the beginning and stopped.

"Amazing," Gualtero said.

"What does it say?" Sullivan peered over Viola's shoulder at the colorful page.

"Here beginneth the tale of Seigneur Luzarches de Morin, Philosophe, Necromancer, and King of superb wisdom and grace," Viola read aloud. She turned the creamy page with great care and they read of his youthful exploits.

"Daring fellow," Gualtero said, as Viola turned the page again. "I wish I'd met him."

They read of his ordeals in training his talents and in honing his mind, and how these ordeals brought him to a throne at a time of troubles. Luzarches de Morin was a strong, but compassionate king and warlord, but not lucky in love.

"Why am I not surprised by that?" Sullivan said, as they pressed on to the next page.

"What do you know," Gualtero said when they set eyes on the grand illustration on the page. "He married after all - to the bounteous, fair and kind Milady Solaine, daughter of the sun, sister of the moon."

"They don't spare the praise, do they?" Gualtero said. "'Nice image of her though."

"She must have been a *'rare'* being," Sullivan said.

"A *rare* being?" Gualtero said.

"He means like the Great Intercessor Ultima and her kindred." Viola turned the page. "They live in the heavens amongst the constellations. I saw the enigmatic Ultima once, when I was very small. She came to the community to celebrate Master Sorcerer Macy's anniversary. She was dark, like him, and very serene and beautiful. She had a tall red fox as her escort. I don't remember his name, but I remember the very fine courtly clothes he wore and that he walked upright as we do. He whittled a wooden animal for me and, hang me, I left it at home."

Gualtero read on. "They reigned together for many ages during peaceful and prosperous times."

"But no children," Sullivan said.

Viola turned the page. "You're right. No children and that was the source of her sorrow. In the end, she relinquished her mortal shell, as they term it here, and returned to the skies."

"Which broke the wizard king's heart. Wait. Look at this picture," Gualtero said. "See, there's the winged horse in the background."

"And Luzarches de Morin is holding a chest in one hand and his orb of state in the other," Sullivan said. "I think we're coming up on the legend. Quick, turn the page."

Viola smiled at his impatience and turned the page. "He took wing on a Zephyr," she read.

"Now, was Zephyr the horse's actual name or was it just the breeze they're referring to?" Sullivan said.

"Judging by the style this manuscript is written," Gualtero said, "Zephyr could very well be the horse's name."

"Good name, eh, Biscuit?" Sullivan said.

Biscuit bobbed her head and continued nibbling on the tender blades of grass beside the stream.

Viola continued. "In his emptiness of heart, he sought the world over for a place of rest..." The illumination on that page showed the winged horse and its rider flying high away from a tall, spired city and castle. The people in the city gazed after him with grief carefully painted on their tiny faces. "...Until he found the wilderness of Nuneau. The beauty of the land and the purity of its beasts pleased his heart and defeated his sorrows. He blessed it."

The illumination on the page showed Luzarches emptying the sparkling contents of his chest over a rolling forest and its dancing beasties. Sullivan smiled at the image.

Viola turned the page. "The beasts and very trees of the wilderness welcomed him and made him a home, where he lived in contentment all the days of his life. Every day, the forest and the animals showed their gratitude and love for their Master and to this day, they protect the site of his eternal rest. Those who would disturb the peace of Luzarches de Morin shall never be seen again, but whosoever should come, who is pure in heart and desolate, shall be given refuge and blessed."

The last illumination depicted a small mausoleum, densely covered with flowering vines before which a pilgrim was depicted offering his sword under the watchful eyes of an owl and a wolf. In the distance behind it, they could see a tiny gray building with a blue rooftop and a tower tucked deep into the forest.

"Enigmatic," Sullivan said.

"What do they mean by blessed? Or desolate? And who would be providing the refuge?" Gualtero said.

"Maybe we'll find it along the way." Viola turned the page and found the plain print.

"I'm not sure I want to," Sullivan said. "I ain't exactly pure."

"Me neither," Gualtero said. "What's that?"

"An official survey it looks like." Viola peered closely at the print along the top of the page. "Macy commissioned it two centuries ago. It was compiled by Sorcerer Ivan the Dark, Warlock Tristan the Pleasant, and Witch Agnetha the Powerful."

"Agnetha?" Sullivan cried. "They never told me anything."

"You were a boy," Gualtero said.

"I'm grown now."

"You're a rogue like me, not a contemplative like them."

"Oh."

Viola skimmed the pages. "This is amazing. This is a survey of every kind of plant and tree that grows here, every animal, and, look: every secret place and dwelling that is hidden here."

"The tomb of Luzarches de Morin is listed," Sullivan said. "Cross me with my own sword, but I have to see it, Gualt."

"I don't think we should go near it," Gualtero said, but he read the description of the tomb closely. "Is there a map in this book?"

"I haven't looked," Viola said. "Look beneath the Tomb's entry. Castle de Morin - abode of late Master Luzarches de Morin. Southern continental Gothic style. Refuge. Occupied. Perilous. Approach with extreme caution, if at all."

Gualtero looked Sullivan dead in the eye.

"Well, we won't be going to have a look at the Castle, just the tomb. It would be a shame to pass through this wonderful wood a second time without paying proper respects to the man who blessed it." Sullivan grinned and went back to Biscuit's side.

Viola closed the book and held it close.

"Do you want to see the tomb?" Gualtero said.

"I wouldn't mind," she said.

"I kind of want to, too, but if you know any protection spells or blessings, mutter a few for us," Gualtero said.

"I know only one," she said.

"Good. Let's hear it."

"May we be worthy. May the journey bring us wisdom. May we seek only good in all we meet. May those we love be kept safe and sound. Permit us to return to them. Grant us these, our dearest hopes, and we shall be content."

"That's it?" Gualtero said.

"Should there be more? We were heard." Viola nodded at their surroundings. She tucked her Omnipedia safely away and mounted up.

"But who heard us?" Gualtero kept thinking about what the elk had said.

As evening approached, Gualtero and Sullivan searched for a good campsite. Enchanted forest or not, spring showers happened everywhere and were notoriously unpredictable. They found a grove between two massive, wide-spreading oak trees. The tree trunks offered ample protection from the elements, but Gualtero and Sullivan strung up a tent between the sheltering trunks anyway. Viola sat next to the tree trunk and copied a map from the Omnipedia.

Gualtero was making sure that their tent was secure against any gusts. "I'm glad you saw these trees, Sully. They're the best protection we could hope for."

Sullivan unsaddled their horses and dropped the saddles in front of the tent. "I'll take the horses 'round back to the stream."

"I'll help you brush them down as soon as I have this last line secured," Gualtero said.

Sullivan nodded and led the horses off.

Gualtero tied off the last knot. "How's the map coming along?"

"I'm nearly done." Viola worked her pencil with care across her short piece of paper. "I found our location already. These oaks are called the Two Brothers."

Gualtero crouched down beside her and looked at the precise map she had copied. "You have a sure hand, like my last navigator did."

"What happened to him?"

"He's captaining my ship now. Good man."

"You had a ship?"

"Yep, the best in the fleet, but I had to give her up."

"Why?" Viola held up her map and compared it with the one in the Omnipedia.

"Because I am marrying your sister the Queen."

"I don't see why you had to give up your ship though."

"Because, when I marry her, I will have to spend more time in Nuneau. I'll be her Prince Consort and when my father dies, I'll be King of the Islands Federation."

"You'll be her equal."

"I already am that."

"Do you really love my sister?"

"I gave up the sailing life for her, so I suppose I must."

"But it sounds as though it is also a marriage of alliance." Viola's direct gaze was disconcerting.

Grinning a little, Gualtero sat down to watch her put the finishing touches on the map. "I wasn't expecting to meet Anna, but when I went there on Federation business, she insisted on coming with her Minister to see me. She felt that if my father could show such trust by sending me to her Court, then she should do him the honor of greeting me. I was impressed with her from the very first. For a royal hothouse flower, she was quite solid, earthy even. She had a very direct gaze and a firm handshake that any captain would appreciate. She talked treaties as well as my father and a little better than I'm inclined to, but she was decidedly friendly. Sullivan swore up and down that her eyes were devouring me, but I was too busy trying to honor my father's trust. Olwen saw the spark though, like Sully did."

"Did she pursue you? Or was it the other way around?"

"We pursued each other finally. It was a happy development for both sides. Your sister and I have insured that the treaty was settled fairly and ratified on both sides. It goes into effect as soon as we marry."

"Hooray."

"Hooray indeed. I'd better go help Sully. He'll be sore, if I don't lend him a hand like I said I would." Gualtero climbed to his feet with another brief groan and a long stretch. "When you're done with the map, could you collect us some firewood?"

"Surely, Gualt. You don't mind if I call you that."

"Call me what you want, Sister." Gualtero bowed and sauntered after Sullivan.

Viola added a few last touches to the map, examined it closely and nodded to herself. She closed the Omnipedia and tucked the book inside her saddlebags. The map she folded carefully and slipped inside Gualtero's saddlebags. Then she wandered into the nearby woods looking for wood for their campfire.

The sun was sinking and a blue twilight began to rise up around her. She trooped through the undergrowth gathering sizable branches in her arms, pausing every odd moment to listen to the leaves rustling or to a birdcall. She saw many colorful birds that she knew only from the books she studied: a cardinal and its mate, a cowbird, a catbird, two blue jays, and what she thought was a titmouse. The woodpeckers she heard were harder to locate, but there were at least two in her area. She saw a pair of does, but they seemed in a hurry to get clear of that area. The anxious looks they cast backwards were not directed at her. She hadn't scared them, but if she didn't scare them, she began to wonder what had.

Her arms were over-burdened. If she tried to add another branch to her load, she would have dropped the lot, so she turned back toward the camp. What snatches of blue sky she could see were deepening from azure to cobalt and she thought she saw the first star twinkling already. She hurried her pace as best she could and stomped back into camp.

The tent stood quiet and full of shadows. The Two Brothers loomed out of the growing night, their stout branches reaching even further out toward her and the surrounding forest. She felt their eyes watching her and stood hesitantly in the stillness. She could hear the stream, but she couldn't see the horses for the foliage. She stood with her arms full and looked everywhere. Everything was as she had left it, except abandoned.

She cleared her throat. "Gualtero? Sullivan?" Nothing.

She dropped the pile and slapped the dirt from her sleeves and front. She still had the feeling that she was being watched and, worse, that the forest was closing in on her. Watching everywhere about herself, she crept nearer to the tent where their saddlebags sat in a jumble. She reached down for her saddlebags and caught a hold of them just as a garter snake poked its head out from beneath the tent. She flinched.

"Sh!" whispered the garter snake. "Don't make a sound."

Viola caught her breath. "Why?"

"There are villains in the woods," the snake said.

Viola's glance roved wildly on all sides of her. "Villains?"

"Yes, conniving ones," the snake said. "They have your two friends and they're watching you."

"What should I do?"

"Act normal. Come into the tent as though you had something to do in here, and then crawl out the back. There's a rabbit in the shrubs on the other side. He'll show you which way to run. I'll warn you if they come after you."

"Thank you." Viola shrugged, picked up her saddlebags and stooped toward the tent.

"Remember, be casual. I'll warn you if they're coming," the snake said.

Viola stepped inside the tent and let the flap fall behind her. She flung herself softly to her knees and crept to the far end, dragging her saddlebags alongside her.

"They're coming," the snake said suddenly.

A brown rabbit poked his head inside the tent. "Hurry. Leave the bags. You won't be able to run fast, if you bring them."

Viola let go of the saddlebags at once and scrambled after the rabbit.

"Stay low to the ground," the brown rabbit said, as he loped ahead into the shrubs.

Viola crawled rapidly behind it. She could hear footsteps pounding and scuffing the ground as they approached the tent. She looked once over her shoulder and saw the garter snake slithering off to her left into the shrubs.

"Knives," the garter snake said in a high, trembling voice.

The rabbit was propping up the shrub branches for her with one paw. The other he had poised before his mouth in warning. She slid rapidly under cover and followed the rabbit on all fours through the dense undergrowth. She caught herself on several thorn bushes, but bit back the pain.

Voices sounded out.

"Where did she go?"

"She snuck out the back. That's what she did."

"Search the forest. She can't have gone far."

She heard a tumult among the leaves behind her as the men spread out in pursuit. She heard them hacking at the bushes and shoving through them.

The rabbit paused once to catch its breath and look back beyond her. "There's a tunnel up ahead. If you can fit in it, you'll be home free."

Viola could only nod. She plucked a thorn from the palm of her hand and hurried after the rabbit.

They shifted around a thorny berry bush and she saw the gaping hole behind it. The rabbit had mounted the exposed root of a spruce tree and stood on its hind legs looking back.

"They're coming this way," the rabbit said. "Can you fit through the hole?"

"I can try," she muttered and she crawled at once into the tunnel. She had not gone far when she stopped. "I can't see."

The rabbit loped past her. "Follow my voice then. This tunnel exits on the other side of this hill. It winds a bit though, so be patient."

"I don't think I like tunnels," she said, as she groped ahead on the cool earth, "so the sooner you get me out of here the better."

"Hurry then." Thumping the ground as he went so she could hear him, he hopped ahead.

"What's your name?" she said as they rounded a corner. She felt mud press up around her fingers as she crawled.

"Vandin," he said. "What's yours?"

"Viola."

"Good evening, Viola. What brings you to our woods?"

"We were passing through. We were going to visit the tomb of Luzarches de Morin before we journeyed to the city by the sea."

"Pilgrims, eh?" Vandin said.

"Sort of," she said, "until now. What happened to my friends?"

"The villains have them all trussed up down by the stream."

"They aren't going to hurt them, are they?"

"'Couldn't say."

"Shouldn't we try to help them?" She stopped.

"They're being watched. If the opportunity arises, my neighbors will do what they can. It's best that you keep going though. Your friends were hoping that you would escape and we mustn't disappoint them."

"No, we shouldn't do that." Viola resumed her cramped pace along the tunnel. "Is this tunnel shrinking?"

"Only a little. We haven't much further to go."

"Why did you help me?"

"We don't like villains around here."

"Who does?"

Vandin chuckled.

"What do you think they're up to?" she said.

"No good. Their leader found that map you drew of our forest."

"Oh, no."

"Oh, no, indeed. He was mightily impressed with it. There's going to be real trouble around here before we've seen the last of him."

"I'm sorry."

"You didn't know he was waiting for you to show up. Jajhara should have been more specific when he warned you."

"Jajhara? Who is he?"

"The elk you guys met by the stream earlier today."

"Oh."

Vandin's voice lost its echo. "We're out."

Viola clambered out into nearly total darkness. The outside air struck her coldly. She sat down outside the tunnel and tried to rub the mud off of her hands. She shivered a moment and climbed carefully to her feet. She could see the stars everywhere above, shining liberally, but not enough to guide her path in the dark. There would be no moon tonight. She was cold and she had no place to sleep and she couldn't linger there overnight without risking capture.

"Where do I go from here?" she said.

"Straight and eventually you'll find the road out of the woods, I think," Vandin said.

"I can't leave my friends behind like this," she said. "Is there anyone I can go to for help?"

Vandin sat up and pressed a paw to his chin. "Well, I could tell you, but I couldn't show you the way. The owls will feast on me, if I go into the open."

"Just point me in the right direction and I'll find the way myself."

"If we wait long enough, the bats will be out and we can see if one of them will show you the way."

"I have the skill to guide myself in the dark. I'll show you." Viola held her hands out before her, one nearly a foot above the other. Both moved slowly in circles and slowly a glowing sphere took shape between them.

"How did you do that?"

"By concentrating and pulling the random energy from the air."

"Nice trick."

"Which way do I go from here?"

Vandin pointed east. "If you look carefully, you'll see our little footpaths. When you come to the great stump in the woods, turn northeast. There are a few folks living up there in the depths."

"Thanks, Vandin, my blessings upon you and yours."

"Thank you ever so much, Viola. Take care." Vandin leapt from the slope into the underbrush and scampered for home.

Viola withdrew her hands from the softly glowing sphere she had summoned. "Show me where I must go. I must find help."

The sphere drifted toward the ground and floated above the narrow path. It moved forward with her first step headed east.

"It was nice of your handmaiden to provide us with fuel for the campfire," Lombard said, as he watched Scudamore and Parslow assemble their dinner in a pot over the flames.

Gualtero and Sullivan were trussed by then to the Two Brothers, one to each enormous trunk. They watched as the bandits settled around the campfire with their saddles and blankets. A coffee pot was passed around between them while they waited for supper. They counted sixteen bandits in all, including their blonde, semi-human leader. They were grossly out-numbered, and, except for the bruises they had received during capture, the Faerie prince and the Elf were unharmed.

They had caught a few names here and there: Hawtrey, Quinzano, De Vere, Suedama...but the leader remained enigmatic. He regarded them with an expression of cool calculation in his eyes. He began to go through his captives' saddlebags with an indifferent curiosity. Even his minions expressed only mild interest in their belongings. Sullivan's hunting knife was lost to the one named Trapnel. The leader had confiscated Gualtero's new map and tucked it deep inside his pocket, but everything else of the prince's returned to the saddlebags. Finally, he picked up Viola's saddlebags and had a long look inside them.

"She doesn't go much for fancies or frills, does she?" Lombard looked at his prisoners.

Gualtero glared. Sullivan shrugged.

Lombard eyed them closely, saying, "But then lackeys usually don't have much to cherish. Still, I've never seen a young female in the service of a prince, unless she was a concubine or some secret love who masquerades as a boy to stay close to her warrior."

"Her glorious hair wasn't chopped though," Suedama said.

"So she wasn't masquerading." Lombard sighed and pulled out the plain clothes, three spare tunics, breeches and stockings. They were clean and whole. Not even one patch or fray to spoil the garments. " 'Comes from a comfortable family, I daresay." He looked at his captives. Neither of them had talked so far and they wouldn't be likely to yet. "Now, here's a fine item for a lackey." He took out the Omnipedia. "Books cost a pretty gold piece, even in the city."

His captives exchanged quick looks. Lombard saw them. He turned the book over in his hands. "I don't see a title. What sort of book is it?"

Their silence was damning, Lombard thought. He opened the book and leaned toward the campfire light. The first two pages were absolutely blank, so he flicked further through it. He snorted. "They're all blank." He held it open for his comrades to see. "The lackey owns a blank book."

"What use is a blank book?" Trapnel said.

The other rogues shrugged and smirked.

"Now, I wonder why a poor snip of a maiden would carry around a blank book?" Lombard focused his stare on the captives.

Sullivan saw writing appear on the pages. The pages began to move, but Lombard shut the book before he could see what his question had conjured.

"Unless," Lombard said, " she isn't what she seems to be."

The Prince stiffened. The elf looked at his feet and feigned boredom.

"I think it's time I introduced myself," Lombard said, "and asked you a few questions." He shoved the Omnipedia back inside Viola's saddlebags and footed it aside. He shifted so that he faced his prisoners directly. "I am Lombard, the Bandit King. I see you've heard of me, Mr. Trooper."

Sullivan nodded once, but the Prince stared back at him, his brow arched

"But you haven't, Prince Gualtero. I'm insulted. You see, I've definitely heard of you, sir. I'm a famous man myself, and yet, you haven't heard of me at all."

"He's lived on the Islands all of his life," Sullivan said. "They don't know much about the mainland at all."

"But you do," Lombard said.

"I grew up on the mainland."

"When my boys Russell and Warwick came running back to tell me that they'd seen you, I was surprised," Lombard said. "Then I asked myself, what could such an important person as Prince Gualtero be doing out in the Nuneau countryside, so far from the seashore and the Queen's city. There are no ships out here, so what could bring him here." He jerked his thumb over his shoulder toward the west. "Then I remembered that Shadow Mountain was nearby. He must have had business with the Almighties up there."

"And if I did?" Gualtero said.

"It makes no difference to me. I don't interfere in their business. 'Wouldn't want to be turned into a newt."

"You're risking that now," Gualtero said.

"Possibly, but I suspect I'm interfering in Queen Anna Marpessa's interests more than theirs. After all, she chose you, Prince, to be her consort. What would she pay to have you back safe and sound?"

The bandits grinned and chortled amongst themselves.

Lombard allowed himself an easy smile. "Let's not forget the Federation. What would your father and his knights pay to secure your freedom? You are his only son, are you not? And if you don't marry the Queen, there goes the peace treaty."

Gualtero scuffed the ground with his boot heel and looked down at the ropes that bound him to the tree trunk.

"A King's ransom twice over, that's what I can look forward to," Lombard said. "And Mr. Trooper, the last of your kind. Both nations would do anything to set you free, too. It'd be like ransoming two kings." He grinned over his shoulder at his men. "We could all retire."

"Then ransom us and be done with it," Gualtero said. "No one will begrudge you your retirement at that price."

"We could retire, but not in style," Lombard said. "And I mean to be comfortable in my dotage."

Sullivan cocked his head to the side. "So you aren't going to ransom us?"

"I'm going to ransom you both all right. I plan to draft the notes tonight and send them off with a pair of my men tomorrow early." Lombard took out the map. "It was particularly fortuitous for both of our sakes that you had this extremely precise map in your possession. It shows me that my suspicions were true and that will save us a great deal of time. I don't have to be afraid of getting lost." Then he returned the map safely to his pocket.

"What are you getting at?" Gualtero said.

"I expect you to do me a favor or two."

"What sort of favor?" Gualtero said.

"You'll find out tomorrow."

Suedama couldn't constrain his curiosity any longer. "Tell me, Prince, is Anna Marpessa as beautiful as her profile on our gold coins?"

Lombard's face lit up. "That is a good question." He enjoyed seeing Gualtero and Sullivan cringe. "Tell us about the Queen and her sisters. We hear that they're the loveliest women in all of Nuneau."

"I've seen better on the high seas," Sullivan said.

"Oh, who?"

"Thetis Megara and her maidens."

"You've seen the Sea Queen?" Lombard said. "She's said to be the most surpassing temptress in the entire hemisphere."

Suedama shifted nearer to catch every word. He was dazzled already.

"It's bad luck to see her," Quinzano said. "That's what I heard."

"Yeah, I heard that she puts the come hither on people if she likes or dislikes them too much," Acton said with a nervous glance at the darkness.

"She can put the come hither on me anytime," Suedama said. "I'd be her lackey all the days of my life, if she'd stroke my face and lay me down in her shell."

"I've heard the stories, too, but she never batted an eyelash at me," Sullivan said. "And I've had to negotiate often enough with her for safe passage through the straits."

"You're lucky then," Quinzano said.

"I suppose so," Sullivan said.

"Until now," Gualtero said, as he met Lombard's interested stare.

"So how does Anna Marpessa and her sisters compare to Thetis Megara?" Lombard said.

Both prisoners fell as silent as stones.

Lombard grins. "I guess, I shall have to see her for myself."

"She's well protected," Gualtero said. "You'll never get close to her."

"As long as I have you under my thumb, I can request her presence to dinner and she won't dare deny me." Lombard left Gualtero and Sullivan to ponder that over, while he turned to set out his bowl for his share of dinner.

5.

Viola wandered deep into the forest, following her conjured orb. She was tired and hungry and cold and there was no sign of any dwelling or settlement. She remembered some of the map she had copied and knew that there were at least three different places up ahead some distance apart from each other. One of the places had been the tomb and castle of Luzarches de Morin. The other two places were something different. One was called the Rose cottage and the other was called Hermit's Maze.

She asked the sphere to guide her toward the Castle Morin. It was commonly understood that castles contained knights or their armories. Her path would take her near Hermit's Maze, but she wasn't in the least bit interested in getting lost there. It had a tunnel at its end and she had had enough of tunnels already.

The forest made too many sounds around her for her to find rest. Although its denizens had so far shown themselves to be her allies, she couldn't shake the feeling that she was being watched by other eyes, so she moved on.

Viola stomped and stumbled after her glowing sphere, until she became sluggish and the sphere dimmed. She yawned and the sphere dimmed a little more. She stopped and wrapped her arms about herself, letting go a shiver. The sphere waited a short distance ahead, its strength fluctuating. "This is ridiculous. I have to sleep. Find me a safe place to sleep."

The sphere darted ahead with renewed vigor and she marched after it with a sigh. It disappeared around a grove of sorts. She ran after it, turning the corner, found it waiting for her within the ruins of an old building. She couldn't tell in the darkness whether it had been a manor or a castle, but it had been made of sturdy granite and vines hung thick around it. She could smell honeysuckle. A nightingale sung nearby. The sphere showed her a deep recess just above the old, overgrown flagstones.

"Perfect," she said with another yawn. She climbed into it and curled up inside. The alcove was bone-achingly cold and hard, so she cocooned herself inside her riding coat. As she pulled her head inside and tucked in her feet at the other end, she closed her eyes upon the sphere. "Good night," she said.

The sphere popped like a bubble and night filled the alcove.

Viola awoke to the sound of hens chatting amongst themselves. She listened to them talk about the weather, point out insects to one another, and scratch at the ground. She eased herself toward the opening and peered out.

"I expected rain this morning," a red hen was saying. Her yellow eye was cocked toward a stalk of corn.

"Me, too," said a white hen, "but look at it now. Clear as a bell. 'Makes one want to just sit and bask."

Viola looked beyond the hens. These were indeed ruins. She leaned out of her alcove even further and saw towering walls, ragged with time and neglect, and the dark gray husk of what had been an abbey. They were picturesque in themselves, but not as picturesque as the sprawling garden occupying every open slot of soil. The lots were all marked with homely little painted signs: corn, pumpkin, squash and grape vines, green beans, tomatoes, eggplant, an herb garden, berry bushes, potatoes, everything a farmer could want. Somebody lived here. Somebody who could help her.

She climbed out of the alcove and landed softly on the ground. The hens stopped their chatter and looked at her.

"Morning," Viola said.

"Yes, it is, a fine one, too," the red hen said.

"Whose garden is this?" Viola said.

"Nobody's," the black hen said. She moved on quickly into the garden.

"Oh," Viola said. "Is it yours?"

"No, not ours," said the white hen. "We just keep it clean." She followed the black hen.

"You're lost, aren't you?" the red hen said.

"Yes."

"Well, you won't be found if you stay here, lass." The red hen seemed eager to catch up with her girlfriends and her girlfriends seemed anxious that she get away from the Faerie.

"Someone planted this garden."

"Someone did, but I'll not be blamed for telling you." She scurried into the corn patch with her friends.

"Thanks for nothing," Viola muttered. Dusting off her trousers and stretching her legs, she ambled toward the abbey ruins. She rounded a crumbling wall before she saw the slender stream of smoke rising from its chimney. Someone did live there and they were home that moment.

Viola ran around the overgrown corner and stopped short. A crooked sign greeted her.

BE YE WARNED. THIS BE CURSED GROUND. GET THEE HENCE UPON YONDER TRAIL.

The sign's paint was faded. It had been a long time since anyone had maintained it. Viola pushed on. She entered the abbey courtyard and stopped short again.

Another sign hung from a low bough directly in her path.

HEED THIS ADMONITION: DANGER AWAITS. HIE THEE AWAY AT ONCE.

Viola gritted her teeth. Saire had told her frequently over the past few months that if she chose to stay at Shadow Mountain, she could easily assume the full rank of Witch and would be permitted to pick out her dragon mount-companion from the new litter of dragon pups. She had enough power to deal with most threats. Straightening her shoulders, she ducked beneath the sign and passed two more crooked ones that barked, *GO BACK* and *NO TRESPASSING!*

Beneath a dense tapestry of dripping vines, stood a stout little door. Another sign that said simply *GO AWAY* peeked out at her, but she pushed the vines aside and gripped the knocker hard as she banged it against the door.

The window beside the door cracked open. "Can't you read?" snapped a male voice.

"In several languages," Viola replied.

"Ha! And what good does it do you when apparently you can't read a simple sign."

"I can too read your signs..."

"Then why are you disturbing me?"

"Because I need your help."

"Go find some valiant knight."

"I don't know any."

"Then you're out of luck, aren't you, miss?" He shut the window.

Viola bit her tongue and beat again on the door with her fist and her foot.

The window opened wider this time. "Stop that racket before someone hears you."

"Then help me." She heard him sigh. "My guardians have been captured by bandits at the Two Brothers."

"You didn't lead them here, did you?"

"No, Vandin showed me a secret way out and I took rabbit trails all the way here. My guardians are important men..."

"Bah!"

"And we have to help them escape."

"If they were stupid enough to get captured, let them pay the consequences." He started to shut the window again.

"No!" Viola grabbed the window and pulled. "It is Gualtero Bainbridge and Sullivan Trooper. They are being held by bandits."

"Then they are worth their weight in gold."

"I expect so."

"A king's ransom each."

"Most likely. Will you help me, hermit?"

"Will there be a reward for their rescue?"

"I expect so."

The hermit disappeared from the window and Viola heard the bolt draw back. The door swung open.

"In that case it would be worth my while to help you."

Viola peered up at a tall, gaunt chap whose dingy red cap perched crooked atop his narrow head and dingy brownish gray and olive clothing hung from his body like sails lacking a stiff breeze. A very long, formerly bluish muffler trailed its scraggly ends down his front and back, and the fat, rounded tips of his shoes poked out from beneath his trousers. The gray man was almost rectangular. Even his face was angular, with small black eyes that burned with inexhaustible impatience, full of crooks and sharp, awkward angles, from his pointy ears to his thin white mouth and his sharp, narrow chin.

"You are a *redcap*?" Viola said.

"Not completely," retorted the hermit as though vaguely insulted.

"Then what precisely are you?"

His crooked mouth took on a crooked smirk. "I bet you're sorry you knocked now."

"That depends. What sort of Unseelie are you?"

"A retired one. These days I spend my time as a conservator-cum-curator. I have quite a collection." He closed the door behind her and gestured down the narrow corridor where light filled a room at the end.

"You have a hoard then."

"A hoard? A 'Collection', thank you very much. I am not some mere gold-counting miserable Troll – although I do have a collection of gold coins that would be the envy of any king if I say so myself. I collect rare and historic antiquities from all over the known and unknown world. Perhaps you have heard of me – *Phineas Brock, Unseelie Redcap Bogle - and Antiquarian.* I am in the Registry."

"I have not read the Registry, but I think they keep one in the library at Shadow Mountain."

They entered an enormous hall where once banquets and fetes had been held, but currently, the place served as a central collection space. It stood crammed in miraculously stately order with statues of bronze, gold, alabaster, and marble from more past and current cultures than she could recall.

"You should open a museum, Mr. Brock," Viola said.

"You think so?" Phineas Brock strutted down the aisle, produced a feather duster and worked it as they proceeded.

"Indeed, such wonders as these should be shared with the world."

"These are just a fraction of my collection. I rotate them once a month. It would take me ten years to rotate through my entire collection of statuary alone."

"That **is** an enormous collection."

"I shall bear your suggestion in mind, Miss-?"

She stopped to gape at the stained glass ceiling. "Viola Marpessa."

Phineas Brock stopped and turned. His black eyes sparked. "MARPESSA?"

Viola cringed at his tone. "No, Marquesa!"

"No, you said **Marpessa** and there is only one family I know of with that name and I know all of their names." He rattled them off. "Anna, Carissa, and Olwen." He fixed a piercing stare upon her as he smirked. "You know about Shadow Mountain on an obviously intimate level or you wouldn't mention that they even had a library so casually. You were traveling with Gualtero Bainbridge and Sullivan Trooper, who are not your run of the mill errand boys. And you just blurted out that your name was Viola Marpessa." Phineas Brock folded his thin arms over his chest and tapped his foot. "Long-lost sister, eh?"

"You should take up detection." Viola shuffled her feet. "I am the Faerie Queen's first sister, but I was raised on Shadow Mountain."

"Whom by?"

"Saire the Ancient."

"A respected sage." Phineas nodded.

"It was time for me to come home, so Anna sent Gualtero and Sullivan to fetch me and educate me about Court life en route."

"Now it looks like you'll have to fetch them back, eh, Princess?" Phineas jogged her in the arm and set off, laughing. "Such good fortune I'm having today."

Rubbing her arm, Viola sighed and followed him down the length of the room, but stopped beside an immense table. Her jaw popped open. "Good heavens!"

Phineas Brock came back and stood beaming at his gemstone and jewelry collection set out on spotless velvet trays. "Exquisite aren't they? The wealth of countless monarchs. The genius of forgotten artisans. Of course, this is only a fraction of my collection."

"Where did you get them all?" Viola leaned forward for a better view of the crowns and tiaras lined up down the center of the table.

"From traders."

"Where did they get them?"

"All over the place. Some of these were plundered and then I bought them to keep them from being broken up and melted down. Some came from gravesites and tombs forgotten by time. All of it is safe here now and will continue to be safe for all posterity."

"That's nice to hear." Viola gaped at the scepters and suits of armor, kept to a blinding polish. "How do you keep this place safe?"

"Well, for one, it's in the dreaded Enchanted Forest. Two, it's hidden and only I know where it is, or did until today." Phineas Brock gave her a quick sharp look.

Viola smiled innocently.

"And three, I've let it be known that a horrible curse lies upon this treasure."

"Does one?"

"Yes, actually. Therefore my collection remains intact. You should see the collection of rare books and historical documents I keep in my library. I'll bet Master Sorcerer Macy doesn't have its equal."

"How long have you been collecting?"

"Over nine hundred years."

"Their collection goes back two thousand years."

"Hmmm..." Phineas Brock headed toward a doorway. "Permit me to collect my effects and then we'll see about making ourselves useful to your illustrious friends." He tramped up a flight of stairs and appeared in the minstrels' gallery overlooking the main collection hall. Muttering to himself, he tucked clothing and various necessities into a drab knapsack.

Viola looked into one of many bronze pots lining the wall. Each pot stood filled to the brim with gold coins from many realms. She examined a few of them and recognized none of them. So she turned to one of several stout little chests on a side table and peeked inside. Emeralds filled it. The next chest contained rubies and the ones beyond that held sapphires in a variety of colors and so on to other remarkable stones.

Phineas Brock stomped downstairs, reached into the coin pot nearest him and pouched several handfuls of golden Faerie Ducros.

"You must be the richest man in the world," Viola said.

"Richest Bogle in the world you mean, and yes, I probably am." Phineas Brock tied his pouch shut and buried it deep in his trouser pocket. "We should be off."

Viola rejoined him.

Phineas Brock gave the place a last fond look and turned his back on it.

Once they both stood outside, he locked the door and muttered a spell. As they walked away, the forest closed in around the old abbey until it disappeared completely from sight.

As they passed the hens beside the garden fence, he said, "Look after the garden for me. I should be back in about five days and then we'll see about having us a real harvest feast, eh? Ladies?"

"Yes, sirree, Mr. Brock," said the white hen. "Have a safe journey."

They even waved their wings at the Unseelie Redcap Bogle as he headed into the Enchanted Forest.

"Do we go back to the Two Brothers and get my protectors?" Viola said.

"Nope."

"Why not?"

"Because for one thing those bandits will have moved on already. Bandits seldom stay in any one place for long. Don't worry we'll find them and start negotiations. But first I need to find us a good horse. The bandits have horses and since I don't have your wings, I'll need a horse to keep up with them or to get away from them at a moment's notice."

His long legs threatened to leave her behind. No matter how quickly she walked, she fell behind. Sighing, she invoked her wings and kept pace with him, flitting just behind him on the trail.

6.

Lombard and his men broke camp. Within minutes everything had been stowed again in the gypsy wagon or in their saddle packs.

Lombard drew out Viola's Omnipedia again and puzzled over it – a very plain book with blank pages, but he couldn't shake the intuition that there was something more to it than that. Perhaps the young woman meant to use it as a journal. It might still be valuable or useful, so he tucked it in his surcoat pocket.

Sullivan and Gualtero exchanged looks. They had hoped he would throw the Omnipedia aside. That much information in Lombard's cunning hands could be devastating, but at least he hadn't figured out what it was yet.

Lombard surveyed their encampment. Soon the Two Brothers would look as deserted as before. Still, he couldn't shake the impression that the birds and animals were watching them out of more than idle curiosity. He turned to his hostages.

"I'm sending two of my men off to Nuneau with my terms and proof that I do indeed have you in my protective custody," Lombard said, "but in the meantime, the both of you will be doing me a small favor."

"And what would that be?" Gualtero said.

"You and the Elf will go into Badenoch."

"What?" Sullivan yelped.

Several birds scattered.

Lombard smiled. "I see you've heard of Badenoch."

"Are you kidding?" Sullivan said.

"No."

"Why in blazes do you want us to go into Badenoch?" Gualtero said.

"Because I don't want to go in myself."

"What is there?" Gualtero said.

"A treasure beyond all treasures and you will get it for me, or I will leave you and the Elf there for all eternity, ransom or no ransom."

"And if we refuse?" Gualtero said.

"We'll take you there and toss you over the walls anyway. King Arvid won't even set foot there, so you'll never get out."

Sullivan started hyperventilating. "Not Badenoch, not the Castle of One Hundred Deaths."

"You can't be serious," Gualtero said.

"Oh, but I am. If you do get this thing for me, I will set you free even before your beloved young Queen pays your ransom." Lombard moved on.

"What could he want so badly there?" Gualtero muttered.

"I don't know and I don't want to find out," Sullivan said. "We have to get loose before he can get us there."

Gualtero nodded.

Lombard's men came for them, picked them up and, stowing them inside the gypsy wagon, bound their legs and arms nice and snug and shut them inside.

"Well, at least they didn't gag us," Sullivan said.

Gualtero grimaced.

"What's wrong? 'Rope cutting off your circulation?" Sullivan said.

"No. Itch." Gualtero squirmed until he could rub the itchy spot against the wall.

At a village on the edge of the Enchanted Woods, Phineas Brock bought lunch and purchased a roan pinto stallion named Meadowlark because he had a lucky pink hoof. In the course of conversing with the locals, he found out that a band of gypsies with a wagon had passed through. In itself, there was nothing unusual about that, but when the local mentioned that the band had consisted strictly of men Phineas Brock's ears keened.

"They had a wagon you say?" Phineas Brock said.

"A gypsy artisan wagon with pots and pans swinging from it."

"Which way did they go?" Phineas Brock tempered his intensity with a smiling remark, "I need a new camp skillet and cups."

"Directly north across the meadowlands. They must have been heading for the northern trade route for the summer."

"Indeed. Thank you. Perhaps I can catch up with them before they reach the hill country." Phineas Brock tipped his redcap at them and turned away, drawing Viola along with him.

"'You think that was them?" Viola led their new horse alongside.

Meadowlark listened to every word they said.

"It had to be. When gypsies travel, they travel as a family." Phineas Brock stopped and checked the new saddle and then climbed into it. He leaned down and held out his hand. "Let's give your wings a rest, shall we?"

Viola took his hand and Phineas Brock pulled her up behind him. They set off at an easy canter out across the meadowlands.

Queen Anna Marpessa, lovely supreme maiden among the Faeries of Nuneau, sat at the head of a long table lined with her ministers and emissaries. They chatted and bickered while she perused several formal documents. Rings decorated each of her fingers; an exquisite bejeweled golden torque surrounding her pale neck, bejeweled earrings hung low from her earlobes, and a delicate tiara to accent her elaborately arranged soft blond locks. She wore a gown of pale blue and a robe of white, both embroidered with gold silk on the borders. As long as she flourished so would Nuneau and that day she radiated well being and serious concentration.

At last her blue eyes rose. Her ministers and emissaries fell silent. "This canal proposal sounds worthy, but will it not drain a marshland and leave homeless the many beings that live there?"

"It will have an impact upon the marshes, Your Majesty, but it will enable the farmers in that region to irrigate their crops year round," said her Agriculture Minister.

"Are these farmers really so desperate?" Anna Marpessa said.

"They get by," he said.

"But this would help them," she said.

"It would immensely."

"But what of all those beings who cannot speak for themselves? The egrets? The marsh rats, turtles, snakes, and fish? Are they to be deprived of their only home and left to suffer and die?"

"Birds can fly, snakes can crawl," he said.

"But the fish are doomed." Anna Marpessa held the documents back out to him. "I will not authorize this unless a balance can be maintained between the farmers and the humblest citizens of my land. Go back and do another survey."

He inclined his head and accepted the documents again. "I will do my best to find a harmonious solution."

"Balance is the key, my good gents," Anna Marpessa said. "However much it may benefit one group or another, I will not see anything done that unduly harms another or deprives it of its rightful living space. We are not the only beings upon this land."

They all bowed. "Yes, your Majesty."

Thimbleby, her steward and all-purpose man about the palace, ventured forward into the sunny council chamber. He peered back once and then bowed to his Queen. "Begging pardon, Madame, but two young ruffians are here to see you."

"Ruffians?" Anna Marpessa half-frowned and half-smiled.

"They say they have important news for you concerning your Betrothed and the esteemed Sullivan Trooper." Thimbleby looked uneasy.

Anna Marpessa turned serious. "Then by all means, show them in." She sat back in her gilded chair and put on a façade of absolute calm.

Her ministers folded their hands over their papers or sat back and drummed their fingers, a useful façade of mild impatience for their visitors.

Despite their mission and their exhaustion after three hard days of riding, Russell and Warwick could not hide their eagerness. They pushed past Thimbleby and rushed down the length of the chamber until they stood mere feet from the seated monarch. There they gaped for a moment.

Anna Marpessa smiled as patiently as the situation merited. "My man Thimbleby says you have some important news for me concerning two dear friends of mine."

"Oh yes!" Russell rummaged through his pouch.

Warwick stood dazzled by her beauty and grace. His grin frozen upon his face.

Russell dug out a sealed document, smoothed out the wrinkles and held it out to her. "This comes from our Master."

"What are your names?" Anna Marpessa said as she took the document and turned it over to break the seal.

"Russell and Warwick Masham," Russell said.

Warwick was useless. Russell prodded him.

"What?" Warwick said.

Russell shook his head at him.

"And who is your Master?" She took her time opening the slender document.

"One you must appreciate," Russell said.

Anna Marpessa cocked a brow. "Must? Who is this man?"

Russell drew himself up to his full height. "Lombard, King of the Bandits."

Anna Marpessa froze and then perused the document. She stood. "I want proof."

Russell nudged Warwick.

Warwick dug in his pouch and produced two gold rings with a braid of hair looped around each one. "We took these from the redoubtable gents so that you would believe." He placed them in her outstretched hand.

"What is amiss?" said her Minister of Defense.

"Lombard has kidnapped Prince Gualtero and Sullivan Trooper." Anna Marpessa studied the rings closely.

"That cannot be," her Minister of the Guilds said.

"I am afraid so. This is the engagement band I gave to Gualtero and this is the ring that Sullivan received from Master Sorcerer Macy the day he left Shadow Mountain. There can be no mistaking." Anna Marpessa laid the rings and their locks of hair upon the table. "Your Master says that terms are forthcoming. When shall I receive his terms?"

"When he summons you into his presence in seven days' time," Russell said. Her darkening glance intimidated him.

"And in the meantime, what am I to do?" Anna Marpessa said.

"Consider how much the Prince is worth to you and inform others who might be interested in the gentlemen's welfare so that they too might consult their treasurers in advance of the reckoning day," Russell said.

"And if we mount a rescue expedition?" the Minister of Defense said.

At least that stupid grin had disappeared from Warwick's face. "Then Lombard will make sure that both the Prince and the Elf become lost to the ages and he knows precisely how to do that too."

"We might keep you hostage ourselves," the Minister of Defense added.

"We will be content then to wait for our Master to reclaim us, and he will when he claims his ransom from you and the Island Federation," Russell said.

"But what of the Princess Vi-?" one of the Ministers blurted.

Anna Marpessa silenced him with a look. "Go back to Lombard and tell him this: If both men are harmed in any fashion, not only will he receive nothing from us, but I shall join with the Island Federation and ask King Arvid of the Wolf Trolls for his assistance in hunting every last one of you down. Lombard will end his days in my prison if he does not heed my warning."

Russell and Warwick bowed.

"I shall tell him, Ma'am," Russell said.

Both young men fled the palace after that. Fearful of being followed, they disappeared down winding alleys and hid out until night. Then they ventured out of the seaside city into the forest to the north, collected their mounts and headed northwest to the rendezvous just south of Badenoch.

As soon as they were gone from her council chamber, Anna Marpessa sat down. "They did not mention Viola. What has become of my sister?"

Between Phineas Brock's natural born cunning and Viola's special, honed skills, they found the bandits and trailed them north. Lombard had some enchanted Faerie rope or they would have been able to free Gualtero and Sullivan in the dead of night and flee for Nuneau. He also had Viola's Omnipedia and she saw him puzzling over its blank pages from time to time before restoring it again to his coat pocket. If he figured out what her book could do, they would be in a jungle of trouble.

As it was, the situation was alarming enough. The night Phineas Brock and Viola crept upon the camp and crawled beneath the wagon to untie Gualtero and Sullivan they found out why Lombard was heading north. After terse introductions to Phineas, Gualtero and Sullivan said that they were being taken to Badenoch, and that Lombard wanted them to go inside and bring back something. Phineas Brock took on a strange look and chewed on his lips.

"Whatever it is," Sullivan whispered, "he's willing to cut us loose if we can get it out to him, so it must be incredibly valuable."

"Yes, it would have to be," Phineas Brock said as he struggled with the knots.

"Why? Do you know what it could be?" Gualtero said.

Phineas Brock scowled instead. "This rope is enchanted. There is no way we'll be able to get you loose."

Gualtero cursed under his breath.

"We'll have to try another way at another time." Already, Phineas Brock was pushing himself back out through the dense grass.

"Hopefully before we reach Badenoch right?" Sullivan said.

"We'll see," Phineas Brock said under his breath.

"We will," Viola said, and she followed Phineas Brock back out into the night.

They crept well out of harm's way before veering off onto the course that would take them back to their camp hidden behind a knoll in the sea of grass.

"What is it that Lombard wants at Badenoch?" Viola said.

Phineas Brock fed more peat onto their fire and glanced at Meadowlark. Faerie horses tended to be very intelligent creatures. This one was no different from the rest of his breed, but it originated from the Enchanted Forest. Phineas noticed that he watched everything and missed nothing, although as yet the stallion kept his own counsel.

Viola squatted down across the fire from Phineas Brock. "You know precisely what it is, don't you?"

Phineas Brock stretched out atop his bedroll beside the campfire, folded his arms under his head and gazed up at the crowded night sky. Sometimes, it was said, if you looked really carefully, you could see the Great Intercessor Ultima, as thin as gauze, crossing the night sky in her sleep.

"You could trust me to stand alone amid your treasures, but you can't trust me with the truth? Is that it?" Viola settled down cross-legged and spread out her bedroll too.

The night wind made the sea of grass roar like an ocean, whispering with its millions of eyes in the night. With no mountains nearby, Viola felt exposed and afraid in the open expanses. Without so much as one stout tree to hold it up, the night sky might fall on them. She made herself lie down and look skywards.

Phineas Brock rolled over on his side and looked her in the eye. "I had thought it was only an object of legend, but apparently Lombard believes it's real enough that he is willing to risk the lives of your protectors to get it."

"What is it?"

"A wish fulfilling entity known as a *jinn*." Phineas Brock sat up and scrutinized her. "I can see by the look on your face that you have heard of them."

Viola sat up straight again. "I have heard of the jinn, but not up north."

"So they are real?"

"Yes, and formidable. I wouldn't want to cross one on a bad day – or any day for that matter." She lay down again on her back and gazed up into the night sky.

Phineas Brock frowned. "Are you sure you haven't heard the legend of a great lost treasure, chief of which is a sealed bottle containing a powerful wish fulfilling *Jinniyah*?"

Viola looked at him and shook her head.

"For ages, the location of this treasure remained undiscovered. It became as I termed it: 'legendary', something you only daydreamed about." Phineas Brock had turned completely earnest. There was even wonder skirting about his expression. He gazed off into the night sky for a moment, before his gaze reverted to Viola's rosy face in the campfire light. "Now it appears that it existed all along."

"And at Badenoch of all places – actually that makes sense," Viola said.

Phineas Brock nodded with her. "What better place to hide the greatest treasure in history than in a place everyone goes out of their way to avoid?"

"Even the fearless King Arvid of the Wolf Trolls gives the place a wide berth," Viola said, "and Sorcerer Alison the Terrible and his brother Ivan the Dark won't set foot near the place."

"Well, it does have a reputation," Phineas Brock said.

Lombard sat beside his campfire, one of two in their encampment, and gazed over at his two prisoners. They had been acting strange earlier, but now they sat quiet again, if watchful. The enchanted ropes held them fast. They weren't going anywhere unless he willed it.

Sighing, Lombard stretched out a little more beside his campfire, tossed on another peat brick, and folded his arms across his chest. Still, he couldn't go to sleep. Half of his men already slept on their bedrolls under the sky, four of them had guard duty, but the rest loitered around the other fire finishing off dinner and talking about their plans. Since he had told them that they were bound for Badenoch, they had avoided even mentioning the place, but it consumed their thoughts as much as it consumed his.

A little distraction was in order. Lombard took that peculiar little book out of his pocket again and flipped through its immaculate pages. Why would anyone carry a blank book? It might have been intended for a journal or a diary, but there wasn't even a name scribbled on the front page revealing the name of the young Faerie woman it had belonged to. He had noticed though that whenever he took the book out Gualtero and Sullivan did their best not to look all that interested and that they relaxed visibly whenever he shoved it into his pocket again.

Lombard turned the book over in his hand, examining it as he had several times already. "What sort of book are you anyway?"

The front cover struggled against his grip. He shifted his finger and it flung open. There on the front pages, in elegant print, appeared the words *Omnipedia, First Edition, Shadow Mountain*.

"Hello!" Astonished, Lombard turned the page and found the succinct answer.

'The Omnipedia is a book of answers. Ask a question, however mundane, and the answer shall appear upon the ensuing pages. If however, you are attempting to cheat on a test, the Omnipedia will provide only WRONG answers, so don't say you weren't warned.'

The rest of the book was still blank. Lombard grinned and closed it. "Omnipedia, eh? What shall I ask first?" He looked toward Gualtero and Sullivan. Neither looked happy. "Who is your owner?" Lombard said.

The book flew open. *'Current or true owner?'*

"True," Lombard said.

The page flicked over on its own. *'Viola Marpessa.'*

Lombard felt a flush of excitement. Marpessa. "And who is she?"

The book closed and re-opened to the same page. *'Viola Marpessa is Anna Marpessa's first sister.'*

"That's it?" Lombard watched the book close again. "What all can you tell me about her?"

The book reopened. Quietly astonished, Lombard read in dry, succinct terms about her upbringing with her guardian Saire the Ancient on Shadow Mountain, her general education , and how she set out with Gualtero Bainbridge and Sullivan Trooper to be reunited with her sisters in Nuneau. It omitted discussing her particular magical skills though.

When the book closed again, Lombard said, "Where is she now?"

The book flew open. The pages he had seen before were blank again, except for one remark, *'Do you really think I am going to tell you?'* Then the book slammed shut.

Lombard flinched and then grinned. "What a remarkable treasure you are."

The book popped open briefly. *'Thank you.'* It shut again.

"Is she planning to help her friends escape?" he asked.

The book opened as before. *'You know better than to ask that.'* And it shut again.

"Fair enough. You're loyal. I respect that." Lombard came up with a new question. "Is the Jinn bottle at Badenoch?"

'Yes, but I wouldn't go there if I were you.' The book remained open. It wanted its admonition to soak in.

"So Badenoch is as bad as its reputation?"

The page flicked over. *'Worse.'*

"Will my plan succeed?"

The page flicked over. *'I am not an oracle. I can only state facts.'*

"Can you tell me then everything and I mean EVERYTHING I need to know about Badenoch? It's terrors, its design, anything and everything."

The book closed. Lombard would have sworn that he heard it sigh and then it opened, its pages flying as words and diagrams filled every page and then it returned to the very first page. There was one last admonition:

'This is one case where knowledge won't necessarily save you. Don't say you weren't warned.' Then it flicked over to the next page. *'Badenoch Castle, its environs, its architecture, its history, and its rare fauna.'*

Lombard made himself comfortable and read well into the night.

Unable to shake the feeling that they were being shadowed, but unable to corner their shadows, Lombard and his men proceeded north until two days later they stood gazing up at the enormous slope leading to Badenoch Castle. It was a comfort that the day was so bright and clear and the hills covered with high grass and wildflowers, the sort of pastoral beauty that painters reveled in capturing. If only that dark, hulking pile of malevolence called Badenoch didn't sit coiled atop the hill, seeing everything and generally spoiling the view. The bandits stood in a line taking it in.

"Go in, get out, and clear out. Don't even bother to build a fire for tea afterwards," was Quinzano's verdict.

De Vere stood beside him, nodding. Normally, nothing intimidated him, but when Lombard met his protégé's glance, De Vere added, "I wouldn't go in there for all the gold in the world."

"Luckily, none of us have too," Lombard said. "Bring our gentlemen here."

While his men watched, Lombard set out a collection of ropes, climbing hooks, a pair of crowbars, hammers, and two long daggers, Montargis and Hawtrey brought Gualtero and Sullivan out of the gypsy wagon.

Lombard cut the ropes binding their wrists. "Welcome to Badenoch, gents."

Sullivan took one look at the vile place and closed his eyes. He knew a few protection spells and he was invoking every last one of them if they would help him survive that place.

Gualtero had no invocations. He took a deep breath and steeled himself. 'My destiny lies elsewhere,' he repeated in his heart as he thought of home, his parents, and of Anna waiting for him in Nuneau.

Lombard pressed a folded piece of paper in each of their hands. "I drew up these maps. If you can avoid the patrolling terrors, the random weaponry, and the insidious traps along the way, the route I marked out should bring you to this chamber deep in the heart of Badenoch."

Sullivan and Gualtero examined their maps.

"All this for treasure," Gualtero sighed, as he stowed his map in his pocket.

"WE are not going to the treasury," Lombard said.

His men reacted.

"You aren't going in there too?" Acton cried.

"I am." Lombard tucked a third map in his own pocket and began dividing up the equipment between the three of them. "I figure this to be a three man operation."

Gualtero and Sullivan exchanged looks as they prepared for the hike.

"And if you don't return?" Kelyng said.

"If Badenoch claims me, Scudamore and Quinzano are your men. Do as they say. They have our band's interests at heart." Lombard grinned, slapped Acton on the shoulder and set off up the slope. "See you later, gents."

Gualtero and Sullivan followed him, looking back at the stunned bandits.

Quinzano propped his hands on his hips. "If someone would be so good as to start us a healthy blaze, I could use some coffee."

By sheer luck, dumb luck actually, Acton and Gripwell came back from their wood gathering mission with a prisoner in tow – a young Faerie woman with long golden brown hair, dressed in plain clothes. They made a big show of their captive, but Quinzano and Scudamore in particular found her lack of alarm disconcerting.

"Following the Prince, eh, Princess Viola?" Suedama said. He jumped at the opportunity to be the one to bind her wrists and ankles. "Lombard has your book."

"Friends don't abandon friends," she said.

Done, Suedama stroked her calves through her trousers as he sat back. She rewarded him with a kick to his chin.

"Do that again and I'll turn you into a slug," she said without anger.

"Steer clear of her," Quinzano said. "Lombard said that she grew up on Shadow Mountain, so she can probably do it."

Rubbing his chin, Suedama gave her a serious look and backed off.

Quinzano's warning was enough to cause the others to keep a wary distance from her, but he stooped down in front of her. "You must be powerful or you wouldn't be so bored with your predicament."

Viola smiled.

"You let them catch you," Quinzano said.

Viola kept smiling.

"Why? Or would it hurt to ask?"

Her expression turned earnest. "I am here to see that my friends come to no harm."

"'Tis too late for that, Princess. Our bold leader has gone up to Badenoch with them."

"I know, but all the same, I am here for their sake." Viola's gaze reverted to the dark place atop the hill.

Quinzano sighed. There was something more to her presence, but she didn't seem inclined to reveal anything more, so he left her alone and started pacing, all the while clutching his good luck piece.

7

If the place hadn't been so blasted spooky, the three men would have thought it strange that its front gates remained unguarded. More than that, the gates stood WIDE OPEN, simply waiting for fresh prey. They peered into the courtyard for a long moment.

"It looks clear," Lombard said.

"What about the booby traps?" Gualtero eyed the flagstones before them.

"There aren't any out here, besides I have them all marked out on your maps," Lombard said. "Those are the least of our concerns."

Sullivan and Gualtero opened their maps and began studying the route Lombard marked out. Every trap and how to avoid it was listed.

Gualtero mused over the list of roving hazards though. "Man-eating demons, phantoms, man-eating bugs – lovely. Hallucination oubliettes?!"

"What in blazes are those?" Sullivan said.

"Places where if you aren't strong of mind, you begin hallucinating and become lost forever or until something terrible finds you and makes a phantom out of you," Lombard said.

Sullivan groaned and beat his forehead against the gate. "I'd rather face an angry pack of flea ridden Werewolves."

"So the phantoms are all the people who trespassed here?" Gualtero said.

"Some," Lombard said. "According to your friend's Omnipedia, Badenoch acts like some kind of magnet for all the malignant spirits adrift in the world. It soaks in all that evil and uses it against any mortal being that dares disturb its quiet."

"Well, at least we know there won't be any rats in there," Sullivan sighed.

"The rats have too much sense," grumbled Gualtero.

"Ready to go in, gents?" Lombard said.

"Do we really have a choice?" Gualtero said.

"Not once we pass the gate," Lombard said. "It's part of the curse. We won't be able to get back out until we either get what we came for, thereby warping the curse or…"

"…Don't come out at all. I get it," Gualtero said. He glanced toward the white clouds coasting across the crisp ultramarine sky. "Hold faith for me and I shall return."

Lombard frowned. "What was that about?"

"A wish and a prayer," Gualtero said. He took a deep breath. "Let's get this over with." He stepped out into the courtyard.

Lombard and Sullivan flanked him. All three froze at once.

"Ohhhh…I can feel it," Sullivan said. "Badenoch is watching us."

Lombard nodded and shuddered once. "Let's not give it time to come up with a strategy."

Instead of heading for the grand entrance that had lured too many adventurers to their doom already, Lombard headed for a low doorway far to the end of Badenoch. Perhaps it had been a servants' entrance in sunnier times, but no one could remember when Badenoch had ever been anything but a terrible, haunted place.

At the door, Lombard stopped and had Gualtero and Sullivan shift to the side. "First of many traps," he said and then he kicked the door open and sprung aside immediately. An array of lethal barbed missiles streaked out past them, shining with bloodthirsty intent in the sunlight before lodging in the stable wall with several deep thuds.

"Actually, I could use that dagger." Gualtero pried one of the missiles out of the wood and rubbed it against his trouser leg before sheathing it under his belt. He pried out two more and handed one each to Lombard and Sullivan.

Lombard gave him a long puzzled look as he accepted the dagger. "If you decide that court life isn't for you, would you consider joining my band?"

Gualtero arched his brow. "Life as a bandit rover?"

Lombard nodded.

"I'd rather be at the helm of my corsair, but thanks for the offer," Gualtero said with a brief grin.

Lombard reached into his rucksack and took out a battered old torch stump. "It has seen better days, but it still serves. Give us some light, old son."

The torch stump sparked up and gave off a healthy blaze. Only then did Lombard step inside. Gualtero and Sullivan followed after casting long looks at Badenoch's deep, dark recessed windows.

Sullivan propped the door open with several loose bricks. When he turned about he saw Lombard hand Gualtero a large spool of string.

"Tie that to the door knob, so we can find our way back out," Lombard said, "and unspool it as we go along."

"Right." Gualtero tied the end several times over around the cold knob and gave it a hard pull. "Only a tornado could undo this one."

"And into the belly of the beast we go." As though the floor might not bear his weight, Lombard crept along holding his torch ahead.

Gualtero and Sullivan followed his steps precisely. Already they felt another presence about them.

Only they didn't know that it was Phineas Brock with his invisibility cap pulled low over his brow. It didn't exactly render him completely invisible. Actually it camouflaged him, causing him to blend in with the shadows or Badenoch's cold, meager light, but it enabled him to follow without being readily discovered.

Phineas Brock didn't like being there any more than Gualtero or Sullivan, but his concern overrode his fear: If Lombard found the infamous legendary jinniyah, who knows what sort of disasters he might unleash? Viola had agreed to his plan at once. She let herself be captured so that the bandits would think she was entirely alone, just another devoted servant girl, and Phineas Brock could sneak in with Lombard. It bothered him more than it did Viola to leave her at the mercy of such ruffians, but between her calm assurances and Meadowlark finally speaking up to say that he would rescue Viola if they attempted to hurt her, he braced himself for his misadventure.

So while Viola set off to intercept one of the bandits and Meadowlark shadowed her, Phineas Brock took out his special cap that he usually used to scout out rare antiquities without being discovered, brushed off the lint and settled it firmly on his head in place of his dingy red cap. He blurred into his surroundings immediately.

Now he followed the three men into the depths of Badenoch and tried not to whistle away his fear.

Somehow Lombard knew where all the traps were and foiled each of them, from the swinging axes and the false floors over the oubliettes with spikes - and that was just on the ground floor. Phineas Brock caught a glimpse of a map when Gualtero stopped with Sullivan to verify their location. Evidently they still had a whole labyrinth of corridors and antechambers to negotiate before they reached the forgotten chamber with its prized relic. This could take hours.

At the end of the low corridor though, Lombard stopped and extinguished his torch with a wave of his hand.

Gualtero and Sullivan drew up close behind him and peered over his shoulders into an octagon shaped hallway lined with several stout doors, all of which were shut as though they never intended to open, and a wide stairwell leading up into darkness. Stillness occupied that space and yet the two lanterns on either side of the stairwell glowed as though they had been freshly lit.

"What's wrong?" Gualtero said.

"This isn't on my map." Lombard took it out and studied it as his frown deepened.

"Could it be one of those hallucination oubliettes?" Sullivan said.

"Either that or the house is re-arranging itself to confuse us," Lombard said.

"Excuse me?" Sullivan said.

"It's just the effect of the hallucination oubliette. We should be able to walk directly through it to the door beyond."

Lombard stepped out into the open, looking every which way, and stopped, looking up. "Odd."

"What's odd?" Gualtero said.

Sullivan looked up with them. "There are doors up there, but no landings. They open onto empty space."

"Hallucination oubliette indeed," Gualtero said.

"The longer we linger the stronger its spell becomes." Lombard moved ahead and tripped on the stairwell. "This isn't supposed to be real." He kicked it.

Gualtero knocked on the banister. "It's real enough."

"This can't be possible." Lombard held his map open under the light.

"Unfortunately it is all too possible," said an irritated male behind them.

They jumped and turned about in time to see a gaunt, sour-faced gray man in drab clothing appear with a blue cap in his hand.

"What are you?" Lombard reached for one of his daggers.

"I beg your pardon, but I am a 'who' not a 'what'," he said as he folded up the blue cap and tucked it inside his frock coat. He donned a dingy red cap.

"Phineas Brock is my name, and no, I am not one of Badenoch's surprises. We have a mutual acquaintance, I believe, Viola Marpessa."

"You're with her?" Gualtero looked past Phineas Brock. "You didn't bring her in here?"

"Of course not. I came here to prevent a disaster from happening." Phineas Brock glared at Lombard. "But apparently I failed since now I am trapped in it with you."

"Where is she? Is she all right?" Gualtero said.

"She's fine. She's with Lombard's bandits."

"What? No!" Sullivan said.

"Hush yourself. She's a powerful lass. They won't meddle with her. I'm wishing now though that I had brought her with me. A girl with her training and talents might have been useful in this accursed place." Phineas Brock drummed the banister with his long fingers.

"We should go back," Sullivan said.

"'Can't, Mr. Trooper," Phineas Brock said. "Look."

They looked back. The low passage had vanished and another stout door stood in its place.

Sullivan reached for it.

"Don't open it," Phineas Brock said. "Any manner of horrors might be lurking behind it now."

"What'll we do then?" Gualtero said.

"Go forward, always forward, right, Mr. Brock?" Lombard said.

"Ah, but which door or should we take the stairs?" Phineas Brock squinted into the darkness seething at the top of the stairs.

They surveyed the six doors. None of them looked welcoming.

"It is supposed to be in a low chamber," Lombard said, "and there was supposed to be a doorway directly ahead that led to it."

"No longer, Mr. Lombard. So what shall we do?" Phineas Brock said.

"Go up."

"Lead on and we shall cover your back," Phineas Brock said.

"How do I know you won't clout me the moment my back is turned?"

"Because either we all get out or none of us will."

That was good enough for Lombard. With a word, his torch sprung to life again and holding it forward, Lombard crept up the stairs.

As if to torment them further, the steps creaked, complaining with each step they made loud enough to wake the dead. Finally they could bear the noise no longer and charged the rest of the way up the stairs onto a small balcony leading to one narrow door.

The balcony groaned beneath them.

Lombard closed his eyes a moment, took a deep breath and turned the handle. The door opened an inch and stopped. "It's jammed."

The balcony quivered.

"Oh, I don't like this," Sullivan said.

From far away the pounding began.

"Where is that noise coming from?" Sullivan said.

"Behind us?" Gualtero said.

"No, it's above us," Sullivan said.

"It better not be ahead of us," Lombard said as he pushed again.

Gualtero cringed. "It is coming from behind, from one of those doors below."

Even Lombard stood stock still as they listened to the sound close in upon one of the doors below. Soft scraping sounds, shuffling, scratching, and sniffing, and then after a moment's silence when they thought it might have faded back into the noxious shadows that birthed it, it beat upon the door. The chamber filled with its echoes. The four men covered their ears. A crack appeared in the door below. Whatever **it** was howled with fiendish glee.

Lombard flung his entire weight against the door. Gualtero joined him. Sullivan drew both of his daggers and braced for an attack.

Phineas Brock took his blue cap back out and held it ready to slap atop his gray haired head.

"It won't budge," Lombard said.

The crack widened. Whatever it was behind it grew fiercer. They could hear it slavering.

Phineas Brock had to shout over the racket. "I have an idea." He unwound his sprawling muffler and tied it once about his waist. "Wrap this once around your waists and climb over the side of the balcony."

Lombard looped the muffler once about his waist and passed it to Gualtero and Gualtero passed it to Sullivan in his turn.

"Knot your end, lad," Phineas Brock said. "Make it tight. If it slips off, you'll be doomed."

Sullivan nodded with one eye on the breaking door and tied on the muffler tight.

"What are you going to do?" Gualtero said.

Phineas Brock raised his blue cap over his head. "Hide us. There. Now climb over the side. I'll be right behind you."

The door splintered apart. Phineas Brock donned the cap and they all disappeared as the room filled with terrible cold. The presence lingered at the bottom of the stairs and then charged suddenly up and burst through the door into the upper hallway. They didn't see it. Except for Phineas, they all hung from the balcony railing with their eyes squeezed shut. Phineas did look, but although he saw nothing he felt its malevolence well enough to suppress a shiver.

After a little while…

"Do you think it's safe to climb back up?" Sullivan whispered.

"That cold is gone," Lombard said.

"Then it is safe," said Phineas Brock.

Gualtero was staring at the door the presence had burst through. The string again stretched back the way they had come. The passageway stood as it had before. The mysterious broken door had vanished. "I just hope I'm still sane when I get out of here."

And in a desolate old throne room, from an obscure corner…

"Badenoch has awakened, Evin."

"What?!"

"Someone has stirred its shadows and awakened this place."

"Criminy, Beolagh! What sort of fool would come in here?"

"A greedy one, I expect."

"Well, 'tis done and there's naught for us to do except scurry for the tunnels and hope no one notices us. Find Conor and tell him to get into the tunnel."

"Right, Evin."

The sound of little footsteps darted across the desolate corridor into a small gap in the opposing wainscoting.

Beyond the little balcony stretched a corridor lined with doors, all of them closed.

Sullivan rolled his eyes. "Tell me we don't have to try every last one of these doors."

Lombard shook his head. "Nope. We're going straight to the one at the end."

"Are you sure about that?" Phineas Brock said.

Lombard folded up his map. "Absolutely. Just you make certain that you keep unspooling the string, Sullivan."

Sullivan grumbled under his breath as he brought up the rear with the spool of string.

The corridor echoed from their trespass. While Lombard headed directly ahead, Phineas Brock had Gualtero watch the doors to their left while he watched those to their right and had Sullivan watch their rear. Although the doors stood silent and still, the Bogle's abiding concern was enough to rattle their nerves.

"'You think something is lurking behind the doors, do you?" Sullivan said.

"Any manner of evil," Phineas Brock replied, "real or imaginary, Mr. Trooper."

"Wonderful," Gualtero muttered.

They reached the door soon enough, but the instant Lombard laid his hand upon the handle, a rumble issued from the distance behind them. The walls trembled. The floors vibrated.

Gualtero and Phineas Brock looked back. Sullivan faced forward, not daring to look back anymore. He knew he wouldn't like it when **it** did show up.

Whatever **it** was, Lombard wasn't about to wait around for a good look at **it**. He turned the handle and pushed the door open. "This wasn't on the map."

"What wasn't?" Gualtero peered over Lombard's shoulder.

A narrow footbridge stretched over a bottomless pit. At the end of it stood another narrow passageway full of darkness.

"Where did you get your map again?" Gualtero said.

"That damned Omnipedia."

"I'm sure it told you the truth," Phineas Brock said, "but where Badenoch is concerned all bets are off. This is a malicious place."

The sound grew. Suddenly, over the top of the first balcony a wave of black water broke. In itself, the wave was frightening enough, but when they saw the spectres entrapped in the obsidian current thrashing about and reaching out for them, it became something truly awful. Their reaction was to be expected.

"Run for it!" Lombard led the dash across the footbridge.

It wobbled and swayed beneath them, but sheer desperate momentum flew them across, leaping the last few treacherous steps onto solid stone again. They turned then, gasping, and watched the black water spout out onto the footbridge and spill down its sides. The specters tried to cling to the footbridge, but the obsidian water spilled into the pit, dragging all of its prisoners with it.

Still, they heard the howling and crying for sometime afterwards, receding further and further into the unfathomable depths.

"What was that anyway?" Gualtero said.

Lombard managed a brave look. "Let's push on, shall we?"

They stooped to get through the passageway and came out upon a winding staircase that grew narrower the lower it went until finally they had to squeeze through one at a time on the bottom.

"Lovely! Another corridor," Sullivan said.

"At least we are back on the correct level," Lombard said as he advanced.

"It feels like a tomb down here," Gualtero said.

"You had to say that, didn't you?" Sullivan said.

Lombard stopped in mid-step and held his torch out further. "Hush it. I think I hear something."

He didn't have to say it twice.

His companions shut up and listened hard.

"Voices," Phineas Brock whispered.

Lombard nodded.

They stood still and strained to hear them better.

"I told you this was a horrible notion," said one small, male voice.

"'Tis not what you said at the start," said another small voice, also male.

"Enough with the bickering. We're trapped here now and King Leith will have our hides for this folly," said a third small, male voice.

The first small voice began complaining most bitterly, but not in plain speech.

Phineas Brock tilted his head and frowned wonderingly. "That's Earthen Gaelic. I'd bet my hat on it."

"Leprecauns?" Gualtero said.

"They're the only ones I've heard tell of in this hemisphere or anywhere else that speak fluent Gaelic," Phineas Brock said.

"Do you suppose they came here for the Jinni too?" Sullivan said.

Lombard shrugged, but he feared precisely that.

"Well, if they had and found her too," Phineas Brock said, "then they'd have been well away from here already. There are other legendary treasures here though and that would be enough to attract anyone with more ambition than sense."

Lombard gave him a dirty look. Phineas Brock smirked, politely.

"Leprecauns are said to bring luck to whomever captures them," Lombard said.

"Oh, you mean the pot o' gold, three wishes and all that?" Phineas Brock said.

"I'd heard that too," Gualtero said.

"So have I," said Sullivan.

"Me too, but I couldn't tell you whether there was any truth to that tall tale. I didn't know that there were any Leprecauns about though," added Phineas Brock more thoughtfully.

"Well, now that we have a fair notion that they are indeed real," said Lombard, "let's see if we can't catch one of them. A little good luck couldn't hurt in this place."

"Indeed it may very well be good luck to catch one," Phineas Brock said. "They might know their way around this frightful place."

It was decided that Phineas Brock would don his blue cap and creep ahead to locate the three little men. Meanwhile, Gualtero and Lombard took the string and fashioned lassos, while Sullivan fashioned a net out of it with his Elven skills. Even as they worked swiftly, they couldn't shake the impression that Badenoch sat in wait. They kept their hands busy with the string and waited for Phineas Brock to return.

Which he did after several minutes had dragged past. They froze. Soft footsteps padded toward them and suddenly Phineas Brock loomed over them, his blue cap in hand.

"There are three swift-footed Leprecaun men by the names of Evin, Beolagh, and Conor. Conor appears to be the leader of the would-be plunderers," he said.

"Plunderers," said Gualtero.

"Evidently there is quite a treasure chamber somewhere in the depths of this unhallowed place." Phineas Brock sighed at the drab corridor walls. "They came to liberate it of a portion of its enchanted treasure as a means of placating King Leith. Apparently, they had the charge of his prize herd of white horses and lost them somehow. They hope to use the treasure to either buy back the King's herd or replace it with better horses somehow."

"Where did you last see them?" Lombard tried his string lasso on the tip of his boot. It worked perfectly.

"Beyond the corridor in something like a pantry, struggling with their little bags of gold. Follow me." Phineas Brock turned and headed back down the corridor.

"Gold, eh?" Lombard said.

Phineas Brock grinned at them. "Large gold coins. They're having a devil of a time lugging them about. It will be tricky snaring them though. Apparently, they've been getting about via old ventilation shafts and sewer lines."

"Thereby escaping the many terrors of this place," Gualtero said.

"Or Badenoch's notice," Sullivan said, nodding.

"Or did, until we showed up." Phineas Brock still grinned. "That's what has got them all knotted up. Our intrusion stirred the place awake."

Lombard grinned.

Phineas Brock whispered, "I'll go ahead and see if they're still in the same place. When I return, be ready."

They nodded. Phineas Brock donned his blue cap again and vanished. They noticed that his careful, steady footsteps scarcely disturbed the dust.

Suddenly Phineas Brock stood before them again, cap in hand. "Go get 'em!"

They charged 'round the corner and surprised all three little men. The lean little blond man dropped his bag of gold coins and ducked into the nearest tunnel. His two comrades failed to escape the net that descended on them and pulled them in tight. Another tug and they found themselves dangling in mid-air, struggling within the net's tight confines. The dark-haired one was a stocky, muscular little man, but his red-haired friend was just plain round.

"They kick like trout," Gualtero said as he held them up.

Lombard held his torch closer to get a good look at them.

"Ayeee! They're fixing to roast us!" screamed the red-haired one.

The dark-haired one punched at them. "You won't toast me without a fight."

When they got a good look at Phineas Brock in the torch's lurid light, both screamed and clung to each other.

"'Tis a goblin come to gobble us down!" cried the red-haired one.

"I beg your pardon," Phineas Brock sniffed, "but I am a Redcap Bogle."

"An Unseelie," gasped the dark-haired one.

"He'll eat us like dumplings!" said his comrade before lapsing back into a Gaelic rant.

"I am an antiquarian. My name is Phineas Brock."

"Bloody tomb robber," said the dark-haired one.

"I am nothing of the sort, but I can't speak for this chap." Phineas Brock glanced at Lombard.

"And who might His Honor be?" said the round red one.

Lombard snorted. "Lombard."

Both lapsed into Gaelic again in a panic.

"Look, if it's the pot o' gold you're wanting, wish for it and be done with us," said the dark one at last.

"Cursed Leprecaun gold - that I can't use," Lombard said.

They retorted in Gaelic.

Lombard was sure that they were cursing him out. "Gold I can pick up anywhere."

"What do you want then?" said the round red one.

"Your names for starters," Lombard said.

"Evin," said the round red one.

"Beolagh," said the other.

"And what was your friend's name?" Lombard nodded toward the tunnel where he saw the blond Leprecaun peeking out.

"That would be Conor," Evin said.

Lombard leaned down toward the tunnel. "Greetings, Conor. I am

Lombard. Your friends will not come to any harm – at least not from us. What Badenoch has in mind for us though I cannot say, but all I want from you is your help."

Conor peered out at him. "What do you want?"

"I am searching for a very old ceramic bottle, possibly a foot high, with these specific markings upon its sides." Lombard held out a separate sheet of paper so he and his friends could have a good look at it.

Conor scratched his chin. "A ceramic bottle?"

"Yes, one ceramic bottle," Lombard said.

"Well, I don't know about one such bottle, but I do know where there's a whole room full of them."

Lombard felt his stomach drop. "A room…"

"…Full of them," Conor said.

"Show us the way."

"Release Evin and Beolagh."

"Show us there and then I'll set them loose."

Conor frowned. "Very well, but when I say run, run. Badenoch is awake and hunting for us all."

8

Viola watched the Faerie bandits pace and fidget, consult their pocket watches and pace some more. Alone among them, Quinzano sat sipping on spiced tea and watched Badenoch as an uneasy sheep watched a wolf lazing in the sun.

"Shouldn't we go in after him?" said Acton.

"He told us to wait here," Quinzano said.

"But what if he is danger?"

Scudamore came back to the campfire to replenish his cup. "Acton, don't you get any fool ideas in your head now. Lombard told us to wait here. If you go in there, you won't come out again."

"But Lombard went in."

"Son," Scudamore said, "he went in with two men to back him up. You go in there alone, Badenoch will gobble you up."

Viola knew all their names by now. Scudamore and Quinzano were toughened leaders, Lombard's chief partners and closest friends. Acton spoke of Lombard as he would a beloved elder brother and suffered the worst for the Bandit King's absence. The Masham brothers, Russell and Warwick squabbled constantly, but no harm ever came of it. Handsome Montargis occupied those tense hours with his ledger, finally announcing that if Lombard came through he intended to retire immediately afterwards to his own vineyard. Hawtrey sipped on tea, but mentioned that he hoped that their first destination after this adventure was a tavern with a worthy stock of refreshments. His expression was one of resigned despair, brightened by only the most fleeting of grins. Parslow sat practicing card tricks and fussing with his brotherhood ring, as though troubled by a lingering sense of guilt for abandoning his chaste reflective calling for this reckless life.

She could tell that Kelyng, Biagio, and Gripwell had been *earthbound* Faeriefolk before they took their detour into banditry. They sat together gazing out across the meadowlands, discussing the quality of the soil, the sort of weather that one might endure there, and the latest farmers' auction catalog, already dog-eared from study, which they passed back and forth as they discussed the price of seeds, land, and livestock. Like Montargis, they had hopes of an agricultural nature.

Trapnel lay sprawled out in the grass with his hat over his face. At least he didn't snore.

Suedama was quite a handsome rogue, she acknowledged, but whenever he attempted to venture near her Quinzano drove him back with a simple stern glance. She did not encourage his amorous delusions, not when he was already fanning them to an alarming degree. A real Marpessa Princess sat in their midst. Who could blame him for attempting to seduce the comely, bright-eyed creature? Still, one didn't dare cross Lombard, Quinzano, and Scudamore – or a maiden who had been raised on Shadow Mountain.

Calderon's hands seldom enjoyed a moment's idleness and then only when he slept. Creativity ruled his nature. Viola watched him craft a silver bracelet beside his fire. The man was inspired. He spoke very little, but seemed pleasant the entire time, if a little preoccupied, despite De Vere's interested presence.

De Vere was a singular Faerie man. Unlike the rest, his wings did not rest folded and mostly transparent upon his back. They did not rest at all because he no longer possessed wings. At that moment, he sat fascinated by Calderon's skill, but Viola had watched him earlier practicing his sword moves in the high grass. Either he had been a professional soldier or he meant to become one someplace else. Without his wings, he could not hope to serve anywhere in Nuneau. Of them all, De Vere fascinated her the most. Now and then she caught him looking her way as though studying her, but the moment their eyes met, he turned away and concentrated on something else. He had dark hair, touched here and there by the sun, and dark, impenetrable eyes set in a strong face. He reminded her of Alison the Terrible and Ivan the Dark, two wizard brothers on Shadow Mountain, only much younger and not quite so intimidating.

"There's that pinto again!" said Russell.

The bandits looked off. In the distance they saw a roan pinto standing.

"I'd swear that it's watching us," Warwick said.

"So catch it," De Vere said.

"We tried that already. The critter runs too fast and if you get too close, it spreads its wings and soars way out of range," Russell said.

"So leave it be then," De Vere said. Both he and Quinzano noticed Viola's reaction: she was smiling.

"'Friend of yours?" Quinzano said.

"You could say that. He promised to keep an eye on me," Viola said, "but you'll never catch him so you might as well get used to him out there."

Meadowlark neighed and trotted into the depths of the meadow until the tall grass concealed him again.

"What do you want from us?" Scudamore said.

"I told you," Viola said, most pleasantly, "I came after my friends."

Scudamore and Quinzano exchanged dubious looks.

"So why don't you go in after them?" Quinzano said.

"I may be loyal, but I'm not stupid," she said.

That provoked a few chuckles from the bandits.

After ducking huge, hungry, hairy monsters with mouths nearly as wide as their bodies and dripping fangs longer than a Leprecaun, specters of darkness that would suck away their living breath or stop their hearts, statues that came to life long enough to attempt to make statues out of the intruders with their poisonous embrace, an entire hall filled with suits of armor that promptly took up arms and pursued them, and too many other unspeakable perils en route, the six men stood in a closed room lined from end to end with shelves that were loaded from floor to ceiling with bottles and amphorae - and every last one of them bore the markings of the bottle that Lombard sought. Even Conor and his friends gazed dumbfounded at the chamber.

"Uhhh," groaned Sullivan as he pressed his forehead against the door.

"This is a nightmare," Gualtero said.

Lombard sighed. "At least we are here now. Let's barricade the door so that nothing can sneak up on us."

Sullivan and Gualtero scrounged some benches from a neighboring chamber. Coughing on the dust, they returned and closing the door, braced the benches against it and then piled some broken statuary swiped from the corridor against the benches.

Lombard spied four torches gathering dust and touched his enchanted torch against the nearest one.

At the very first spark up flamed a Jinni. It coiled and swelled, glowing like a bright orange lantern, until it filled the ceiling and then it turned upon the intruders. Smoke and flames resided within his eyes.

"Crikey! A Jinni," cried Sullivan.

The being fumed. "I am no mere Jinn, pointy-eared one. I am the Ifrit..."

"An Ifrit?" Phineas Brock groaned.

"What's an Ifrit?" Gualtero whispered.

"The most powerful of the Jinn and one of the more malevolent branches of these spirits of fire," Phineas Brock muttered.

"... Jalil Futaih and you are now in my custody," he thundered.

Conor, Evin, and Beolagh ducked behind the tall men and struggled with the barriers on the door. When nothing budged, they began to look for gaps in the walls they could use. They cursed and fretted in their native tongue the entire time, except for when Evin moaned in plain tongue that the orange Ifrit would surely roast them on the spit for his luncheon.

"Fine," said Lombard. "What do you require of us, Jalil Futaih?"

"Strike your torch upon my companions."

Lombard met Phineas Brock's stern '*I told you so*' glance.

"Might as well, lad. We aren't going anywhere anymore without his say so," Phineas Brock said. He kept a canny eye on the surly Ifrit.

The surly Ifrit scrutinized the tall gray fellow too. "You are an Unseelie, are you not?"

Phineas Brock bobbed his dingy red cap. "I never had much stomach for mischief, but I am a Redcap Bogle."

"If you are not satisfying the causes of darkness, what do you do?" said Jalil Futaih.

"I am an antiquarian, sir."

"Then you came for treasure. Fool!"

"No, sir. I came at the request of my young friend Viola to look after her two friends in this man's control."

Lombard stilled his shaking hand long enough to touch upon the next torch and out rolled a blue Ifrit in sinuous bellows of smoke.

"Finish," said Jalil Futaih.

Lombard touched the last two torches in the sconces and out streamed a green Ifrit and a golden yellow one.

"At last we are free again," said the blue Ifrit as he regarded the last two.

"Now what do you want from us?" Lombard said.

Gualtero and Sullivan had to give him credit. Lombard kept his genuine fear in check. The Leprecauns huddled behind Gualtero. Failing to spy a hole, they had to sit this crisis out and hope the fierce Jinn couldn't see them, or wouldn't bother with such tiny creatures.

"Now who are you?" said Jalil Futaih.

"I am Lombard…"

"Just Lombard?" said Jalil Futaih with an arch of his brow.

"Lombard de Montfaucon," he said gravely.

"Very well." Jalil Futaih's glance shifted toward the others.

"Phineas Brock," said the Redcap Bogle with a formal bow to the Ifrits.

"Sullivan Trooper." He too managed a bow although he perceived the quick interest in the Ifrits' eyes.

"Trooper? That is an unusual name," said Jalil Futaih.

"I am a member of the Seelie Court of Trooping Elves," Sullivan said.

"A noble if restless people."

"Who have all vanished," said Gualtero, "all but our friend here."

"Truly?" said the blue Ifrit. "This is dire news indeed. What became of them?"

"No one knows," said Sullivan. "A dragon found me as a babe crying outside a deserted village and carried me to Shadow Mountain."

"Ah." Jalil Futaih looked upon Gualtero.

"Gualtero Bainbridge."

"And you little ones?"

After a short outburst of Gaelic cursing, Conor edged out of Gualtero's shadow long enough to say, "I am Conor, and this is Beolagh and Evin. We are the subjects of King Leith of Meath."

"Meath is far, far away, Conor."

"Do not I know it!" Conor said.

Lombard pointed his torch at the other three Ifrits. "Might we know your comrades' names?"

The blue one smiled and said, "I am Aziz Faruq. I can see into all lies so it is best to speak only truth in my presence."

The green one remained solemn and dignified. "To Kings, I have lent my might to win great wars and my wisdom to rule their realms. They call me Karim Jubran."

The golden one that shone like morning sunlight smiled and bowed. "Those who see me do not regret it. I, Yumni Mubashir, am the bringer of good news, good luck, and great success. Just make sure you know what you want."

"What do you do then, Jalil Futaih?" Gualtero said.

"I commanded legions of jinn of the water, sky, fire, and earth. None can withstand my might as a conqueror. Many great kingdoms have I laid waste, many are the proud and vainglorious that I have brought low."

"Okay," said Sullivan.

"Why have you released us?" said Jubran.

"It was not intentional," Sullivan said. "It was dark and we needed to see."

"What are you searching for?" said Aziz.

Phineas Brock crossed his arms over his lean chest and fixed a long hard look upon Lombard. It would be interesting to see what sort of answer he would give.

"A rare and old object," said Lombard. "People believe it's a myth, but I think it does exist."

Aziz the truthful one nodded. So far so good. "And you think it is here?"

"Wherever here is," said Yumni the luck bringing one, eyeing their surroundings.

"Yes," said Lombard.

"You are in Badenoch," said Phineas Brock.

"Badenoch?" said Jubran the wise one. "I know of no such place."

Gualtero saw Conor and his friends shake their heads.

"What is the last thing you recall before this moment?" Gualtero said.

The Ifrits exchanged looks.

"Sun, warmth, palms and dates, an ocean the color of cerulean and turquoise," said Jubran.

"And white and golden sand," said Aziz.

"Well, it sounds as though you are very far from home too," said Evin.

"What is this Badenoch?" said Jalil Futaih.

"A great horrible pile o' stones," said Beolagh. "Except for us fools, no other souls would come within range o' the sight of it."

Aziz frowned.

"He tells the truth?" said Jalil Futaih the fearless one, destroyer of kingdoms.

"Unfortunately, he does," Aziz said. "Moreover, I perceive that they all stand in great dread of this place."

"Certainly, or why else would they barricade themselves in this dusty place with frightful entities such as ourselves," Jubran said.

As if in response, an elusive roar echoed from the corridor beyond the door. It roamed about. They heard a great crashing and smashing of things before it gathered beyond the barricaded door breathing the chill of death and oblivion through the cracks in the door.

"I wish we had a boulder," said Evin.

"I remember a dark and fierce mage," said Yumni with an air of total nonchalance, "who could weave doom out of words."

"I too remember such an accursed necromancer," said Aziz.

Jalil Futaih and Jubran did too.

"He enchanted us and banished us to this abominable place," said Yumni.

"Brace yourselves." Sullivan covered his ears.

Pounding erupted upon the door like fists made of stone.

The intruders jumped and quailed at the sound - but not the Ifrits.

"I will deal with this menace." Jubran disappeared through a crack in the door scarcely wide enough for a slip of paper to slide through.

They waited to hear the terrible sounds.

Instead Jubran returned, looking puzzled and a little disappointed. "There is nothing there after all."

"Except evil," Lombard said. His eyes scoured the shelves. Where to begin?

"I saw nothing," Jubran said.

"Yes, but it had a full look at you," said Conor. "Badenoch knows that you are here now too."

"Since we are trapped here, might we continue our search for this relic?" Lombard said.

The Ifrits exchanged looks.

"We see no harm in that," said Jalil Futaih. "After all, you cannot leave without our say so."

"I thank you." Lombard bowed and motioned to the others to go ahead of him.

The Leprecauns made it a point to keep the much taller men between themselves and the Ifrits.

"What are we looking for?" Conor said.

Lombard took out a sheet of paper. "I copied this from an ancient text and the Omnipedia confirmed that this is what it looks like." He held open a drawing of a large ceramic wine jug with a long thin neck and a very wide, round base and a very strange exotic series of markings painted upon its sides. "It is somewhere lost among all these similarly marked containers."

Conor turned to Evin. "You stay here and listen to what the Ifrits say. Beolagh and me, we're going to help find this blasted jug."

Evin cast an unhappy look at the Ifrits locked in their close conference. "If you wish it, Conor, I shall stand my post."

"If you find it, do not open it on your own. If we're to get out of here unharmed, we need to open it together." Lombard glanced over his shoulder at the Ifrits.

Aziz was frowning at him.

They split up. Conor and Beolagh worked through the highest shelves on both sides while Phineas Brock and Sullivan worked the lower shelves on the left and Lombard and Gualtero worked the ones on the right. Shifting the containers about and examining each one, they moved with care and efficiency.

Meanwhile, Evin puffed on his pipe, watched his comrades' progress deeper and deeper into the storeroom, and listened to the Ifrits trying to figure out why that accursed mage would banish them to Badenoch. None of them had crossed the mage, so there could have been no vendetta. All those who had crossed Jalil Futaih and Jubran had been obliterated with all their relations and retainers, so it was doubtful that any survivors had anything to do with their exile. Finally they figured that the mage, by his reputation as a worshipper of power, had stolen something of great unimaginable worth and had captured and cursed the four great Ifrits with the guardianship of this object. And that object had to be the antique that these seven strange individuals sought.

At that moment, Sullivan spied the object, tucked inside a niche in a far recess. "I see it," he said under his breath.

Phineas Brock hissed at the others. "We found it."

They gathered behind Sullivan.

"I can't reach it though," Sullivan said.

"We'll push it out." Conor clambered down to it and Gualtero lifted Beolagh onto the shelf.

Both little men walked into the shadows, pushing their sleeves up and tilting their hats forward.

Gualtero felt a slight rap on his boot and looked down.

Evin looked up at him. "How goes it?" he called. Then he whispered. "You had best make haste. The Ifrits are curious about your quest."

"Thanks," Gualtero whispered. Then he said normally, "Conor has his foot caught. As soon as Beolagh can get him loose we'll be able to continue."

Evin moseyed back to his original post and puffed on his pipe as though he hadn't a care in the world, but he listened to every word the Ifrits said.

Gualtero leaned in and said lowly, "Remove it as quietly as possible. We can't let the Ifrits see it."

Conor and Beolagh exchanged looks.

"We rather figured that out already," Conor said.

Sullivan spoke up. "Maybe there is some oil in one of these amphorae. We can unplug it and put some on your foot so you can slip out of there."

"No, I think I've figured how to wriggle out of it," Conor replied, loudly.

Meanwhile, he and Beolagh pushed and shifted and pushed again and gradually the jug came loose from the niche. Then they got behind it and pushed. The object moved with more ease than they expected.

"Are you sure this is what it was supposed to look like?" Beolagh hissed.

"Precisely," Lombard hissed back. "Why?"

"Because it feels empty. It has no weight to it at all."

"Just get it over here quickly," Gualtero said. "The Ifrits are looking our way."

Lombard leaned in and snatched the jug and concealed it under his coat. In his other hand he held Conor. "Let's have a look at your ankle."

Beolagh followed on his own and watched Lombard go through the charade of checking Conor's foot and ankle.

"I am fit, I tell you. Now set me down so can finish the hunt," Conor said.

"All right. All right. Stop fussing." Lombard set Conor down. In a low voice, he added, "When we get to end of this shelf, gather close to me and I'll open the bottle."

"Found it yet?" said Jalil Futaih.

Lombard chose his words with care. "We're close to it now. I can feel it."

"What was all that fuss about?" said Aziz said.

"Conor. He was having difficulty in a niche back there," said Lombard.

Both statements, however vague, were true enough to foil Aziz's lie-detecting instincts.

Evin listened to them discuss again what possible treasure they might have been sent to guard and what they should do once they left Badenoch. The Leprecaun made it a point then to tell them in lavish and lurid detail about

Badenoch's many terrors and that none who entered it had ever returned from it. That gave even the powerful Ifrits pause.

"Could it be that we have merely escaped from a prison cell only to be trapped in the prison itself?" said Jubran.

"So it might be," said Yumni, "but we should make many valiant attempts to see the sunlight again."

"We shall," Jalil Futaih said.

Lombard stopped at the end of the first shelves and stood as though getting his bearings before pushing on to the next section. He rested his forehead against his forearm and the others gathered round.

"You two lads, hop on Gualtero's shoulders and hang on," Lombard said. "When I open this we don't know what will happen, but it could be violent."

"Violent?" said Sullivan.

"Winds, thunder, lightning, who knows what all accompanies this being. Brace yourselves."

Conor and Beolagh clambered onto Gualtero's shoulders and took a firm hold of his pouch straps.

"What about Evin?" said Beolagh.

At that moment, Evin ambled up to them. "The Ifrits wish for you to tell them how you got in."

"Why?" said Lombard.

"So they too can escape." Evin shrugged.

Sullivan snatched him up. "We'll tell them to follow the string."

"Unhand me, Pointy Ears!" cried Evin.

"Hush-t, Evin," said Conor. "Lombard is about to unleash the unholy being."

Lombard took a firm grip of the stopper and…it wouldn't budge.

"Twist it first," said Phineas Brock with absolute authority. "Then pull."

Lombard gave him a long look. Phineas Brock shrugged harmlessly.

He gripped it again and twisted. His knuckles whitened. His palm and fingertips reddened. Finally the stopper moved, then turned and he pulled and out it came.

Out rose a stream of smoke, pale lavender smoke. They breathed in the scent of jasmine and honeysuckle that came over them so strongly that if they closed their eyes they would have thought themselves lost in an overflowing garden.

The Ifrits fell silent and gaped.

Out of the smoke an entity formed, wonderfully rounded as women were, with dark, almost blue skin, as luminescent as a pearl, and coiling black hair rising into a gem-studded headdress. The smoke settled around the entity, forming her garments of rich blue, green, and lavender that shifted and flowed at the slightest breeze. She smiled with closed lips, but the look in her obsidian eyes was fathomless.

"La Questa!" said Aziz.

Her glance shifted toward the Ifrits. They gathered at once about her and bowed.

"What have you found?" Gualtero whispered.

"A most powerful Jinniyah," Lombard said, "La Questa, the legendary one."

"Something tells me that we are going to regret this," Phineas Brock said.

"Why are they bowing to her?" Sullivan said. "Is she a monarch of some sort?"

They noticed that the Ifrits did not dare touch her person beyond the hem of her robes. La Questa beamed upon them though.

"Maybe she's their mother," Gualtero said.

"You might have something there," Lombard said.

"Rise, my guardians," she said in a husky voice.

The Ifrits rose and gathered behind her.

"Who is my liberator?" she said.

Lombard shrugged and tilted the jug.

"What do they call you?" she said.

"Lombard de Montfaucon."

She tilted her head. "You are a Groundling Faerie."

"My father was a mortal knight and my mother was a Faerie Princess."

His companions cocked their heads at him.

"Is there anything more we should know about you, Lombard?" Gualtero said.

Lombard gave him a dirty glance. "They call you La Questa. What does that mean?"

"*The Song of the Nightingale*. The great sad king to whom I brought comfort from his grief gave me that honorific, Lombard de Montfaucon, but my name is Khuzama Zamurrud. Since you have freed me, I shall permit you to address me as Empress Zamurrud."

"You are most kind." Lombard bowed at once. This was not how he had visualized the moment. He had freed her, but suddenly it seemed as though the Jinniyah was very much in charge of him.

"Since you have freed me from my terrible prison, you may abide with me. Bear his companions out of harm's way and then return to me," she said.

"Yes, Empress," said the Ifrits.

"But how shall we leave? Badenoch is a wicked prison and we are in the beast's belly," said Jalil Futaih.

La Questa glanced at the ceiling.

It exploded skyward and each succeeding floor gave way, as though the cellar had spit out a boulder. Suddenly into the deepest darkest space of Badenoch fresh daylight poured. Lombard and the others had to shield their eyes.

Out on the meadow, Lombard's men jumped at the rumble and then ducked beneath the caravan as debris rained down. Viola curled into a ball, covering her head, when suddenly she felt someone cover her with his own body. She looked over her shoulder and saw De Vere with his eyes squeezed shut.

"What do you mean take us out of harm's way?!" yelped Sullivan, but then Aziz had him in his grip and flew up through the hole into the sky, taking Evin along for the ride. "Gualtero!"

Gualtero uncovered his eyes. "Sullivan?"

Then Jubran had him tight and carried him off too, with Conor and Beolagh hanging on for dear life.

Viola peered up and saw a man made of blue smoke soaring off to the southwest with Sullivan kicking and pummeling in his arms. A man formed of green smoke zoomed from the depths of Badenoch next and veered north toward the mountains of the Wolf Trolls. She sat up and stared.

"Something has gone wrong," she said.

De Vere watched with her as a smoke-made man of golden yellow carried off a lean gray fellow directly over them, bearing south. The man had his arms folded across his chest and a look of placid disgust on his face.

"Who was that?" De Vere said.

"My ally Phineas Brock," Viola sighed. "He was supposed to watch over them and help them get back out."

De Vere watched the golden being disappear to the south. "Well, they are out, but heaven knows where they'll end up."

Quinzano and the rest came out of hiding. De Vere untied Viola and helped her to her feet. She stood in time to see Meadowlark soaring southward after Phineas Brock. Doubtless he would return for her once he knew what had become of his master.

"What fresh crisis is this?" Scudamore shouted. He kicked at a tile from Badenoch's roof. "Where's Lombard? Who were those beings?"

Russell and Warwick eyed a gargoyle that had been blown off of Badenoch. It was quite an exotic, fine sculpture.

"What do you suppose this would be worth?" Warwick said.

"They pay in gold for sculptures of this quality," said Trapnel said, drooling at the notion.

"Whatever they would pay, it wouldn't be worth the bad luck that thing would bring," Viola said. "Just bear in mind where it came from." She nodded at Badenoch. "And leave it where it is."

"She has a sound point," De Vere said.

"Warwick, are you daft? Don't touch it!" Russell slugged Warwick in the shoulder.

Warwick slugged him back. "I wasn't going to."

A great spiraling plume of bluish purple smoke rose from Badenoch, accompanied by a smaller one the color of fire. It swooped east, but instead of accompanying the greater entity, the man of fire paused and looked back toward the encampment.

"Now what," said Quinzano.

"Uh oh," said Acton.

"Nobody panic," said Quinzano.

The entity of flame rushed toward them.

Scudamore shook his head. "Ah, hell."

9

It took Sullivan and Evin a little while to figure out that they were in the valley – Radiant Valley - beyond Shadow Mountain. After that their spirits lifted. Shadow Mountain stood a substantial distance away, but as long as they could see it, Sullivan felt certain that eventually he could flag down one of the dragons and go look for the others from there. Evin was more dubious.

While Evin rode on Sullivan's shoulder grumbling about the trustworthiness of dragons, Sullivan began the long march across the verdant valley to Shadow Mountain's western gate, the only way in.

Phineas Brock had a perfectly amiable chat with Yumni the affable one and consequentially he was able to talk the golden Ifrit into dropping him off back in the Enchanted Woods. Yumni did not take him home though, but left him within sight of a forlorn castle deep in the Enchanted Forest. For awhile, Phineas Brock was torn between simply setting off for home anyway or lingering about to explore the castle. Curiosity got the better of him. Blue cap on head, he crept into the place.

The Wolf Troll scouts spied Gualtero and his two little companions stranded atop a precarious peak. After they were done laughing, they sent word to the King. King Arvid could not come, but he sent his right hand man Archduke Balthazar to look into the situation. Conor and Beolagh gawked at Balthazar's gleaming helmet with its grand set of bighorn sheep horns behind his ears slots, at his furry pointed ears, and his glowing orange-amber eyes.

"Who are you and what are you doing on our mountain?" Balthazar shouted.

"I am Prince Gualtero Bainbridge and I was stranded here by an Ifrit," he shouted back.

"What in blazes is an Ifrit?"

"'Something you should hope never to meet. Can you get us down? I have some rope, but I don't think it's long enough."

"Sit tight. We'll get you down," Balthazar said.

Gualtero nodded and began preparing his rope. A blue eagle kept circling over them, so Conor and Beolagh hid in the Prince's coat pockets. Despite their situation, Gualtero had to admit the view was breathtaking.

After the whirlwind died away, Viola and Lombard's startled band looked about and found themselves standing in the center of a seemingly endless plain filled with high grass and wildflowers as high as their waists. There wasn't one hill in sight and other than the sun's gradual transit overhead, not one indicator of direction to be seen anywhere. The Ifrit had picked up their entire encampment and removed them to a place that Viola suspected he had chosen purposefully to confuse them. They stood amid the rippling flowers and grass and gazed for a time in all directions.

"Lombard betrayed us!" cried Trapnel.

"No, he wouldn't do that." Quinzano rested a steadying hand briefly on Acton's shoulder. "I wager that he has no idea of what has been done to us any more than we know what those beings did with him. Our mission now is to try to get back to civilization."

"And hope it's one we recognize," said Calderon as he reassured his horses.

"We'll cross paths with Lombard again, I promise," said Scudamore.

"Fine, so which way do we go?" said Montargis.

Viola raised her hand. "I have an idea."

"Speak it," said Quinzano.

"Send men out in each direction and see if they can find something while they're out there. If they find anything, they then return and tell us."

"You're reading my mind, Princess." Quinzano surveyed the band. "Montargis, you take Russell and fly east."

"Drop your pack and let's wing it, son," Montargis said.

Russell sighed as he handed his pack to Warwick and shot after Montargis eastward.

"Kelyng, you and Hawtrey fly south."

"Right," they said and they set off.

"Biagio, you and Suedama go north."

"See you later," Suedama said as he and Biagio took flight.

"Gripwell, take Parslow and go west."

"Off your duff, Parslow," Gripwell said. "We've a range to cover."

Parslow tightened his cravat and took off beside Gripwell.

"In the meantime," Scudamore said, "we'll make camp and cook up some stew. The lads will be hungry when they return."

Warwick and Acton were assigned to making the biscuits over the fire Scudamore built. Quinzano, Trapnel, and Calderon began chopping vegetables for the stew. De Vere took charge of their horses and tended to them. Viola joined him.

"You have magic abilities," De Vere said after awhile. "Why don't you help us find our way out?"

"Simple logic - first you have to know where you are, before you can chart a course away from there. Flying blind is the most dangerous thing a person with my capabilities can do. Now, if I had my Omnipedia, I could have figured out where we were and we'd be already on our way back to find the others."

"Where is your Omnipedia?"

"Lombard has it."

"Oh, that's right." De Vere grinned. "Inconvenient, isn't it?"

Viola smiled. "A little, but if he consults it, which I think he will the first minute he's free, he'll figure out a way to resolve this situation. Why exactly did he want to go to Badenoch?"

"There was supposed to be a great wish-fulfilling treasure in there. If he found it, we all could have retired in peace and comfort for the rest of our lives, if that is what we wanted."

"Somehow I get the feeling that peace and comfort are the furthest things from your mind."

De Vere locked gazes with her. "I'm not ready for the peaceful life. I burn still and cannot be peaceful, not yet."

"If you aren't careful, you might not survive to even dream of a peaceful life."

"So long as I am in Nuneau, I will not know peace, but perhaps in the southern realms I can find a place for myself." De Vere sized her up anew. "What sort of powers do you possess?"

To answer or not to answer? Viola folded her arms across her breast and kicked at the turf a moment. "Let's just say that if I had had my Omnipedia, I would have had no problem whatsoever getting us back into familiar terrain. Even all the way to the Queen's city if I so chose."

De Vere arched his brow. "Really?"

Viola grinned. "Truly. They raised me on Shadow Mountain for a reason, you know." She turned away and walked off through the grass, gazing off into the distance after their scouts.

When all the smoke and incense faded away, Lombard found himself standing in the palace by the sea.

"Uh-oh."

"Uh-oh? Surely this is what you wanted, Lombard de Montfaucon." La Questa strolled past him, gesturing airily at the marble pillars and domed ceiling glowing pure in the reflected sunlight. "Majesty, power..."

Lombard was shaking his head.

A willowy blond woman in flowing garments of creamy yellow and azure blue rounded the corner at the far end and froze. "Who are you?"

"...Beauty," said La Questa, appraising her.

Lombard's eyes widened.

"Who are you?" she said again.

Lombard did have some manners. He bowed deeply. "I am Lombard de Montfaucon, but you would know me as the King of the Bandits."

Her breath caught in her throat. "You had best leave at once or I will summon my sentries."

"They will not come, Faerie Queen," said La Questa.

"They will if I shout for them," Anna Marpessa said.

"Let me rephrase that then. They cannot come. They are back in the city where you are not," said the Ifrit Empress with a polite smile.

Anna Marpessa frowned and rushed past the two intruders to the balcony. She gasped. "What happened to the land?"

"It is where it always was," La Questa said.

Lombard rushed to the balcony and peered over it beside the Queen. Through intermittent breaks in the clouds both glimpsed Nuneau and the waves crashing against the white cliffs on the eastern shore below.

"Only part of the palace is here," Anna Marpessa said, peering about at the solitary tower and the structure attached to it. "The family wing." She glared at Lombard. "What sort of evil is this?"

"It wasn't my idea," Lombard said.

The clouds held tight to the domestic wing and drifted eastward.

Anna Marpessa scowled at him and turned on the exotic woman watching them. "This is an outrage. I demand that you restore me to my realm."

La Questa smiled and shook her head. "Sorry."

"Fine, I'll fly home."

"With what? I have deprived you of your wings, Beautiful One."

Anna Marpessa glanced over her shoulders. She strained and attempted to summon her wings into useful sight, but they had vanished. "What sort of villainy is this?" She put distance between herself and both intruders.

"This is what my liberator wished," La Questa said.

" 'Tis not!" Lombard snapped. "You didn't give me a chance to say what I wanted."

La Questa sighed and shrugged. "Ah well, there is no pleasing some." She sat upon a gilded cathedral chair and arranged her garments.

"Anna! Anna?" Carissa rushed around the corner, trailing Olwen by one hand and clutching a letter opener in the other. "The rest of the palace is gone."

"I know," Anna Marpessa said.

Olwen threw her arms about Anna Marpessa and hid her face. "We can't find anyone."

"I know," Anna Marpessa said. "They are all down in Nuneau. It seems as though we are prisoners of the Bandit King and his Sorceress." She glared at him.

"This wasn't my idea," Lombard said, but Olwen was sniffling and the Queen and her sister Carissa were glaring at him, so he turned to the Empress. "We need to restore everything and then discuss what I truly wanted."

"You wanted wealth, did you not?" La Questa said.

"Yes, but…"

"And authority, did you not?"

"I have authority enough, thank you," Lombard said.

"And beauty to companion you?" La Questa motioned to the three sisters. "I have even given you a choice in the matter or you might indulge yourself with all three."

The Faerie women gasped. Carissa held her letter opener ready.

Lombard flinched and turned red. "Now listen here, Madame, I never ever took a woman against her will, and I don't plan to start now. All I wanted was enough wealth for my men and me so that we could disband and retire in comfort for the rest of our days. What we did after that would have been entirely up to us and after you had given us that you would have been free." He waved the jug at her.

"But I am free now," La Questa said.

"What sort of Jinni are you?" he said.

"I told you. I am the Empress Khuzama Zumurrud, called La Questa, and I think you have more need of me than I have of you this instant."

"I will ask you politely – return me to my men in the meadowlands and return these royal ladies to their proper place and I shall consider the obligation fulfilled."

La Questa smiled instead. "Your men no longer await you and your brave friends have been scattered to the winds as well."

"What have you done to them?"

"Wherever they are, I promise you, they are fine, but I hear my guardians upon the wind. I must meet them and thank them for their service. Faerie Queen, do not come into your Throne Hall until the doors stand open again. Some things are not meant for others' eyes." She rose up high above the floor. Her slippered feet turned translucent as she veered down the corridor. The doors opened just wide enough to admit her and then closed tight.

Lombard shook his head and suddenly he felt the cold tip of Carissa's letter opener against his throat.

"Start explaining or we toss you over the balcony so the Sea Queen can have you," Carissa said.

"And she likes handsome rogues like you too," said Anna Marpessa. "You'll have fins and gills before she's done with you."

One after the other, four glowing spheres of blue, gold, green, and fiery red rushed in and vanished into the throne hall, without so much as a trace of incense or smoke to mark their trespass. Sinuous music trailed from the hall. Olwen ventured nearer to the doors, her head tilted toward the sounds.

Lombard stood with his hands extended out from his sides. "Look, I'll explain everything, just please put the knife away." Instead she pressed it closer. "Really, this wasn't my idea. I'm afraid I'm just as much her captive as you are, so perhaps we should plot together how to get out of this situation. Does that sound right to you?"

Carissa and Anna Marpessa exchanged looks.

"Fine," said Anna Marpessa.

Carissa lowered the letter opener. "What do you propose?"

"That we get away from here before we discuss anything. Do you have a room where they can't sneak up on us?" Lombard said. "A room with one entrance and no windows, a secret chamber would be even better."

"I have one," Carissa said.

Anna Marpessa stared at her. "Since when?"

"Anna…" Carissa said, blushing.

"Oh, heavens!" cried Anna Marpessa. "Just take us there." She turned and saw Olwen peering through the large ornamental keyhole into the hall. Immediately, she pulled her away. "Come away from there. You might have turned to stone."

"I don't think so," Olwen said. "They weren't doing anything frightful."

"What were they doing?" said Lombard.

"Well, not what Carissa does in her secret room."

Carissa's jaw dropped. When she caught Lombard's sharp glance, she turned a bright cherry red.

"Why is it that everyone knows about your secret room except me?" Anna Marpessa said.

Carissa opened her mouth, but Olwen had the answer.

"Because you just aren't nosy, Anna."

"I see," Anna Marpessa said. "Well, you and I are going to have a word about snooping, Olwen. As for your secret room and everyone you've entertained in there, I don't want to know so long as HE wasn't..."

"No, I promise, Gualtero has never set foot in it. He's yours and yours alone, Anna. Sullivan though..."

Anna Marpessa raised her hands. "Don't say another word. Just lead us there." She met Lombard's bemused look and rolled her eyes. "Perhaps our captor may have a point after all. You and my adventurous sister might be perfect for one another."

Carissa turned a fresh shade of crimson, but she didn't avert her glance quickly at all from Lombard's.

Lombard took on a subtle smile before he realized it. Clearing his throat as he brought up the rear, he said, "What were the Ifrits doing, My Lady Olwen?"

"They were sitting in a circle conferring, but they spoke so lowly that I couldn't hear a word."

"That can't be good," Lombard said.

Behind a seemingly solid wall stood a door and beyond that door stood an octagonal chamber, arranged for comfort and designed to seduce the senses. A wide, low bed waited atop a dais behind three curtained screens. The fourth set of screens stood open in expectation of immediate use. A chaise longue waited against another wall, backed by a tapestry. Other than the bed and the chaise longue, the only other significant piece of furniture was a dresser with a mirror, but the room overflowed with rich tapestries and carpets.

Carissa lit a taper in the outer room and lit the lanterns in her secret room.

"Well, at least it is clean," Anna Marpessa said as she drew Olwen in behind her and sat with her on the edge of the bed.

As soon as Lombard came in, Carissa shut the door tight. "Now, they can turn the place upside down and they won't be able to find us."

"But how would we breathe?" Lombard said.

"See those grills along the top of the walls?" Carissa said. He nodded. "They lead to secret vents."

Lombard sat on the chaise longue and folded his hands together.

Carissa sat beside him and set the taper aside. "How did you find out about this room, Olwen?"

"Sound travels," Olwen said.

Carissa turned red again.

"Then we should keep our voices down," Lombard said.

"We are prisoners in a floating palace," Anna Marpessa said. "What can we do?"

"Make a very long rope?" Olwen said.

"Out of what?" Carissa said.

"Any fabric you can find," Lombard said. "Just weave it all together in one rope." He stirred, sitting back a little and felt something hard against his back. Shifting his frock coat a little, he felt the Omnipedia inside his pocket. "Wait! I have something that might be useful." He tugged it out into the light.

"An Omnipedia!" Anna Marpessa seized it from him. "Where did you get it?"

Lombard swallowed. "It belongs to your sister Viola."

All three sisters turned sharpened eyes upon him.

"What have you done with her?" Anna Marpessa said.

"She's fine or was when I last saw her; however I suspect that she has suffered the same fate that my men have." He took the Omnipedia back. "With this we might be able to find out what became of everyone and we might even find a way to escape too."

Lombard regarded the front cover, took a deep breath and said, "All right, Omnipedia, we're in dire straits here."

The Omnipedia's cover flipped open and its first page flicked over. *'Why am I not the least bit surprised? Maybe next time you'll listen…'*

"We need help to escape. We need to know anything you know about the Jinn peoples, in particular the Ifrits Jalil Futaih, Aziz, Jubran, Yumni, and the one called Khuzama Zumurrud," Lombard said.

The next page flicked over. *'I warned you, remember? Didn't I warn you about what lurked in Badenoch?'*

Carissa repeated its words for her sisters' benefit.

Lombard sighed. "You did. I wish you'd been more specific about the item I sought."

The page flicked over. *'You only asked me about how to find the object, not the object itself. If you had asked me about the object itself, you wouldn't be in this situation now. You could have asked me about alternative treasures that would have been all you could ever need, but you didn't, did you?'*

"Fine. Fine. Don't rub it in." Lombard closed the book. "This is a first. I'm being scolded by a book."

"Where is my sister?" Anna Marpessa said.

The book opened and turned to the first page again: *'Viola Marpessa is in the heart of the great Sherka Plain.'*

"Where is that?" Olwen said.

The page flicked over. Carissa read its response: *'Far, far to the west, nigh upon the opposing coast of this continent.'*

"Heavens," said Olwen.

The page flicked over at once. *'Fear not. She is with Lombard's men.'*

"What? I swear, Lombard, if they harm my sister…" Anna Marpessa snapped.

"They won't. She is too important to harm," Lombard said.

Another page flicked over. *'Your sister has joined forces with Quinzano and Scudamore. FEAR NOT.'* The book closed itself.

Lombard took a deep breath. "What became of the others?"

The book flew open to its front page. *'Phineas Brock is back in the Enchanted Forest exploring the lost refuge of the Necromancer.'*

Carissa's eyes widened as she read that aloud.

"Necromancer?" said Anna Marpessa.

"Luzarches de Morin," said Lombard. "Phineas Brock must have been dropped off at the Castle de Morin instead of his own refuge. That was lucky."

"And who is this Phineas Brock?" said Carissa.

"An Unseelie Redcap Bogle," Lombard said.

"Unseelie!" cried Olwen.

"He's a decent chap, really. He's actually an antiquarian, and he's a friend of your sister's." Viola's sisters arched their brows. "Truly," he added, "Viola sent him into Badenoch solely to look after Gualtero and Sullivan and to help us out."

"Gualtero and Sullivan were in Badenoch?" said Anna Marpessa.

"All four of us were."

Looking up from the Omnipedia, Carissa cast a long look at Anna Marpessa. "Well, Gualtero is now stranded atop a peak in Wolf Troll territory with two chaps named Beolagh and Conor."

"Oh dear, that could be a complication," Anna Marpessa said. "King Arvid and I had something of a disagreement last week." She hugged Olwen closer so that her sisters would not see her wring her hands.

A page flicked over immediately. *'Have faith in Arvid's goodness.'*

Anna Marpessa nodded when Carissa relayed that to her.

Then the page flicked over again. *'Sullivan and Evin are on the far western slope of Radiant Valley headed for Shadow Mountain.'*

"Well, that's a relief. It would be horrible if something happened to Sullivan Trooper," said Anna Marpessa. "They are all brave and resourceful, so we should not waste any time fretting over them."

"But who are Evin, Beolagh, and Conor?" Carissa said.

"Three Leprecauns in the wrong place and then they ran into us." Lombard shrugged and closed the book.

"The question is – what can we do to escape?" Anna Marpessa said.

The book opened and all the pages rushed past before it returned to the front page.

"It seems that the book has given us plenty of options," Carissa said. She peered down with Lombard as he turned the first page.

'Ifrits and How to Deal With Them…'

Lombard sighed and took turns with Carissa in reading passages aloud while Anna Marpessa sat stroking her sister's soft hair and frowning at the far wall.

"You and your shortcuts! Ow!" Sullivan stood upright again, tugged free of the thorns, and began plucking them out.

Evin strolled ahead, hands in pocket, cap tilted forward on his brow. "I can't help it that you're a giant."

"I am not a giant, you little rodent." Finally Sullivan was free of them. Moving forward briskly, he scooped up Evin and held him up high above his head. "What do you see?"

Evin got a good look. "I see a cottage on yonder hill." He pointed off to the left.

"Does it look inhabited?"

"There is a trace of smoke coming from its chimney, so somebody must be at home."

Sullivan lowered Evin onto his shoulder and let him rest there. "I didn't think anyone lived here."

"It seems a fertile, pleasant valley," Evin said.

"Let me re-phrase that. I didn't think the community on Shadow Mountain let anyone live here."

"Well, that's a different matter altogether."

"A cottage you say?"

Evin nodded.

"Let's go see if anyone is at home. Perhaps we can chop wood or sing for our supper."

Evin grimaced. "I'll chop the wood. I've no voice for singing, for scaring Banshees perhaps, but not choiring like proper folk."

"Very well then." Sullivan grinned and they set off toward the cottage where it stood stalwart atop a gentle slope.

Meadowlark traced Phineas Brock's footsteps directly into the Castle de Morin and found his master standing before a tomb admiring it.

He gave the Faerie horse a quick look. "Oh, 'tis you. Fold your wings up. This is a hallowed place."

Meadowlark folded up his wings and eyed the chapel with its marble tomb. "Whose place is this?"

"This is **the** final resting place of Seigneur Luzarches de Morin – Philosopher, King, and Necromancer to whom you owe your gift of speech."

"Oh?"

"He so loved the beauty of this Forest that he emptied his magic chest over it, endowing it with his powers. Because you were conceived and born within his domain, you unlike most of your fellow winged equines can express your thoughts with as much eloquence as any farmhand."

"I thank you for the compliment at any rate," Meadowlark said. "Shouldn't we go back for the Princess now?"

"Not yet, I have yet to search the Castle propre."

"Why do you want to do that?"

"Because Badenoch isn't the only castle with hidden treasure. I think I might be able to find something that will be supremely useful to us, particularly in dealing with those pesky Ifrits." Phineas Brock bowed to the tomb and turned away. "Come along. The sooner we find it, the sooner we can help the Princess."

"Very well." Meadowlark turned and followed him, his long tail swishing. "Lead on."

10.

"You are a long ways from your domain on the sea. How is it that you wound up perched atop my mountain?" said Arvid, King of the Wolf Trolls.

Caught in the shimmering afternoon sunlight that poured through the opened windows behind the King's throne, Gualtero, Conor, and Beolagh stood in the center of Arvid's Throne Hall, pinned to the spot by at least one hundred pairs of curious Wolf Troll eyes. Four scholars had already come forward to measure the visitors. Seldom did they see Faerie people or Leprecauns in their neck of the woods, so they did not want to miss the opportunity to examine these unexpected visitors for their encyclopedic almanac of the native peoples of the western hemisphere. It was not such a terrible ordeal, but Conor and Beolagh had fumed and groused that they were not produce at the market as the scholars weighed them.

"'Tis a long story, your Eminence," Gualtero said.

The powerful gray Wolf Troll, in a courtly silken ikat robe of blue, purple and green and a long-sleeved blue tunic edged with elaborate embroidery, smiled, giving them a good look at his sharp teeth. "Bring some refreshments." He rose from his massive oak throne with its carved paw feet and the bear heads carved into its crest and stepped down from the granite dais where the open shuttered windows gave everyone an ample view of the valley. Instead of a crown, Arvid wore a knitted skullcap with holes for his ears to poke through. His bejeweled gold crown stood on a marble pedestal, closely guarded by two very fierce looking black-furred Wolf Trolls, who narrowed their yellow eyes at Conor and Beolagh when they gawked too long at the ancient crown.

A servant nodded and ducked down the passageway leading into the mountainside.

The hall they stood in had been cut out of the side of a mountain and had the benefit of fine, strong glass windows so that the King could look out over the mountain valley where their herds grazed in summer and where he could watch the snow collect over the glacial peaks in winter. In the winter, one would think the region devoid of all but wildlife, unless they peered carefully along the mountainsides and along the peaks, then an intruder would have seen the windows and balconies carved from solid stone in one vast mountain. Within that mountain the Wolf Trolls had created their city Eskanderon, a well-organized maze of tunnels, aquaducts, and chambers, where they spent their winters and where King Arvid held court year round.

A great fire blazed in pit against the far interior wall. Most of its smoke billowed up a hole in the ceiling and wound up through a vent into the wind. Arvid headed for it. At a motion from him, servants brought forward many stout chairs and sturdy little tables. The King sat and motioned to the Faerie

Prince and his two companions to sit with him.

"We will have refreshments and you shall tell me of your misadventure," Arvid said in a rich, mellifluous voice. He sat back in his high-backed chair and folded his hands over his belly.

Refreshments arrived at once for everyone, but the King and his visitors were served first. Archduke Balthazar stood behind the King's seat and sipped on his mulled wine. Arvid preferred to have fresh-picked herbal tea when it was in season, but Conor and Beolagh helped themselves to the strong spiced wine while Gualtero sipped carefully on his. Wonderful aromas drifted up from the kitchens already.

Gualtero took a fortifying drink from his cup and told them all about Viola, Lombard, Badenoch, and the terrible, whimsical Ifrits.

By the time he had finished, servants bearing trays and platters of food filed into the hall and set the food upon the tables around the fire pit. Gualtero glanced back over his shoulder as blue shadows rose upon the slopes and the sky bloomed gold and red.

Arvid smiled as he watched Conor and Beolagh divide up a pot pie and then bicker over who got which half. Finally he looked across at Gualtero. This was the gent who had won Anna Marpessa's heart. He was certainly a handsome rogue, but even better, he was the sort who faced danger with common sense. Obviously also, the sages at Shadow Mountain respected and honored the man enough to entrust the Princess Viola to his protection.

"Well, that was an adventure," Arvid said.

Gualtero turned back around.

"And you have no idea what became of the others?"

Gualtero shook his head. "But if what they did to me was any clue, then I expect they all were marooned in some out of the way place. I was lucky. Your men spotted me."

Arvid smiled. "Well, your fiancée and I had a slight difference of opinion a week ago."

Gualtero froze.

"So I've been thinking about sending an Emissary to talk to her. However, now that you are here, I have another idea."

"Which is?" Gualtero said.

Even Conor and Beolagh stopped eating momentarily.

"It is time that her and I met face to face. I shall deliver you to her and we shall see whether her gratitude will make her more amenable to our concerns."

"That sounds fine to me. When do we leave?" Gualtero said.

"In the morning. You will travel with my entourage. Tonight, we shall see whether we can figure out a way to find your friends. I have a few things tucked away in the Treasury that might be useful to us."

Phineas Brock and Meadowlark stood in the subterranean chamber directly below the tomb. A granite effigy of Luzarches de Morin gazed out at them from a niche at the end of the narrow chamber.

"Tell me again," whispered Meadowlark, his eyes not leaving the effigy's face for an instant, "why we are here." The horse would have sworn that the effigy took in a deep breath as they had trespassed its threshold.

"This is the Oracle," Phineas Brock said. "Show some respect." He removed his redcap and bowed.

Meadowlark inclined his head too.

"We ask questions and hopefully it will provide us with the answers we need," Phineas Brock said.

"Okay," said Meadowlark.

On either side of the effigy, water trickled into two stone basins and yet it never seemed in danger of overflowing. Its sound filled the awful silence.

Phineas Brock stopped again a short distance from the awful effigy and bowed again, deep and long. "Great Necromancer, we are in dire straits and require your assistance."

The chamber took a deep breath. Meadowlark's ears pricked as he looked about.

A sound emerged from the effigy. "Like dust you are scattered."

"Yes, indeed," Phineas Brock said.

"One stands in the heart of an endless plain. One sits atop a mountain. One crosses a valley wilderness. One paces in a castle in the clouds, imprisoned by beings of fire and air."

"That doesn't sound good," Meadowlark muttered.

"Indeed," said Phineas Brock. Then he cleared his throat, "How might I best help them?"

"The one upon the mountain has fresh allies. The one in the valley wilderness is not far from home. The one in the endless plain is resourceful and has new allies enough as well. These ones need no help. Take wing to the cliffs south of Nuneau and search out a ship sailing the cloudseas. Give its Captain a sack of gold, and he will bear you to the stolen castle among the clouds. Proceed with care. Approach only in darkness lest the entities of fire and air see you and make you captive as well."

"But what of my cohorts?" Phineas Brock said.

"Go first to the castle in the clouds. Events will unfold, as they must from there. Go with good intentions. Go in the Palm of Providence." The effigy let go one last sigh and fell utterly silent again.

"The cliffs south of Nuneau," Meadowlark said, his white tail swishing back and forth.

Phineas Brock turned about, hands on hips. "That's what the oracle said and there we shall go, but first we must stop at my home. I need more gold to pay the mercenaries in the clouds."

"Right." Meadowlark turned about and plodded all the way outside. Blinking at the sunlight, Phineas Brock climbed into the saddle and the horse stretched out its wings.

"Home, old son," Phineas Brock said.

In three bounds, the Faerie horse was airborne and swooping southwest toward Phineas Brock's stomping grounds elsewhere in the Enchanted Forest.

Moss and vines attested to the cottage's lengthy existence on that secluded hilltop and the well-worn footpaths Sullivan and Evin crisscrossed confirmed that the place was not some hideout, especially not when smoke persisted from the chimney. Someone was at home within Radiant Valley, so, obviously, the Mountain's powerful residents not only knew about this intruder, but also tolerated, if not welcomed them. Therefore, Sullivan figured, whoever lived there couldn't be too scary. Eccentric? Maybe, but not scary, and maybe they could even throw together a decent meal for two weary travellers.

Ready to scurry into the undergrowth at the slightest sign of danger, Evin let Sullivan lead the way.

Sullivan marched right up to the cottage, peered inside over the half door and knocked on the open upper half. "Hello, is anyone home?"

"Tristan?" came a man's voice from within a low doorway. A lean, tall man with thick black hair ventured out of the inner shadows and hesitated. "Oh! You aren't Tristan the Pleasant."

"No, I'm Sullivan Trooper."

The man smiled and came up to the doorway. "I've heard of you. Welcome to AErmish Cottage." His brown eyes took in the gangly Elf with real warmth and he extended a well-worked hand to shake his.

"I wish I had the same honor, Mr. - ?" Sullivan said.

"Arthur Mudor."

Evin leapt upon the half door in one bound.

"And who is this?" Arthur Mudor said.

"Evin, at your service." The Leprecaun removed his hat and scratched his red head. "You wouldn't have any refreshments for a pair of parched wanderers, would you? Punch, a spot o' tay, spring water, anything that is cool and refreshing?"

"On a warm day such as this, my spring water is best. It is the coolest, sweetest water a body could crave." Arthur Mudor pulled the bolt on the lower half of the door and swung it open. "Come in and rest your feet. It is early yet for supper, but you can have some buttermilk biscuits and jam, or honey, if you prefer, to tide you over."

"What sort of jam?" Evin said as he leapt down and strolled with Sullivan behind their host.

"Strawberry, crinkleberry, cranberry, greenberry-mint, these hills overflow with wild berries and fruit every spring and summer. Pull up a chair. It's so seldom that I get any company that isn't astride a dragon."

Evin sprung into a chair and from the chair onto the table. Sullivan helped him improvise a chair and table out of a brick, covered with a soft folded tablecloth, and two more bricks topped with a colorful tile that Arthur Mudor wiped off and handed to him. Then Sullivan sat down and eased his feet out of his boots.

"So you know the people on the Mountain too?" Sullivan wriggled his toes. He had a hole in his right stocking. His heel felt odd poking through it.

Arthur gave Evin a small tin cup filled with water and handed Sullivan a glass brimming with water. "I went ahead and started boiling some water for your tea." He opened a container on his counter and took out some fat buttermilk biscuits. He set them on a plate and set several small ceramic pots around it. "There, you can try each one until you find one you like." Lastly he gave them spoons and knives before he sat down too.

Evin took up his spoon and peered into one of the little pots of jam. "Smells scrumptious." He dipped his spoon in and covered half a biscuit with some of the jam.

Sullivan made for the crinkleberry jam first. "You mentioned Tristan. You're friends with him?"

"He's my son," Arthur Mudor said.

Obviously this was a surprise. Evin noticed that Sullivan's jaw dropped and that his spoon nearly did too.

"But you don't look a day over thirty and Tristan came from another land," Sullivan said.

Arthur Mudor nodded and glanced over his shoulder at the kettle on his cast iron stove. "Yes, he came from Caermon like his parents. You didn't know about that practice?"

"If you mean the practice that they have on Shadow Mountain of bringing gifted children here to raise, yes, but usually, the parents don't come," Sullivan said.

"Master Sorcerer Macy brought us here as a family - Henriette, the baby and me, so that Tristan would grow up on Shadow Mountain, and so Henriette and I could have a life together after all." The water was boiling. Arthur Mudor stopped to add the tea and bring the pot to the table with cups, cream, and honey. Then he sat down again while the tea steeped.

"You have to tell me the story," Sullivan said, "that is, if you don't mind."

"Did Henriette make these biscuits?" Evin said, already slicing his second one in half. "If so, they're delicious."

"No, I made them," Arthur Mudor said. "They come from a recipe that Henriette learned from Madame Sanger up on Shadow Mountain. Actually, she learned everything about cooking from Madame Sanger, and I learned everything I needed to know to survive in this wilderness from the Necromancer Griffith the Moody."

Sullivan grinned. "His green thumb is miraculous."

"Griffith even gave me a copy of his Agricultural Omnipedia." Arthur Mudor motioned toward a fat little book sitting in a place of honor above the pianoforte beside the window. "Thanks to him, I know all about the soil and everything that grows from it."

"I'm impressed." Sullivan glanced at Evin.

Evin nodded vigorously.

Arthur Mudor poured tea for them. "It's a special blend. Walton the Watcher blends it."

Sullivan breathed in its particular perfume. "Red and black tea, but only particular leaves. I've had it a couple of times. So when do we get to meet Tristan's mother?"

Arthur Mudor met Sullivan's glance. "She died many, many years ago."

"I'm sorry."

Evin stopped slurping daintily on his tea. "My condolences, Mr. Mudor."

"It goes back to the circumstances that brought us here. Henriette Amazo was a princess, the only daughter of a powerful king - his youngest child. The Mudors served the Amazo Kings hand in glove and my beautiful aunts were the King's mistresses. Wherever the King went with his Queen, my two aunts went as well. My cousins were his children and all of us were close, but I was closest to the King's eldest son Artair Amazo. We were like brothers, until Henriette and I fell in love. She was carrying my child and we married in secret. Evidently, although a Mudor was good enough to serve as the King's right hand man and as his mistress, a Mudor was not good enough to marry the King's daughter. The King imprisoned both of us for a year. My son was born inside a prison tower. I did not get to see him until the day I was released and then it was so the King could bring Henriette and me together one last time before he sent us into exile – her to the mountains of Norgel County and me to the kingdom of Gobelin in the south. We were never to see each other again."

Arthur Mudor smiled in a quiet, thoughtful manner. "Fortunately, Macy had other plans in mind. Tristan had gifts, so he belonged here, so Macy sent Alison the Terrible and Valeria the Grand across the vast ocean to find him – and his parents. It was terrifying. One minute, I was riding Mercy south to Gobelin and the next both of us were in the grips of Alison the Terrible's dragon Hubert. They brought us directly to AErmish cottage. Henriette and my son were waiting here for me with Valeria the Grand and Macy. Here we made our home. When Tristan was old enough, he went off to school on Shadow Mountain, but he came home every week to see us. We were happy, but Henriette missed home and the King's brutal treatment of her had wounded her deeply. She could not let go of the past and I could not make her happy enough, so whereas I survived and become rooted to this bewitched realm, she grew ill finally and died when Tristan was twelve. Here I have remained ever since. I go herb hunting with Griffith the Moody, Edmund the Healer, and Agnetha the Powerful when the hills are in season. Tristan still comes to stay with me once a month. We collect fossils and mineral rocks for the students on Shadow Mountain." He sighed. "What brings you two to my door now?"

"Now there's a tale of adventure," Evin said, wiping his mouth on the handkerchief he whipped from his coat pocket.

"I should love to hear it," Arthur Mudor said.

"Be my guest, Evin," Sullivan said.

"Well, it all started at a creaky old pile of evil called Badenoch Castle…"

At the end of Evin's recounting of their grievous misadventures, Arthur Mudor sat back and tucked his thumbs inside his pockets. "What you went through could turn a young man's hair white."

Evin nodded.

"So you have no idea what became of your friends?" Arthur Mudor said.

"Not at this moment, but Walton the Watcher might be able to pry some clues out of the Flame of Prophecy once we reach Shadow Mountain in a few days," Sullivan said.

"We can be there within an hour," Arthur Mudor said.

"How?" Sullivan said.

"Take Mercy."

"Your horse?" Evin said.

Arthur Mudor nodded. "Like his master, my charger has also endured a subtle transformation. He is a Seven-League horse. He can cross in hours what it might take a normal horse to cross in a week. Only Faerie horses can come close to matching his speed and even they must rest their wings."

"We would love to go with you on your Seven League horse," Sullivan said.

Evin nodded energetically.

"Good. I shall surprise my son," Arthur Mudor said.

"But let us finish this wonderful tea first," Evin said.

"Certainly," Arthur Mudor said.

The scouts returned an hour before sunset, winded, but otherwise unaltered from when they left. Viola, Scudamore, Quinzano, and the rest gathered round them to hear their report.

"What did you see to the south?" Quinzano said.

Kelyng spoke for Hawtrey and himself. "Some villages, most of them along the sea coast and beyond that miles and miles of ocean. None of it looked familiar."

Hawtrey added, "They certainly did stare and point at us though."

"Then they've never seen Faerie folk before," Viola said. "That is not good."

"Biagio, what did you and Suedama see up north?" said Scudamore.

"Forest, mountains, and tundra," Biagio said.

"And more scattered people pointing and chasing after us," said Suedama.

"They shot arrows at us," Biagio said.

"We definitely don't want to go that way then," Quinzano said.

"How about to the west?" Scudamore said.

"Meadows, farms, fishing villages and vast ocean," said Parslow, after exchanging looks with Gripwell, who nodded.

"That leaves the east," Viola said.

"We are at the far western end of a very vast plain," Montargis said. "We saw tents and teepees and herds of buffalo on the way east and then we hit some rolling hills and in the distance we saw some mountains that only got higher the further north they went."

"But we saw nothing familiar," said Russell.

"That Ifrit dropped us on the far end of our own continent," Viola said.

"How can you be sure it didn't drop us on another continent altogether?" said Calderon.

"Because I paid attention in geography class," Viola said. "Shadow Mountain and its community guard the gateway, the only mountain pass between the special peoples of the eastern lands and the other people in the western lands. This is not a safe place for us to be."

"So I noticed," said Suedama.

"Therefore we must head east as swiftly as possible before one of the natives captures or harms one of us," Viola said.

"I'm with you on that," Biagio said.

"Is everyone agreed on that strategy?" Quinzano said.

A chorus of earnest nods and muttered agreements followed.

"Then we go east at once," Scudamore said.

"No," said Viola. "Let us eat and rest until nightfall. I will need the stars to steer us."

"Excuse me?" said De Vere. "Did you say 'steer'?"

Viola nodded. "I did indeed. I have talents remember? And we dare not cross overland. Someone will capture us, so I will fly us back as far as our home territory. Then you'll have to hoof it the rest of the way."

"Good. Have your supper and wake me in an hour." Viola saluted them with a brief smile and climbed into the vehicle.

"You heard the Princess," said Quinzano. "Get out your ropes and then we'll have stew and flatbread."

Precisely an hour later, De Vere climbed into the back of the gypsy wagon. He found Viola stretched out lengthwise inside, her hands folded over her heart and her eyes closed. For a moment, he wondered and leaned down to make certain she still breathed.

Instead, she opened her eyes. "What?"

"I thought something was wrong," De Vere said as he leaned back.

"Why would you think that?"

He imitated her pose. "Because of the way you were sleeping."

"Oh, sorry about that." Viola stretched and grinned. "Spooked you, did I?"

"You really shouldn't sleep like that." His grin widened. "What sort of tea am I supposed to bring you?"

Viola fished out a slip of paper. "I wrote it down." She slapped it into his palm.

"I'll be back shortly." De Vere read the ingredients as he climbed back out.

Five minutes later, he returned with a cup that trailed an aromatic steam behind it. "Here you go, Princess."

"Thank you." Viola sat up and breathed in the aroma. "Tell everyone to mount up and stand ready. As soon as I finish this fortifier, I'll begin work, but I need someone to ride in here and watch over me, make sure I don't stop breathing or some such rot."

"You might stop breathing?" De Vere stared.

"It's a possibility. Magic is more than spells. It's concentration, meditation, mind over matter, the understanding of the true nature of things – what is and what is not," said Viola as she took the first sip and made a slight face.

"Well, in that case, I'll ride in here and if you stop breathing?"

"Pinch my ear."

"I'll do that."

"How do you suppose she's going to do it?" Acton whispered to Russell. Russell and Warwick shrugged.

"Exciting though, isn't it?" said Suedama.

The young men nodded and tightened their grip on their reins.

Quinzano and Scudamore exchanged looks. All around them the bandits waited on horseback, except for Calderon, who sat on the wagon's seat humming a calming melody to his horses. De Vere's horse stood tied to the back of the wagon while he sat inside, keeping watch over the Princess, as he had explained to the rest.

Suedama had smirked at that, but one dark look from De Vere had wiped it off his knowing face.

Within, De Vere sat on Calderon's bed, the emptied cup in his hand.

Viola remained stretched out. She had closed her eyes again and her breathing deepened.

The soft glow from the lantern flickered and went out. De Vere stared at it. There had not been one draft to cause it and although the lantern had gone out, a soft light suffused the interior, emanating from around Viola. De Vere wondered at it, but dared not utter a sound.

"Where did that fog come from?" yelped Kelyng.

"Stay calm," Quinzano said.

Everything within the wagon vibrated and then went still.

"Whoa! Where did that wind come from?" Biagio shouted.

"Stay calm," shouted Quinzano.

"I can't see a thing," Gripwell said.

The wagon creaked. Outside, the horses neighed. The wind whipped the sound around them. It seemed to last for hours until startlingly, it stopped.

Viola opened her eyes. "Hello?"

De Vere jumped. "Hello, yourself! Is it over?"

"Where in blazes are we?" Trapnel said.

"I'll go ask our little witch," Scudamore said.

Viola and De Vere heard his footsteps and suddenly the night air burst in.

"Cozy and dark, I see," Scudamore said.

"Oh, pardon me." Viola glanced at the lantern and it flared to life.

Scudamore squinted in its sudden brilliance. "Where are we?"

Viola held up her hand to De Vere. He helped her up. "We are on the western border of the Enchanted Forest, pretty much where we all first crossed paths." She edged out for a look at the forest ahead of them. "I couldn't focus on an abstract location, so I focused on the last place I remembered clearest before this whole rigmarole began." She sat down in the doorway and took a deep breath. "I'm still a little weak. This was my first big, independent spell."

"Congratulations," said Scudamore. "Rest yourself. We'll take care of everything from here."

"Where do we go from here?" said De Vere.

The other bandits rode around to join in the conference.

"Badenoch?" said Acton.

Viola shook her head. "There is only one place to go."

"Shadow Mountain?" said De Vere.

She shook her head. "Nuneau – to see if we can't enlist my sister's help."

"But we are wanted men, Princess," said Quinzano.

"I'll vouch for you. Besides, I think powerful Ifrits will be considered a much greater concern than a bunch of bandits looking to retire," Viola said. "If you help her get Gualtero and Sullivan back safely, the Queen will do more than pardon you."

"I'm with Viola," said De Vere.

"Well, for the lack of a better plan, I say we go to Nuneau and hope for the best," Quinzano said.

"A show of hands, all in favor?" Scudamore said.

All, but two raised their hands.

"Off to Nuneau. I'll take the point," Scudamore said. "It'll be dark in that forest. We'll need lanterns."

"No, here," Viola said. She cupped her hands together and whispered words into them. Opening her hands, a sphere of light rose into the air. "It will last until dawn. Tell it where you want to go, Quinzano, and it will lead the way."

"You're handy," said Scudamore.

Viola shrugged. "I was raised to make myself useful."

"Well, then, little sphere, lead us toward Nuneau," said Quinzano.

The sphere bobbed once and then glided off. They set off at once at a steady pace, heading into the deep, dark forest.

As the wagon lurched forward, De Vere climbed out and mounted his destrier. He rode directly behind the wagon, guarding its rear. He exchanged looks and comments with Viola for some hours, until she settled back and curling up within his sight, slept off her fatigue.

11.

The Ifrits seemed to come and go with alarming frequency. Whenever they returned, La Questa shut herself up with them in the throne room for yet another secret meeting.

Anna Marpessa remembered that there was a concealed chamber above the throne's dais where, long, long ago, widowed consorts and their uncrowned children or special guests observed formal proceedings. So while, Lombard and Anna Marpessa crept up into the private chamber behind the throne to listen in to their conferences, Carissa and Olwen sat out in front of the throne room staring out at the clouds passing their balcony. They watched seagulls flap around outside. Some of them roosted on the balcony and stared in at them. They heard that many more outside. No doubt they were hitching rides on the rooftops and windowsills.

Carissa watched yet another seagull preen and groom. "I think they're making themselves at home."

Olwen grinned. "Thetis Megara always said that they were the keenest opportunists she had ever seen. Thanks to our floating castle, they don't have to fly across the ocean."

Carissa groaned. "Where are we anyway?" She went out to the balcony. The seagulls eyed her up and down and didn't budge. "Don't get too comfortable, fellas. Someday we'll be grounded again."

As it glided eastward, the castle rotated gradually as though the wind were grasping the turreted towers and giving them an idle spin. To the west, lay endless ocean. The same was true of the north and south, but as Carissa stared east she saw...

"Land! Olwen, come look. We're approaching land."

Olwen put down her embroidery and ran to the balcony.

The seagulls shifted to make space for her, but otherwise showed no inclination to leave.

"What place is that?" Olwen said.

Carissa shrugged. "Wait! Aren't you holding the Omnipedia for Lombard?"

"Yes, in case La Questa and the Ifrits catch him and Anna." Already Olwen dug in her apron pockets and brought out the stout little book. She exchanged looks with Carissa.

Carissa glanced back at the closed throne chamber doors. "Ask it."

"What land are we approaching?" Olwen said.

The Omnipedia flew open. *'The former Rand-Flanion isle – now called Fernare'*.

"Never heard of it," Carissa said.

The page turned. *'Of course you haven't. Your ancestors fled this region centuries upon centuries ago – long, long before even King Arvid's ancestor gave up too and moved his entire nation across the ocean. The people here think you're imaginary.'*

"Oh," said Carissa. "I expect then that we shouldn't attempt to contact them."

The page turned. *'You could, but they don't have any flying dragons in these parts. There is however an individual who might be useful.'*

"Well, don't keep us in suspense," said Carissa.

The land grew larger on the horizon.

The page turned. *'Sethrida de Sarc of Fernare - she possesses the Amulet of Sorcerer Barnaby. If she notices you, you will meet her.'*

"But what about the Ifrits? They might harm her," Olwen said.

'The Amulet makes her their equal. Although she has not their magical powers, they must respect her all the same.'

"So then perhaps she might be able to intercede on our behalf with that intractable Questa," Carissa said.

'She might. Or she might be able to assist your friends as they come to rescue you.'

"Our friends are coming?" Olwen said.

'One by one they are streaming to the Nuneau coast where they shall join forces.'

"I hate violence," Olwen said.

'Violence is useless against these entities. Reason and cunning, as I have told you before, is the only way to deal with them.'

"Fine, we remember," Carissa said, "but what about this Fernare place and how do we signal this Sethrida person?"

'Fernare is an island recently convulsed by war and bloodshed…'

"Lovely," Carissa groused.

'It was and remains governed by Queens of the de Sarc line – the newest one is very nearly the last of her line – Gavra de Sarc. Sethrida de Sarc is her cousin. As the weather is particularly fine, she will see you, as will just about anyone on Fernare who happens to look up today.' The book closed.

"Somehow I don't like the sound of that," Carissa said, "but since there's nothing we can do about it, we might as well enjoy the view."

"What are you looking at?" Anna Marpessa said.

Olwen and Carissa jumped and turned.

"We're approaching land," Olwen said.

Lombard held out his hand for the book and Olwen restored it to him. "What sort of land?"

"According to the handy, dandy Omnipedia," said Carissa, "it is an island named Fernare."

Lombard and Anna Marpessa stared at the blue-green landmass lengthening across the horizon. They exchanged looks.

"If only we had our wings, we could make a run for it." Anna Marpessa glanced back where her wings once existed. "I wish I knew how to get them back."

The Omnipedia flew open. *'Your wings are in a jar in La Questa's keeping. If you can find the jar and open it, your wings will be restored to you.'*

"In a jar?" said Carissa. "What are we? Butterflies?"

"Where is the jar?" Anna Marpessa said.

'I expect SHE has it in her pocket. Good luck getting to it.' The book closed.

"Thank you for your confidence," Carissa grumbled. She met Lombard's glance and saw his bemused smile. She narrowed her eyes, but his grin widened. "You're a thief. You could get our wings back."

"No, I'm a bandit."

"What's the difference?" Carissa said. "You both steal."

"A thief is good at slipping in and out of places and in and out of people's pockets, whereas I'm good at robbing and kidnapping. Slightly different skills, your Highness, you see."

"You're useless. That's what you are," Carissa said.

Lombard grinned. "I wouldn't say that exactly."

"This is no time for flirting," Anna Marpessa said. "We have to get our wings back."

"Someone has to sneak in and get them," Carissa said.

"I'll do it," Olwen said.

"You shall do no such thing," Anna Marpessa said.

"I shall. I am the obvious candidate," Lombard said.

"Yes, you are," Anna Marpessa said. "Now, how do you mean to go about it?"

"Through that private chamber. I'll wait until they take their siesta and then clamber down and see if I can't spot anything containing little fluttering wings."

Anna Marpessa exchanged looks with her sisters and put her arm about Olwen's shoulders. "Fine. Do what you can, but do be careful. You have been a valuable ally and I should hate to think of what those Ifrits would do to you if they caught you."

Lombard bowed. "I will, your Majesty." Walking soundlessly, he crept off.

"Perhaps by the time we are over that island, we shall have our wings and can make our escape," Anna Marpessa said.

"What about Lombard?" said Carissa.

"You like him, don't you?" Anna Marpessa said.

"Already!" Olwen grinned.

Carissa propped her hands on her hips and tilted her head. "And if I do?"

"If we get our wings back, we're taking him with us," Anna Marpessa said. "I wouldn't leave a snail at the mercy of these Ifrits."

Carissa sighed and turned to watch the distant island realm of Fernare rise higher and higher, filling the horizon.

King Arvid's caravan stood ready within an hour of sunrise. Gualtero had been expecting a rather grand and cumbersome assembly, but instead he surveyed a restless collection of twenty packhorses and one hundred cavalry soldiers and the King and his Archduke as they inspected the assembly. The Wolf Troll monarch was a master of efficiency. Beolagh and Conor surveyed the scene from Gualtero's shoulders.

"It looks as though he's done this kind of thing before," Conor said.

"It does indeed," Gualtero said.

Beolagh nodded and puffed placidly on his pipe.

Conor cast Beolagh a look. "Take care you don't set the Prince on fire."

Beolagh frowned at Conor and continued to puff contentedly.

Arvid and Balthazar approached Gualtero.

"Are you ready, Highness?" said Arvid.

"I'm ready," Gualtero said. "This is impressive."

Arvid turned and gave the caravan an approving look. "My duties require that I make annual progressions through my realm, so I had to develop the knack for traveling light and swift through a variety of terrains."

"Ah," said Balthazar, "it's ready."

A Wolf Troll matron handed him a set of small baskets connected by a strap of woven cloth. "For the little men," she said as she smiled at Gualtero and the two Leprecauns, turned and went back toward the cavern entrance.

"I had this made for Conor and Beolagh to ride in," said Balthazar. "You hang it over the saddle like you would saddlebags or you can hang it over your shoulders, and your friends will ride cozy and safe too. They have lids, in case you see any prairie hawks or woodland owls."

Conor cast another look at Beolagh. "Don't you set this aflame either."

Beolagh scowled at Conor and continued as before puffing on his pipe.

"If you don't mind my asking," Gualtero said, "did something happen, Conor?"

Conor tilted his cap forward, a not so subtle rebuke at his friend. "Beolagh set my shoes on fire last night."

Beolagh rolled his eyes and extracted the pipe from his mouth momentarily. "I said I was sorry. If I had known that you had put your shoes there, I wouldn't have cleaned out my pipe over them."

Arvid and Balthazar exchanged looks.

Balthazar grinned and shook his head as he walked away. "I'll get our mounts."

By the time Gualtero had Conor and Beolagh situated comfortably in their baskets and had climbed into the saddle behind them, Arvid was in the saddle and at his customary place immediately behind the front bodyguard. Balthazar escorted the Prince to the place beside Arvid. After a simple, single whistle from Arvid, they set off at a hearty gallop southeast across the great meadowlands.

In honor of Sullivan's sudden visit to Shadow Mountain, Head Sorcerer Macy sent at once for the Elf's former guardians - the witches Elspeth the Brave and Olivia the Gracious and the wizard Chauncey the Romantic. Tristan the Pleasant was just down the corridor, so he came at once into Macy's study to greet his father Arthur.

"It's about time you came here for a visit," Tristan said. "You never come here enough."

"I am partial to my cottage and to the woods." Arthur stepped back from his son's embrace and looked him up and down as he always did. No matter how many years passed he could never get over the fact that this wise young man was his offspring, but it was always comforting to see his late wife's Amazo eyes gazing out at him from Tristan's Mudor face. "My new acquaintances needed a ride here, so here I am as well."

Macy shook Arthur Mudor's hand. "Welcome again all the same, good sir."

Walton the Watcher peered through the doorway. "Ah, so he is here." Then he came the rest of the way in and stood beside Macy gazing at Arthur Mudor.

"Is something amiss?" Macy said.

"The Flame was just telling me that fresh immigrants shall be arriving on our northernmost shores," Walton said. Then his eyes lighted upon Evin. "Where in blazes did that little chap come from?"

Macy smiled. "Evin came with Sullivan. His friends are stranded with Gualtero somewhere else."

"Indeed, but I did not know that the Leprecaun folk were in this realm," Walton said.

"Indeed, they live in Meath and other such realms a VERY LONG WAYS AWAY from here." Macy beamed steadily at Evin perched atop Sullivan's shoulder. "It is just as well that he did find his way here to us. His native-born world is changing in drastic ways and soon there will be precious space left to his kind. I intend to give him a message to bear home to his lord and all the rest that there is more than ample room here for them should they decide to emigrate."

Evin inclined his head. "Indeed, Dark Master..."

"Macy," the Head Sorcerer said.

"Dark Master Macy..."

"No, Mr. Evin, it's simply Macy."

"My apologies, but I shall tell King Leith what you said. Our domain is increasingly trespassed upon by beings without care for lesser lives." Evin removed his cap and bowed.

Macy reached into his pocket and drew out a silver medallion. "This shall enable you to return here to Shadow Mountain with ease. Give this to your lord and tell him that if he needs to speak to us, he is to put this around his neck and give it a rub."

Evin held out his hand. The instant his fingertips touched the medallion it shrunk to his size and he hung it easily around his own neck.

A commotion of footsteps and eager voices announced the arrival of Sullivan's guardians, the handsome copper-haired and green-eyed Elspeth the Brave, the blond voluptuous and sweetly pretty Olivia the Gracious, and the dignified, tall and reserved poetic Chauncey the Romantic whose light brown hair made him look more like Sullivan's brother than his guardian and tutor. Evin sprung onto the reading table so that Sullivan could embrace his family. Elspeth and Olivia kissed Sullivan's cheeks and made much of his height and health as they always did, while Chauncey ruffled Sullivan's unruly mane and smiled.

"What sort of mischief are you into now?" Chauncey said.

"I got separated from Gualtero. We both lost the Princess Viola. Everything is in such a mess," Sullivan said with a wayward grin.

"You lost Viola Marpessa?" cried Elspeth. She looked to Macy.

Walton cleared his throat. "The Flame says to go to the cliffs south of Nuneau and look for a thin gray man with a talking horse. It says that she'll turn up eventually."

"Ah, Phineas Brock," Sullivan said nodding.

Three apprentices came in bearing trays.

"Tea!" said Macy. He motioned toward the reading table. "Let us all relax and have some refreshments."

Naturally, Evin and Sullivan were game for seconds.

Macy stirred honey in his spiced tea. "So, Walton, what was it you were about to say before the reunion got under way?"

Walton stirred his tea and grabbed a cinnamon muffin. "The Flame was just telling me that a ship of refugees will be landing on our northernmost shores within the next two weeks. They're refugees from your end of the world, Arthur."

"Oh?" Arthur paused stirring his tea.

Tristan held out the basket of muffins to his father and exchanged significant looks with him.

"There has been a great war between Caermon and Fernare, the result being that Fernare no longer enjoys complete independence," Macy said.

"So an Amazo King has reclaimed Rand Isle from the de Sarcs?" Arthur Mudor said.

"A Mudor King," said Macy.

"Mudor!" Arthur's brows rose. "What became of the Amazos?"

"The Mudors took over the throne a generation ago. This Mudor King is half-Amazo though. He has brought Fernare into a necessary alliance with his kingdom and that of his consort to the east," said Macy, "my ancestral people in Gathlon to be precise."

That impressed Arthur and Tristan. Never once had they heard Macy mention the country of his birth. Once he had been brought to Shadow Mountain as a child, the outside realms no longer held any thrall over him.

Elspeth listened also with keen interest. "So my sisters must rejoin the greater world again."

Macy nodded. "They would have sooner or later, one way or another."

Arthur and Tristan exchanged looks with Sullivan. Now they knew whence fierce Elspeth claimed her ancestry – the Fernarians.

"A new Queen reigns," said Walton, "but her forlorn nieces travel here with a crew of exiles - their countrywomen, and an Ermish navigator. They will need a place to call home." He met Macy's glance and both looked to Arthur Mudor.

"Of course I will be more than happy to be their host," Arthur Mudor said. Tristan nodded eagerly.

"We will have to construct a place to shelter them," Macy said, thinking swiftly. "We shall send a party of engineers and architects home with you, Arthur. Find a goodly site in Radiant Valley where there is ample access to water and good land to farm where they can live unmolested by outsiders. Build there a settlement and place at its crest a fine lodge for the two Princesses de Sarc."

"There is a perfect site on the northernmost end of Radiant Valley," Arthur Mudor said, "where they can also serve as guardians of the valley in exchange for the hospitality."

"Let us hope they are so grateful," Macy said. "Walton, we must send word to Thetis Megara not to sink their vessel."

"Of that we need not fear," Walton said a little strangely. When Macy gave him an odd look, he added, "The Sea Queen has had an eyeful of their Ermish navigator and is fair besotted with him. They will reach our shores unimpeded."

Macy sighed and arched his brow at Sullivan. "Now that we've resolved that, what shall we do about you, Mister Trooper?"

"I hope to rejoin the Prince and find the Princess and get to Nuneau relatively intact." Sullivan glanced at Walton. "Is that possible?"

Walton scratched his beard. "It's just a matter of getting from point A to point B."

"I can't borrow Arthur's seven league horse and I don't know where Biscuit is," Sullivan began.

"If I might be permitted," Elspeth the Brave said, "I might at least reunite Sullivan with Biscuit."

"Why not just send me to Nuneau to see the Queen?" Sullivan said.

Walton and Macy exchanged looks.

Macy cleared his throat. "Because the Queen is no longer in Nuneau."

"And neither is a good chunk of her castle," Walton said with a sigh.

Sullivan voiced enough alarm for everyone. "Whaaat?"

"Your good acquaintances the Ifrits," Macy said, "have carried off the Marpessa family quarters among the clouds,"

Walton added, "By our estimations, it should be crossing over Fernare within the next two hours."

Sullivan sat down.

"We would send you directly to the Queen, but you would only end up a captive as well," Macy said, "and that would do no one any good. Let your Mamma Elspeth drop you off with Biscuit and go from there to the meeting place on the cliffs south of Nuneau. Can you do that, Sullivan?"

Sullivan managed a nod. He met Evin's awed glance. "Do you want to come with me?"

"You are welcome to wait out the situation here," Macy said.

"No, 'tis best I go and help my friends Beolagh and Conor. Beolagh will have scorched Conor's shoes by now as it 'tis."

"It's decided then," Elspeth the Brave said. "When you're ready, simply step out on the balcony and I'll send you both on your way."

Evin and Sullivan finished having further refreshments and accepted two bundles stuffed with more food and a bag of tea leaves. They shuffled out onto the balcony. Scarcely did they have a moment to ponder how the Witch would transport them when they turned and saw a great shining bubble bounce out onto the balcony. Then they were within it and Shadow Mountain's precarious peaks loomed below them. They didn't get to enjoy the view for longer than a minute when the dragons began swooping and hovering about them peering in with their large expressive eyes.

Evin clung to Sullivan's leg and shouted in his native tongue.

"They won't hurt us," Sullivan said. "They're just curious."

Then one of the dragons batted the bubble with its nose.

Sullivan and Evin screamed.

"Oh, dear," Elspeth said, "they think it's a toy."

Macy looked out across the peaks until he saw his dragon, a panther-black dragon named Andreev Eliathan. He whistled a peculiar short melody.

The dragon's long ears perked up.

Macy whistled again.

Stretching its long enormous body, Andreev Eliathan swooped down from its perch and alighted upon the rooftop. It lowered its head.

"Stop the others from playing with that bubble," Macy said. "If they break it, Sullivan and Evin will suffer a most perilous tumble."

Andreev Eliathan lifted his head, craned his long neck and rumbled. In one leap he soared eastward.

The bumping and batting stopped abruptly. Sky and land swept uninterrupted on all sides of them again. Fleetingly, Sullivan and Evin saw a black dragon peer in at them with yellow panther eyes and then swoop back toward the mountains.

Propelled by intention, the bubble swooped eastward toward the Enchanted Forest.

Viola had reclaimed her horse Arcadia from the bandits and was riding beside De Vere and Calderon and the gypsy wagon. Tied to her pommel by long ropes Gualtero's palomino Navis and Sullivan's buckskin Biscuit followed. Their missing masters' saddles were in the wagon. Scudamore and Quinzano had been talking about selling the two horses, but Viola had persuaded them to let her have them back for her friends' sake.

"What are you going to do once this crisis is behind us?" Viola said.

De Vere gave her a long look. So far their conversations tended toward the inconsequential. He hadn't seemed to be the most forthcoming of individuals, but he gravitated toward Viola as much as she did toward him. Brick by brick his defenses were coming down.

"If this ends well, I will journey to the Land of Many Kingdoms and take part in the great tournaments. If I can display my courage and skill, hopefully someone shall take me into their service as a knight," he said.

It was Viola's turn to give him a long look. "You'll make quite a dashing knight. There'll be all sorts of damsels, ladies, and princesses throwing themselves in your path begging you to rescue them and whatnot."

Beneath the serious demeanor, the youth emerged briefly. "You think so?" De Vere said, grinning.

Viola nodded. "Wait and see."

They regarded one another for a long friendly moment.

Whump!

"Whoa! Ow!"

De Vere's horse reared. Arcadia sprung forward, ears laid back. Viola reined in Arcadia with some effort and turned about. De Vere had managed to get his destrier under control again and was stroking its neck and speaking softly to the horse.

"What was that?" De Vere said as he met Viola's glance.

"I don't..." Then Viola saw Biscuit jumping and bucking through a clearing beyond the trees. Navis had darted after Arcadia and waited beside Viola.

"What is that racket?" Scudamore shouted from the front.

"One of the horses has gone loco, I think," Calderon shouted.

The bandits turned back.

Viola handed Navis' lead to De Vere. "I'll go see what startled Biscuit."

Doubling back, Viola rode into the clearing. One last kick from Biscuit and a large object flailed in the air and landed amid the shrubs.

"Ow!"

"Horse thief!" Viola shouted. She used Arcadia to block Biscuit from escaping and re-captured the buckskin's lead. "Easy now. Easy."

Biscuit stood shuddering.

From out of the bushes came a voice. "Viola?"

"Sullivan?"

The Elf popped his unruly head out of the bushes. "It IS you."

Viola dismounted and held her hand out to him. "Where did you come from?"

Wincing, grimacing Sullivan let her pull him to his feet and out of the shrubs. Biscuit tilted her ears at him and sniffed. Making a whickering sound, Biscuit nudged him.

"Fine. NOW you remember me." Sullivan stroked the mare's nose.

"Where did you come from?"

"From Shadow Mountain via magic bubble." Sullivan stretched and grimaced again. "We're in the Enchanted Forest right?"

"We'll be out of it by sunset."

"Pretty good aim." Then Sullivan looked about. "Uh oh."

"Uh oh what?"

"Where's Evin?"

"Evin who?"

"A little round Leprecaun with red hair and a tendency to lapse into his native tongue when he gets overwrought."

"I didn't see him."

"Where is my saddle?"

"In Calderon's wagon, we'll get it out for you." Viola led him back to the road. "Look, De Vere, it's Sullivan Trooper."

Sullivan paused at the number of bandits gazing back at him. Not a smile in sight.

"How did you get here?" Quinzano said.

"A witch sent me," Sullivan said.

"Where did the Ifrit take you?" Viola said.

"I was dumped on the far western slope of Radiant Valley and lucked into a ride to Shadow Mountain. Good day, gents. Anyone see a little red-haired man?"

They exchanged looks.

By response a branch let out a crack and a little voice yelped.

Acton looked up at a diminutive figure dangling from a small branch. A small green cap, sporting a bright red cardinal feather, plummeted. Acton caught it in his hat and immediately afterwards caught the hat's owner as well. "I didn't know that people grew so small," he said.

Sullivan came straight up to Acton and peered into the young man's hat. "Evin! Are you sound?"

Evin lay gaping at the faces peering in at him. The instant he saw Sullivan's amiable face, he grabbed his hat and clambered out onto Sullivan's shoulder. "Sound enough. Get me clear of this lot, Sullivan."

"Easy now, Evin. Here, this is Viola Marpessa." Sullivan turned so that Evin got an eyeful of the Faerie Princess.

Evin twisted his cap and inclined his head. "So this is your misplaced Princess."

Viola let go a laugh. "That's a polite way to put it. Hello, Evin."

After a round robin of introductions, they conferred.

"So are you off to the cliffs too?" Sullivan said.

"Cliffs?" Viola said.

"The cliffs south of Nuneau."

"No, we were going to Nuneau," Scudamore said.

"My sister is at Nuneau and I figured she could help us."

Sullivan was already shaking his head. "No longer. The Queen and both of her sisters have been abducted along with part of her very castle. According to the knowledgeable folk at Shadow Mountain, they are floating eastward over the ocean and should be crossing over Fernarian land before too long."

"Fernarian?" Montargis exchanged looks with his comrades. "Never heard of it."

"Well, it's a place way across the ocean from here." Sullivan waved his arm off in that general direction. "Apparently, they are all prisoners of the Ifrits."

"What else did Macy and the others tell you?" Viola said.

"They said to go to the cliffs south of Nuneau where I would meet up with a gray man and a talking horse."

"Phineas Brock and Meadowlark!" Viola smiled.

Sullivan nodded. "Apparently that is why Elspeth the Brave reunited me with Biscuit. Biscuit was with you and I was supposed to tell you where we had to go."

"Did they say what we had to do once we got there?" Scudamore said.

Sullivan shook his head. "From there on, it's all up to us."

"Unless you got it in you for another transportation spell, we can be there by tomorrow afternoon," Quinzano said. "Otherwise, we should leave now and travel fast."

"Let's get to it then," Viola said.

12.

Sneak-thieving was always a nerve-wracking endeavor. It had never been his forte. Lombard felt certain that the Ifrit would hear the slightest creak from his over-experienced bones and rising up in a great fury, banish him to oblivion somewhere beyond the horizon. He had no idea what the very formal throne hall looked like before the Ifrits and La Questa made it their domain, but it looked mighty comfortable now.

Tapestries covered the walls and the carpets covered the floors, overlapping everywhere, so that every surface was cushioned and every sound muffled. Wide pillows, fat pillows, thin ones, round ones, square ones, embroidered ones, large and small covered the corners where the Ifrits rested – at that very moment. Aziz lay facing the wall, breathing regularly and heavily. Karim lay sprawled out on his back with his hands folded across his chest and a placid smile on his sleeping face. Jalil lay upon his back with a blanket pulled over his face. Yumni had converted the wide chandelier into a very cozy nest. From where Lombard peered down into the hall, he had a full view of Yumni with his feet sticking out over the room. Of La Questa there was no sign until Lombard shifted his perspective and saw her lying behind the throne on a carpet covered bed beneath a canopy veil.

Taking a deep breath, whispering a prayer in his heart, Lombard opened the secret casement and clambered down the pillar. The carpets absorbed the sound of his feet landing on the floor, but Lombard stood still all the same to make certain that the Ifrit still slept. Not daring even a sigh of relief, Lombard turned away from the Throne Hall and edged toward where La Questa made her bed.

Once he stood where he had a full view of the Jinniyah, he surveyed her boudoir for the jar containing the Faerie wings. The Omnipedia hadn't said what the jar looked like, or how big or how small it was, but it had said that she would be keeping it about her person most likely. 'Which means it could be as small as a perfume bottle,' Lombard thought, as his gaze followed a slender golden chain around La Questa's neck, trailing it to a slender little iridescent purple and blue vial resting on the cushions beside her. He smiled. 'Eureka.'

Sticking close to the shadows along the wall, Lombard circled around and then crept along the floor until he came even with the Jinniyah's bed. He peeked to see whether she still slept and eyed the vial for a long moment.

It hadn't occurred to him that he should have brought cutters with him.

Lombard rested his chin on the edge of the bed and eyed the chain. He couldn't see a clasp and it was certainly long enough that it wouldn't necessarily require one, but he couldn't just yank the vial loose. Lombard gazed into that beautiful dark face with its peaceful expression. Nope, he didn't dare yank it free. La Questa would be awake in an instant and his proverbial goose would be cooked to a crisp.

Lombard dropped low again and rested his chin on his hands a moment. He looked up again. The chain looped through the vial's handle and the handle was delicate. He would snap the handle. That easy. Keeping his eyes on La Questa, Lombard raised up on his knees and slid his hands around the vial. He got a grip of the dainty handle, took another long look at the Jinniyah, and snapped the handle.

Her cool hand closed around his hands and the vial. Lombard looked deep into her eyes. She was smiling.

"I was just…" Lombard whispered.

"I know what you were doing and now you must pay the penalty."

Fearful of the worst, Anna Marpessa retired to her sitting room and took Olwen and Carissa with her. Olwen had been peeking through the Throne Hall's rather large ornate keyhole again and reported seeing Lombard go behind the throne. He had not re-emerged and it had been two hours since. Anna Marpessa and Olwen kept their hands busy with projects so that if the Ifrits came in they would not see their hands shaking.

Carissa sat closest to the open door with a book open in her hands, but she read scarcely a word of it. She was too busy glancing down the corridor for a trace of Lombard or their captors.

"Quit looking," Anna Marpessa whispered. "They'll suspect us. Better yet, Carissa, why don't you sit beside my balcony? The light is much better over here and the Ifrits won't think you're our lookout."

Carissa stood and stared again down the corridor. "What do you think has happened to him?"

"I couldn't begin to say," Anna Marpessa said, "but do come away from there. If they catch him, we have to look innocent."

"That's a futile endeavor," Olwen said.

"Futile or not, it might spare us the brunt of their wrath. Come into the light, Carissa, and have a seat. It's a lovely day outside." Anna Marpessa glanced toward her balcony where she fully expected to see an endless vista of cerulean blue sky and fat fluffy clouds. She saw as well a slender young woman with shoulder length dark brown hair and pale azure eyes wearing a long brown tunic and a black riding coat intricately embroidered along its cuffs and hem.

Letting out a cry, Anna Marpessa jumped between the stranger and her sisters. "Who are you?"

Olwen peeked around Anna.

Carissa rushed to Anna Marpessa's side and took her arm. "Are you another Ifrit?"

The woman tilted her head at them. "What is an Ifrit?" Her accent was different. It had a lilting country roll to it. She had her hands clasped together over her heart.

"An entity of fire and air, very powerful, you wouldn't want to meet one," Anna Marpessa said.

"We are the captives of five such beings," Carissa said.

The woman looked past them at the doorway and then at the shadows in the far corners of the room. "Well, in that case, I shall make an effort to avoid them."

"Are you the one the Omnipedia called Sethrida de Sarc?" Olwen said.

The woman looked kindly at her. "My friends call me Seth."

The three Faeries exchanged looks and lunged toward her.

Anna Marpessa gripped Sethrida's right arm. "You must help us."

"Of course I will do what I can," Seth said, "but what has happened? I didn't know that castles could fly."

Anna Marpessa and her sisters laughed helplessly.

"Please sit down," Anna Marpessa said.

Seth sat in the Queen's vacated chair and the three Faeries gathered close about her on other chairs.

"You saw us from all the way down there?" Carissa said.

"Yes, and so did half the countryside," Seth said. "Commander-General Yulya Ranum thought it might be some strange omen. I had the thought that I should come up to investigate and here I am!"

"How did you get here?" Anna Marpessa said.

Seth opened her hands and let them see the Amulet beaming a tranquil yellow light. "Apparently, if I focus my thoughts on a destination, the Amulet of Visions can bear me there."

Anna Marpessa and her sisters exchanged excited looks.

"Close the door and stand guard by it, Carissa," Anna Marpessa said.

Carissa closed the door, but for a crack through which she watched the corridor.

Meanwhile, Anna Marpessa explained their situation to Seth and concluded by saying, "Is there any way you can help us to escape?"

Sethrida sat back in the chair and rubbed her bottom lip with her thumb as she gazed out at the clouds. "I haven't the ability to transport you myself. I am still an apprentice to the Amulet's powers. If your friend can get your wings back, I can distract your captors so that you can escape."

"Would you do that?" Anna Marpessa said.

"I am not afraid of them, not much at any rate. The Amulet shields me from their powers, I suspect," Seth said.

"The Omnipedia said that although you lacked their powers, having the Amulet made you their equal and that they would respect you," Olwen said.

"Then it's worth a try," Seth said. "If your friend can steal your wings, you can fly down after me. I know of the perfect hiding place for you."

"Therein lies the hitch," Carissa said softly from the door. "Two hours ago Lombard crept into their sanctuary to steal our wings back and he hasn't returned."

"Take me there," said Seth.

The Throne Hall doors stood wide open.

"This is not good," Anna Marpessa said, as she peered out from behind a pillar.

Seth peered out as well. "Good or not, we must make the most of whatever the circumstances present to us." She took a deep breath, adjusted the Amulet, and stepped out into the open. "Give me enough time to introduce myself to them and then wander in."

Straight of back, firm in purpose, Seth strode directly up to the Throne Hall doors and rapped on one of the doors. "Good day! Is anyone at home?"

Immediately she saw a dark, exotic figure sitting upon a thick arrangement of cushions, a woman with dark almost bluish skin and a bemused look on her face. Behind her, Anna Marpessa's Faerie throne basked, neglected, in a solitary ray of sunshine.

"Hello." Seth entered. "My name is Sethrida de Sarc."

"They call me La Questa," she said in a rich, deep voice.

"An honor to make your acquaintance." Seth bowed briefly.

"You wear an Amulet of Power."

"It came with the position, it seems."

"And what position would that be?"

"As counselor to the people of these three realms."

"And what three realms would those be?"

"Fernare, Caermon, and Gathlon. This castle is flying over our territory as we speak."

"So you have come here in your official capacity then?"

Seth thought a moment and nodded. "You could say that. We don't see flying buildings in these parts too often, so I came up on behalf of my people to investigate."

La Questa nodded. From the long tapering fingers of her right hand a golden chain dangled and swinging idly from its end hung a small iridescent vial. La Questa noticed her glance at it.

"Interesting bauble," Seth said. "I like the way it captures the light. Is it antique glass?"

La Questa held up the vial so that the light could play off it. "It belongs to me and as I am old so it too must be old."

"Where did you get it?" Seth moved nearer. Based on the few clues the Faerie women had conveyed to her and the Jinniyah's infatuated attachment to the elegant little object, she suspected that it contained the Faeries' wings.

"It was given to me many ages ago." La Questa lowered the vial into her palm and smiled at it as she closed her fingers around it.

"You are fortunate then to have such a delicate beautiful object." Seth stood a short distance from the potent entity. Of the four other entities and the Faerie man she saw no trace. She looked about the chamber and gave its new arrangements an admiring nod. "This is an interesting place."

"It is not mine."

"Oh?"

La Questa eyed her. "It belongs to the hereditary Queen of the Faeries Anna Marpessa, but I expect you have met her already."

Seth didn't flinch so much as an eyelid. Casually gesturing behind her, she said, "I encountered her out on the balcony. She was looking for someone and was becoming quite upset that she could not find him."

Anna Marpessa ventured into the doorway – alone. Wringing her hands, she stopped just across the Throne Hall threshold and exchanged glances with Seth, before regarding her captor. "I beg pardon for disturbing you, Powerful One, but we can't find Lombard anywhere."

La Questa's eyes gleamed with thoughts and suspicions. "Have you looked for him?"

Anna Marpessa nodded and brushed a loose lock of golden hair back from her forehead.

"Are you sure he isn't in your sister's secret chamber entertaining your sister?"

Anna Marpessa faltered, blinked, and then vehemently shook her head. "He is nowhere about." The question had to be uttered. "Have you seen him?"

La Questa let the vial dangle in the light again. "I have."

"Where pray tell?" Anna Marpessa said.

La Questa smiled and reclined with a sigh, idly fanning herself with a fan made of peacock feathers.

"What have you done with him?" Anna Marpessa said.

"Nothing so terrible as you imagine. He is comfortable enough." La Questa fairly purred with contentment.

If Carissa had witnessed La Questa's behavior, jealousy would have incinerated her on the spot. Although the thought occurred to her, Anna Marpessa doubted that Lombard had betrayed them, at least not willingly, but there was no telling what La Questa had coaxed from him through the force of her voluptuous wiles. She was certain though that he had failed and was now her prisoner, very possibly keeping their forlorn wings company in that vial the Jinniyah dangled from her fingertips.

"How can you treat him thus? He liberated you and you reward him by taking him prisoner, tossing his friends to the four winds, and further captivating him in my very own home. You are an ungrateful…"

La Questa's eyes flashed. "Careful now, Your Majesty, or I shall find a new home for you." She held up a bejeweled hand mirror. The sunlight reflected off it across Anna Marpessa's face.

Anna Marpessa flinched at the light and covered her mouth. Taking a deep breath, she clasped her hands together. "What have we done to deserve this? What can we do that will appease you so that we might return home?"

Seth cleared her throat. "Compassion might emerge with a little forthright understanding. Speak to us."

"I am sorry that you find me such a poor hostess." The Jinniyah tilted her head. "Perhaps a trade might be in order."

"What sort of trade?" Anna Marpessa said.

"Your wings for Lombard."

"Do you mean, you will give us our wings back if we leave Lombard behind?"

"A more than fair trade, I should think. He is responsible for this mess you find yourself in after all. You cannot have any loyalty for him. He is just a troublesome bandit. Leave him to me and you can have your wings back to go where you must." La Questa swung the bottle idly to and fro.

"Give me leave to consult with my sisters?"

La Questa nodded.

"Thank you." Anna Marpessa exchanged furtive looks with Seth as she sped from the chamber.

Seth faced the entity again. "I'm sorry, but this begs the question – what can you possibly want with a Faerie bandit?"

La Questa settled back amid her cushions and smiled as she fanned herself again. "He crept in here to steal back their wings, so here he stays to amuse me. I was sincere when I said that I would trade him for their freedom."

"What would your Ifrit companions say to that though I wonder?" Seth said.

La Questa stopped fanning herself. "They do my bidding. They can have no say in how I amuse myself. How did you know he was a bandit?"

"During the course of introductions, the Faerie Ladies told me about him. Where is he by the way? They told me a little about him and perhaps I might be able to calm their nerves if I can see him and speak to him."

The entity tilted her head slightly and narrowed her gaze. She sighed and relaxed. "You may speak to him." A mere glance upwards at a bright lamp caused it to lower from the domed ceiling.

Midway down the lamp stopped. The light within intensified and then flashed. The lamp went dark and between La Questa and the visitor stood a blond man, tall and strong of limb, if a little bewildered. It was hard to tell which person startled him more – La Questa or Seth, but finally his frantic glances settled on the stranger.

La Questa reached out and took his wrist. "Lombard, this is Sethrida de Sarc, a potent emissary from the land beneath us. This is Lombard de Montfaucon, King of Bandits."

Lombard pulled his gaze from the Jinniyah's firm grasp to meet Seth's concerned look. "Charmed I'm sure." He noticed the Amulet and recalled that the people of Shadow Mountain wore ones like it when they had attained their full rank and stations.

Seth saw the sharp light pass into his eyes and read his thoughts as though he had spoken aloud: 'Help me.' She inclined her head ever so slightly. "An honor to be sure," she said, extending her hand.

La Questa tugged briefly on his other arm. The arm Lombard had half-raised he lowered immediately.

Seth smiled apologetically and closed her hands over the Amulet. "I will tell your friends that you are indeed well."

"Thank you." Lombard's eyes darkened.

La Questa pulled Lombard closer to her.

Seth bowed. "I must be off then. My own people are fretting over me by now for certain."

La Questa smiled, maintaining her firm grip on Lombard's arm. As the doors swung shut behind Seth, she caught one last glance from Lombard and nodded one more time.

As soon as the doors closed, Lombard pulled free and began pacing.

La Questa watched him, smiling all the while at his turbulent discomfort. "I have offered a deal to the Faerie Queen."

"Oh?" Lombard stopped.

"You for their wings and their freedom."

"Some bargain. Even with their wings, how far can they go? The ocean is too wide for them to cross and the realm below is bound to be hostile to them."

"How hostile can it be when they already have a powerful ally?" La Questa gestured at the doors.

"They will be exiles and that is no life."

"And you would know what that is like?"

Lombard resumed pacing. "My heritage arises from two realms, but neither one is home, so, yes, I do know what it is to be an exile."

"Poor half-breed."

"Spare me your pity crumbs. I'd rather you throw rocks at me and get it over with."

"But why should I do that when I am so very fond of my new pet?"

Lombard stopped and cocked his brow at her.

She protested, "But I am, Lombard de Montfaucon, my dear liberator."

Lombard shook his head and rolled his eyes. "Puppet, more likely."

La Questa grinned. "You are so amusing."

Lombard narrowed his eyes at her and resumed pacing. "All I wanted was to retire. That's it. This was going to be my last enterprise, and then I could have spent the rest of my days in front of my hearth, watching my crops grow and the seasons change."

"What about the Princess Carissa?"

"I'm your plaything now, remember?"

"True, but I detect something latent between the two of you."

"She is a princess and I am a bandit."

"King of Bandits as I recall hearing."

"And a wingless half-breed, as you so politely described me."

"It was meant out of affection."

"It felt more like an insult."

"I apologize. She must be having fits now that she knows I have you in my keeping."

Lombard stopped pacing again and stared at the doors. "I couldn't say, but they all understood the risk I was taking on their behalf."

"If you had gotten them their wings back, they would have left you behind."

"Possibly and I wouldn't blame them, since this is sort of my fault."

"Now you look sad. Come and sit by me and let me console you."

"Aren't your companions due back yet?"

La Questa sighed. "It will be awhile yet."

"What are they doing out there?"

"Searching for our homeland, if it still exists."

"And if you don't find it?"

"Then we shall be exiles too."

Lombard saw genuine sadness in La Questa's eyes and understood.

Seth returned to Anna Marpessa's chambers.

Carissa jumped up. "Have you seen him?"

"He is well," Seth said.

Anna Marpessa caught Carissa's hand to steady her. "He is a prisoner?"

Seth nodded. "Will you accept her offer?"

"Of course not," Anna Marpessa said.

"Well, suffice to say he serves you still in diverting her attentions. I must leave, but I will find a way to communicate with your friends. Keep alert for anything that can help you escape." The Amulet around Seth's neck was ablaze with orange and red as she backed toward the balcony. "Take care and have faith." She bowed and disappeared.

"A ship in the clouds indeed," groused Phineas Brock. "Have you ever heard of such a thing?"

Meadowlark shook his mane. "Not until the Oracle mentioned it."

They looked skyward in all directions. To their east stretched a seemingly boundless ocean. To the west, north and south lay their known world.

Meadowlark continued to scan the horizon for a wisp of a cloud. "It said that it would be among the clouds."

"Of course, if they flew in the open, everyone would see them," Phineas Brock said, "and that would cause all sorts of problems."

There wasn't a cloud in the sky. The Redcap Bogle and his horse exchanged looks.

Phineas Brock removed his cap and scratched his head. "We might as well make some sort of rudimentary camp while we wait."

"Right." Meadowlark reached around and pulled the saddlebags off. He dropped them at Phineas Brock's feet. The leather sack containing the required gold coins made a solid chink sound as it landed on the turf. Meadowlark sighed and then pulled on the cinch until he could shake the saddle off. Setting his right hoof atop the reins, he pulled the bridle off and let it lie on the grass beside the saddle. He shook himself off all over. "Much better."

"You collect the branches and twigs and I'll help you after I've sorted out our shelter," Phineas Brock said.

"Yes, sir." Meadowlark turned about and, tail swishing, he walked off toward a grove of trees further inland.

Phineas Brock had his eye on an outcrop further off to the south. If there were a cave there, they would have a ready-made shelter. He dropped his blue cap on top of the sack of gold, watched it disappear from sight, and set off toward the outcrop, whistling an ancient air.

Not five minutes after he disappeared around the outcrop a great whirlwind settled upon the site. When it died away, the bandits sat aboard their horses looking about.

Sullivan dismounted at once and climbed into Calderon's wagon.

De Vere sat keeping an eye on Viola. He looked at Sullivan.

"We're at the cliffs beside the ocean," Sullivan said. He grinned. "Amazing."

De Vere grinned and peered down into Viola's face. "You did it."

Viola opened her eyes and accepted their help in rising. "Goody." She groaned. "I think I shall have no difficulty sleeping the night through tonight."

When Viola rounded the wagon with a little help from Sullivan and De Vere, they saw the bandits walking about taking in their surroundings.

"We are beside the ocean and – look! There are Nuneau's castle towers way off to the north," Quinzano said. "You did it."

"Fortunately, Sullivan was able to describe the area well enough for me and his map helped me visualize our destination, so we should thank him as well," Viola said.

"I don't see the gray man you described or a roan pinto though," Biagio said.

"There is a saddle here though," said Kelyng. He picked up the bridle and examined it briefly. "They're still warm."

"I need to sit down," Viola said.

De Vere and Sullivan eased her to the ground.

"Here, so you won't catch a chill." De Vere put his coat about her.

"Thank you."

Sullivan noticed the quiet smile that passed between them.

"Two sets of tracks," said Quinzano. "A rather long set of footprints going off that way and horse hooves going toward that grove."

"Phineas Brock and Meadowlark," Viola said. "They'll be back. Perhaps we should make camp. I could use some tea if someone would make some."

Acton scampered for the wagon. "I'll have some made right away."

Viola gazed out across the ocean. Evening gloom already hinted on the distant horizon. Off to the north she saw Nuneau's tallest spires. Far off to the southeast, she saw the bluish outline of the northernmost island belonging to the Federation, Gualtero's home territory. A solitary schooner headed north. They would be safe in Nuneau harbor by sunset. If the sky remained clear, they would have a night full of stars and they might hear the Sea Queen Thetis Megara and her sea nymphs singing on the rocks below. The world was more marvelous than she could have ever imagined.

Meadowlark came back with a mouth full of branches. He took one look at the strangers and Viola peering over her shoulder at him and dropped the branches. "I presume you are responsible for this intrusion, Princess."

Viola grinned. "I am. Where is Phineas Brock?"

"Off looking for shelter." Meadowlark nodded in the direction of the outcrop.

Acton grabbed up the branches. "Thank you. I need these for the campfire. The Princess needs tea. She is quite drained."

"You're welcome, stranger." Meadowlark watched the young man dart back to where Viola sat and followed. "There's plenty in that grove yonder."

Scudamore grabbed Trapnel, Gripwell, Suedama, and Hawtrey. "You heard the talking horse. Go get more fuel. Night is coming."

Tossing their reins to Scudamore, they darted through the high grass toward the grove.

Meadowlark peered down at Viola. "Are you well?"

"I'm exhausted that's all. Casting these transportation spells took a bit more out of me than I expected."

"It'll get better the more you get used to it." Meadowlark smiled.

"I certainly hope so." Viola winked.

"If no one minds," Meadowlark said, "I feel a need to roll in the grass."

"Do as you please," Quinzano said casually enough. He, like the others, had not quite wrapped their minds around the fact that the horse could carry on a perfectly civilized conversation.

Meadowlark plodded several yards away, plopped down and rolled and rolled and rolled.

"The gray man is coming," Russell called.

Phineas Brock came back over the hillock and hesitated.

Viola raised her arms in the air and waved at him.

"Ah, tis you, Princess." Phineas Brock came the rest of the way back and stooped beside the saddle. "Using your skills I see."

"Time is of the essence. Sullivan told me that the Ifrits kidnapped my sisters and apparently, Lombard at one fell swoop."

Phineas Brock met Sullivan's glance.

Sullivan saluted him.

Riding atop Sullivan's shoulder, Evin tipped his cap.

"We meet again. I understand you wound up on the far slope of Radiant Valley." Phineas Brock grinned crookedly.

"How did you know that?"

"The Oracle of Luzarches de Morin told us where you all wound up."

"That was nice of it." Sullivan grinned. "The only one missing is Gualtero."

"He's en route," Brock said, "and with reinforcements of sorts. There is nothing for us to do, but wait for the clouds to bring the pirates our way." He glanced at the sky.

"Oof!" Russell tripped.

The blue cap fell off Phineas Brock's leather sack.

"Owwww." Russell rubbed at his right ankle and scowled at the sack. "Damn sack." He kicked it with his left foot. "Ow!" He clutched his toes. "What is in that?"

Phineas Brock picked up the sack as though it were a bag of marbles. "Gold coins."

"Gold coins! It felt like iron bars."

"What are the gold coins for?" Quinzano said.

"According to the Oracle, the pirates won't give us a ride for free." Phineas Brock gave them a peek and tossed the sack onto his saddlebags.

"All right," Quinzano said, "no one touches that sack. Do I make myself clear?"

"We got you, but you'd better have yourself a sit down with Trapnel," said Parslow. "You know those sticky fingers of his."

Quinzano nodded. "I'll go help bring in fuel for the fire and I'll corner the gents while I'm out there."

Phineas Brock picked up his blue cap, dusted it and tucked it in his belt. "So the gold will be safe, right?"

"If Quinzano says leave it be, the men won't go near it," Scudamore said.

"Very good." Phineas Brock exchanged looks with Viola. She looked weary.

Once they had enough fuel, Evin used his sure-fire incantation to provide them with an immediate campfire. While the Faerie men prepared their supper, Evin sat beside Viola, gazing out at the ocean, and puffed on his pipe.

The flames suddenly shot up into the air, twice as high as a man could stand and when they dropped again, a figure had formed from the flames, a figure of a woman attired in simple habiliments.

"Friends of those imprisoned in the Castle in the clouds," the fiery specter said.

The bandits uncovered their heads and faces and sat up again.

"We are," Viola said.

"I am Sethrida. I speak for them. They are well, but they are far away."

"No kidding," grumbled Warwick.

Russell nudged him sharp in the ribs.

"You wait for a ship that sails the cloud seas," the specter said.

"We do," Phineas Brock said.

"It will appear two days hence. When you are aboard, fly westward until you meet with the castle, but do not approach it until after nightfall. Take with you the Portal Mirror of Solaine, Milady de Morin. The entities desire to return home. The mirror is the portal they need to take them home, but make certain to exact a promise from them to restore all that they have undone before you let them gaze into the mirror."

"Did you get that?" said Scudamore.

Viola, Sullivan, and Phineas Brock nodded.

"Who is Solaine, Milady de Morin?" Acton whispered.

"Good luck and peace to you," Seth said. The flames shot up high again and dropped as they had been before.

"That was impressive," said Suedama. "Who is this Solaine anyway?"

Viola exchanged looks with Phineas Brock.

"She is the former consort of the legendary philosopher king and necromancer Luzarches de Morin, guardian of the Enchanted Forest, the place wherein he invested his powers," Phineas Brock said. "He is the reason my trusty steed Meadowlark can converse with you gents."

Meadowlark bobbed his head.

"Fine," said Montargis. "Where is her abode?"

Viola glanced up at the starry sky. "She lives up there somewhere."

"You've got to be bloomin' kiddin'!" Hawtrey said. "How do we contact someone who lives among the stars?"

"Through her sister the Great Intercessor," Viola said. "Ultima."

"Who?" said Montargis.

The bandits all sat either exchanging looks or staring at the night sky.

Viola said, "We need to create the pattern of a bird on this cliff that will burn all night. She sleeps in the night sky and if she sees the pattern, she will know that we are requesting an audience with her and she will appear the next day."

"You heard the Princess," said Scudamore. "Create the outline of a flying bird over yonder. Make it big so that this Ultima can see it. Evin, if you'd be so gracious, could you light the fires for us with your incantation when we're ready."

"I'm grateful for the opportunity to make myself useful," Evin said.

"Good. The Princess must rest so that she'll be able to help us later," said Scudamore. "De Vere, stand guard over the camp."

De Vere unsheathed his sword and laid it beside his feet. "Yes, sir." Then he met Viola's gaze across the campfire and smiled.

Viola smiled back. "My hero." She crossed her eyes and made a face.

De Vere tossed a twig at her. "Behave, or I'll ask Suedama to take my place."

"No, thank you. I've no interest in being seduced tonight."

Sullivan and Phineas Brock exchanged looks.

An hour later, twenty small bonfires laid out in the outline of flying bird blazed into the darkness and throughout the night until.

13.

The last embers in the bonfires died out as the sun's first light broke across the ocean horizon. A graceful form draped in all the colors of soft twilight stood where there had been only chill morning air a moment before. The brighter the dawn shone the more solid she became, gathering her substance from the receding night. She surveyed the location from behind a lavender tinted veil.

Before her, in semi-orderly arrangements on either side of a gypsy wagon slept several Faerie men, cocooned in drab, but thick blankets, a lanky Elfin gent, with a fawn-brown mop of hair, propped up in his poncho against a wagon wheel, a long gray gent with a dingy redcap settled firmly over his face and his blanket pulled up snug under his pointed chin, a very little, if stout red-haired gent using the wagon's driver seat for his mattress, and behind the seat, just within, slept a young Faerie woman with long brown hair and a peaceful expression. Bemused, she observed that even the horses drowsed quite steadily.

"Such weary travelers," she said.

A roan pinto snapped to, looked at her a long, close moment before succumbing to a yawn. "You must be the one they call Ultima."

The dark woman extended her arms from her sides and smiled. "I am, for you have summoned me with the flaming sigil."

"Pardon me a moment." Then Meadowlark whistled.

All about the sleepers flinched and jumped. Russell and Warwick sprung to their feet and stood looking wild until they remembered where they were. Then they got an eyeful of the dark woman in her rich robes and pearl and amethyst studded black hair and stood mouths agape even as she regarded them kindly.

"And who might you charming youths be?" Ultima said.

"Russell and Warwick Masham," Russell said, while Warwick stammered out a "good morning".

"Yes, it is certainly a mild and gentle one even with such stiff ocean breezes," Ultima said.

The rest of the band scrambled to their feet and tried to assume some semblance of propriety in the Great Intercessor's presence.

"A chair for the lady," Scudamore barked. "I know we have one. Find it!"

Calderon scrambled around behind the wagon to untie it.

Viola climbed out around Evin and jumped down. "You came!"

"You requested my presence," Ultima said.

"Welcome, Ultima. My name is Viola Marpessa, Anna's sister."

"You have certainly grown. When I saw you last, you were but an infant in bundling." Ultima noticed that the elfin man kept his distance. "Is something amiss?"

"You wouldn't happen to have a sister called Zamurrud La Questa?" Sullivan said.

Phineas Brock gawked. "They could be sisters, except that she doesn't have the Jinniyah's bluish tint."

"There are jinn hereabouts?" Ultima said. Her sudden, deep concern rattled them further.

"Five of them," Sullivan said.

"Oh dear." Ultima looked about.

"No, I'm sorry," Sullivan said. "They aren't HERE. They are holding Queen Marpessa and her sisters, and Lombard the bandit king captive in the Queen's own castle," Sullivan said.

Ultima looked north toward Nuneau.

"Actually," added Sullivan, "they're up there somewhere, flying around the world, we think."

Ultima glanced at the sky. "That must be a most striking sight."

Sullivan shrugged. "It probably is for those who don't run in terror from it."

Calderon set out their chair, gave it a thorough dusting, and backed away with a bow.

"Thank you so much." Ultima sat upon it, and after arranging her garments, regarded the motley assembly. "How can I help you?"

Viola glanced about at the others. They returned her gaze expectantly. She cleared her throat. "We need to borrow something from your sister. A spectral messenger named Sethrida told us last night that the jinn wanted only to return home and that your sister Solaine possessed a portal mirror."

"Then by all means they must be assisted in leaving," Ultima said. "They do not belong in this realm and let us hope that their appearance does not signal the beginnings of a mass migration."

"Oh?" said Quinzano.

Ultima leveled a stern look at him. "It is not that the jinn are so very terrible. It's just that they whimsical as well as tremendously powerful. Look at the mischief they have caused already."

"Say no more, we believe you," Scudamore said.

"I shall contact Solaine." Ultima glanced at the sunrise. "I am sure she will be more than happy to help. In the meantime, if someone would fix some tea, I should love to have some."

"You're going to stay then?" Sullivan said.

"Only until my barouche comes for me."

"Stroke up the campfire. Tea for the lady," Scudamore barked, sending bandits running every which way.

Kind as she was, the bandits were too intimidated to chat with her, so diverting Ultima fell to Phineas Brock and Viola. Sullivan refused to come too near her although she assured him that she was not even remotely related to La

Questa. Evin though made himself quite comfortable upon a log and had himself a lovely chat with the lady.

After a little while, Ultima gave Evin a long look and said, "Your kind are not native to this realm, I think."

"No, ma'am. Conor, Beolagh, and myself, we came through a secret place so small that a hare could scarce fit through it. To be honest, we could not tell you how we got here. One minute we had entered the hole and the next we were tumbling out into a forest of grass, too dizzy to walk."

"Well, you're a harmless little gentleman, aren't you?"

"As harmless as a newborn calf, ma'am."

Acton brought her the first cup of tea in a plain camp cup.

"Thank you, young man."

Acton blushed and smiled as he retreated.

Ultima and Viola were conversing about Viola's education on Shadow Mountain, when in the distant southwest they heard a boom in the sky. Ultima paused, her cup midway to her lips, and looked.

"What in blazes was that?" Kelyng said.

Ultima smiled. "That would be my ride home." She sipped. "This is lovely. What is it?"

"Jasmine and green," Biagio said, "with a trace of honey."

"It's perfect."

The bandits watched the southwestern sky and saw finally a barouche the color of sun-burnished red and gleaming gold plummet down toward them.

"It's going to crash into us!" Gripwell ducked away from their campsite.

The bandits fled. Viola and Phineas Brock stepped aside from Ultima and Evin ducked behind the log.

Ultima was shaking her head.

The extraordinary vehicle with the golden seahorse on its prow landed with a bounce and then skidded and skidded and skidded right off the cliff.

"Whoops," said Scudamore. "I think you lost your ride, ma'am."

"Give him a moment," Ultima said as she sipped again.

The barouche popped back up over the edge of the cliff and landed with a chastened little thump. The Seahorse grinned sheepishly, its emerald eyes twinkling.

Ultima's brow arched though. "What did I tell you about these 'crash landings' of yours?"

"Not to do them," the Seahorse figurehead replied.

"Next time you will land in a more civilized manner, yes?" Ultima said. She handed her cup to Viola and stood.

"Yes, ma'am."

"Good." Ultima turned, saying, "You shall have the Portal Mirror quite soon."

"Thank you," Viola said.

The barouche's door opened and Ultima climbed within, closing the door quite firmly behind her. The Seahorse winced.

"Take me home," she said.

"Yes, ma'am." The barouche backed up as far as it could go.

Ultima waved at them as the barouche rushed past them for the cliff, swooped off the edge high above the ocean waves, swerved southwest and vanished with another sonic boom into the distance.

"Just when you think there is nothing left in the world to surprise you," Phineas Brock said.

De Vere stalked past him, muttering, "Just when you think the world couldn't get any stranger."

Anna Marpessa stood out on her balcony. Below stretched a great wilderness continent. The wind had shifted and instead of flying directly east, her castle now headed southeast. Already, she detected an ocean on the horizon. Sitting just within, Carissa and Olwen had their breakfast, but disinterestedly. The Omnipedia waited on the table for someone to consult it.

Anna Marpessa strolled back inside. "Where are we now?"

The Omnipedia flipped open. *'Leaving Gathlon, for Valennce and the Valenncian Sea. You should see the Forbidden Continent by this afternoon.'*

"The Forbidden Continent?" Olwen said when they had read it.

"We'll have circled the world soon." Anna Marpessa sat to the table again. She read the gloom in Carissa's face. "He's fine."

"How can you be sure?" Carissa said.

"Because if they had harmed him, I'm sure they wouldn't have hesitated to tell us."

"That's comforting to know." Carissa took a bite out of her toast and gazed out at the endless blue sky.

Olwen was reading the entries, "Ultima lives on the Forbidden Continent. Perhaps she will see us and help us."

"There's something to hope for," Carissa said. "A castle floating in the clouds – she can't miss us."

"That much is certain," Anna Marpessa said.

"What is certain?" La Questa stood in the doorway.

The sisters exchanged looks.

Anna Marpessa cocked her head to the side. "Have you heard of Ultima the Great Intercessor?"

A troublesome frown flinched across the Jinniyah's serene blue brow. "Should I have?"

Carissa's brows arched. "I guess she hasn't."

"And who is this **Great One**?" La Questa said.

"Well, it's kind of hard to describe her," Anna Marpessa said, "but she is a kind of mortal immortal. When people, kings, whole nations sometimes too, have insurmountable problems they contact her and she intercedes with Fate on their behalf or finds some other working solution to their problem."

"She has great powers then," said La Questa.

"Helping people in dire straits? I'd call that a great power, wouldn't you?" Anna Marpessa said.

La Questa looked toward the window. "It is indeed. Perhaps she will pay us a call."

"How fares Lombard this morning?" Carissa blurted.

"Cranky, but he has not had his breakfast yet. I don't think he likes being confined in tight spaces." La Questa smiled and glided back out.

Carissa threw her toast over the balcony.

"Patience," Anna Marpessa said. "Patience."

They rode too swiftly to converse, but Arvid made up for lost time whenever they stopped to rest that afternoon. The Wolf Trolls broke out the supplies and started up campfires with expert ease. Those who weren't stretching their legs or seeing to their mounts and the pack animals settled around the fires and worked on supper. Gualtero squatted beside the stream and dipped his bandanna in the cold water. With languorous care, he wiped the dust from his face and gazed out across the bucolic terrain blooming in the gentle sunshine.

Arvid brought him a camp cup brimming with a sparkling golden liquid. "Here you are, son. Drink your fortifier."

Gualtero dropped his bandanna on the rock he stood on and accepted the cup. "Thank you, sir. You are a most gracious host."

"Cheers." Arvid tapped his camp cup against Gualtero's and both took a long drink.

"You brew a savory drink, sir. I feel my blood percolating already."

"You seem distracted, son."

"Worry will do that."

"No point in worrying. We'll be there tomorrow and then we'll see what there is to truly worry about."

Gualtero grinned. "I like the way you put things."

"Pragmatism comes with the position." Arvid's glowing yellow eyes took on an amused gleam. "Interesting."

"What?"

"Here I thought this was a diplomatic match to get the Island Faeries to stop harassing the mainland Faeries, and instead, I see that it is a love match."

"Blame Princess Olwen. The nice thing is that both of our nations benefit."

Conor and Beolagh ambled down to the stream and sat down to hang their feet in the water.

"Careful you don't get eaten by a fish," Arvid said.

"So much for cooling off." Conor withdrew his feet and pulled on his shoes and stockings again.

Beolagh stared into the swirling water and shrugged and sat back to bask in the sunshine. He squinted and then frowned. "That cannot be a hawk."

"What? Where?" Conor scrambled back under Gualtero's shadow.

Arvid and Gualtero peered up into the sky.

A human figure zoomed and circled above them. A second, slightly shorter one joined it. They seemed to be bickering.

"I don't see any wings on them," Conor said. "What sort of birds can they be?"

"No regular birds - that's for certain," Arvid said.

"What sort of birds are they then?" Beolagh said.

"T'would be Ultima's pets – Rockwell and Spurlock. They're called

Mercury Birds, but some call them a bloody nuisance," Arvid said.

Gualtero grinned. "What would you call them?"

"Visitors. Here they come." Arvid continued sipping on his tea.

The gangly, dark-haired male-looking one swooped down first and smacked directly into the stout oak behind them. He collapsed onto the deep cool grass with a groan. A large oval object wrapped in red velvet was strapped to his back.

"That would be Rockwell," Arvid said, his mirth showing.

"Whoever that is, he has the ears of a jackass," said Beolagh. "Very strange – a big-eared young man, who can fly without use of wings." He sat up.

"Hang it!" shouted the shorter, dark-haired, long-eared female as she landed easily on a rock in the stream. "Rockwell, you could've broken it."

Rockwell opened his eyes. "It's impossible to break a diamond mirror, Spurlock."

"Well, you could've bent it," Spurlock said. "Hello, Arvid."

"Hello, Spurlock." Arvid found his companions' gaping reactions to Spurlock immensely amusing. "To what do we owe the honor of this visit?"

"We were supposed to deliver that mirror to someone named Viola," said Spurlock. "Where is she?"

Arvid and Gualtero exchanged looks.

"She isn't with us," Arvid said.

Rockwell clambered to his feet and staggered up to them. The wrapped mirror bumped on his back and shoulders with each step. "I knew we had the wrong place. I told you this wasn't the right location."

"Where were you supposed to go?" Gualtero said.

Rockwell and Spurlock exchanged looks and threw their arms in the air.

"Heck, if we could tell you now," Rockwell said.

"Why did she need a diamond mirror?" said Gualtero.

"It's called the Portal Mirror and it belongs to Ultima's sister Solaine." Spurlock pointed at the sky. "The Princess needs it to send the Ifrits back where they belong and get her sisters back."

"Sisters? What happened to her sisters?"

Arvid put his hand on Gualtero's shoulder. "Tell us what has happened."

Rockwell nodded at Spurlock. He was busy untying the straps that held the mirror to his back so he could flex his arms freely and let the blood circulate more.

"Okay, let's see if I have this straight..." Spurlock's dark eyes rolled skyward.

Gualtero did not take the news at all well. His fiancée had been abducted in her very own castle along with her sisters Carissa and Olwen by the powerful Ifrits and were floating somewhere in the sky with their captors. Heavens knew what sorts of torments they were enduring. By the time Spurlock finished explaining everything, the Faerie Prince was sitting on the ground with his arms about his legs and his face pressed against his knees, sucking in breath.

Arvid stood beside him patting his shoulder. "Just keep taking long deep breaths, son."

Gualtero nodded.

"Leave the mirror with us," Arvid said. "We will take it to her."

"All right," Rockwell said.

Gualtero's head shot up. "No, wait. You said that this was a portal mirror, right?"

"That's what our Ulti-ma said," Rockwell said.

"Then theoretically we could use this mirror to get to Viola and the others, right?" Gualtero said.

"Theoretically," said Spurlock.

"But the mirror would remain here," Rockwell said.

"It wouldn't travel with us?" Arvid said.

Rockwell and Spurlock shook their unruly long-eared heads.

"Can I see it?" Gualtero said.

"Sure." Rockwell untied the knot and pushed the velvet sack down.

The diamond Portal Mirror's oval frame gleamed a sapphire blue and amethyst purple, but the mirror itself sparkled and glowed where the sunlight struck it, refracting about beneath its smooth surface.

"That is truly a marvelous object," Arvid said.

Conor and Beolagh gaped.

Gualtero touched it with his fingertips and the light within shimmered. He withdrew his hand.

"So that mirror could bear us home, if we asked it to?" Conor said.

Immediately, Conor and Beolagh saw their rolling green homeland appear as a dreamscape in its shimmering depths.

"Obviously," said Beolagh.

"I have a plan." Gualtero spun about. "I will use the mirror to join Anna and her sisters."

"That's too risky," Arvid said. "If you become a prisoner too, you'll be of no use to us, son."

"Yes, but I'll be of service to Anna simply by being there."

Arvid sighed.

"I will step through the mirror and then you must take the mirror to Viola and tell her what I've done."

"There's no dissuading you I see," Arvid said.

Gualtero grinned. "No, Sir."

"I will take this to the Princess then on your behalf."

Gualtero ran off and came running back with his saddlebags over his shoulder. "I'm ready. How does this work?"

"Simply say where you want to go. The place will appear in the mirror's depths and all you have to do is step into the mirror. At least that's how it was explained to us," Spurlock said.

Rockwell shrugged.

"Mirror, bear me to Anna Marpessa's side," Gualtero said.

The mirror began shimmering.

"Hold on a moment, Gualtero," Conor said. "We're coming with you."

"We are?" Beolagh said.

"We are. We can go places he can't. The Ifrit aren't likely to notice us."

Deep in the bright depths Gualtero saw pale clouds form in an azure sky and then amid the clouds, the pale turrets of Nuneau castle.

"I am not going on this mission," Beolagh snapped.

"Indeed you are." Conor pushed Beolagh ahead of him just as Gualtero stepped into the mirror.

The image cleared. The Prince and the two Leprecauns had vanished into the mirror.

Arvid sighed. "Best wrap that up, Rockwell. I'll tie it to the Prince's horse."

"Yes, sir," Rockwell said.

14.

Anna Marpessa strolled through the corridor, a favorite book in her hands, when soft, urgently in her left ear…

"Beloved."

Anna Marpessa let out half a yelp before slapping her hand over her mouth. A strong hand pulled her into the conservatory.

"Gualtero!" Anna Marpessa flung her arms about him.

Beolagh and Conor had to jump aside to avoid being hit by her book.

Gualtero glanced down at them. "Gents, keep a weather eye out for the Ifrits, would you please?"

"Certainly," Conor said, dragging Beolagh with him to the edge of the corridor. "Leave them some privacy," he added, pushing Beolagh's cap over his eyes when his friend kept looking back.

The corridors shadows remained still and the air soundless.

"I cannot see the purpose of this, Conor," Beolagh whispered. "What can we do if one of those entities shows up anyhow?"

Conor rolled his eyes. "What did you do when you had to fool that old farmer?"

"I turned meself into a little brown rabbit."

"And that is what you do if one of those entities comes 'round. Let those Ifrits chase a little brown bunny so that the Prince can hide."

"And where shall you be while I'm hobbing all over the castle?"

"I shall be a little white rabbit and I'll be hopping the other way." Conor pointed down the corridor.

"Oh."

They continued watching the unmoving shadows.

Gualtero extracted himself from Anna's trembling embrace and pulled her across the room to the window. He popped the shutters and peered out onto endless blue sky and high clouds, building up strength with their size. "'Looks like a storm is brewing."

Anna Marpessa clung to his hand and caressed his face. "Where did you come from?" She didn't wait for an answer. "Oh! You must leave."

"I'm staying."

"No, you must go before you end up like poor Lombard."

Gualtero hesitated and grasped both of her hands. "What happened to him?"

"La Questa keeps him prisoner in a lamp in my throne room. If they find you, you'll join him."

"They won't find me. I came to help you."

"How?"

"We'll fly away."

"Take a closer look, Gualt."

"Where are you wings?"

"La Questa took away our wings. She keeps them in a bottle about her neck. That's how Lombard ended up her prisoner. He snuck in there to steal our wings back and she caught him."

"Well, that was decent of him."

"La Questa has offered to give us back our wings, but only if we let her keep Lombard."

"Then why didn't you accept the offer?"

"Because Lombard is a prisoner as much as we are and has been one since this whole mess started. It wasn't his idea to come here and kidnap us and La Questa disregarded his objections from the very first. Besides, Carissa is smitten with him and I think he feels the same about her."

"You're kidding."

"We can't abandon him."

"And negotiation is useless."

"Only if you are willing to pay her exorbitant price and we are not willing. We all leave or none of us do."

"Help is coming. The same Portal Mirror that delivered me to you King Arvid is delivering to your sister Viola."

"King Arvid? How did he get tangled in this?"

"His people pulled me and Conor and Beolagh off of a mountain peak, saved our lives."

"I didn't think he had much use for us."

"Consider this a good will gesture on his part." Gualtero closed the shutters again. "Now, are the Ifrits about?"

"Only La Questa is here. Every morning she sends the other four out to search the world for their old homeland."

"Hence the need for the Portal Mirror. Can you get me into the throne room?"

"No, don't try it."

"I just need a look inside to get a lay of the land and then I can have a plan ready when the reinforcements arrive. Will you take me?"

Anna sighed, closed her eyes and nodded. "There is a secret gallery, but we have to be absolutely quiet."

"Lead on, milady." Gualtero tweaked her chin gently, prodding a smile onto her worried face.

Anna led him by the hand. Conor and Beolagh fell in behind them.

"I have a dangerous mission to do," said Gualtero, "but I would love some assistance, chaps."

"What is it you need?" Conor said.

"I may need you spy for me. Maybe even steal something back for us."

"A gentleman never turns away from the opportunity to perform brave and noble deeds," Conor said. "Right, Beolagh?"

Beolagh dragged his heels. Conor elbowed him.

"Indeed," Beolagh grumbled. "Two orders of rabbit stew - coming up."

"Where are your sisters?" Gualtero said.

"They were trying to find a fishing pole. Carissa had a plan for stealing both the lamp containing Lombard and the bottle with our wings if she could find or make one."

Creeping so quietly that they could hear their clothes scraping, Anna Marpessa led them up into the concealed gallery.

There they lay upon the floor in silence, looking down into the chamber. La Questa reclined on her pillows before the vacant throne and smiled as she whispered into a glowing lamp.

'Lombard?' Gualtero mouthed.

Anna nodded.

La Questa let the lamp go and watched it float gently about the room by her whim. Only then could Gualtero see the little irredescent bottle hanging from about her neck. The Marpessas' wings sparkled as they fluttered inside it.

Gualtero nodded at Anna. They withdrew as soundlessly as they had arrived into the private stairwell. He pressed the door shut and leaned upon it, saying, "I have an idea."

"I'm all ears," Anna said.

Gualtero met Conor and Beolagh's looks. "I would like to use Carissa's fishing pole idea, except that we will lower my two brave little friends Conor and Beolagh here to steal back your wings and Lombard. That is, if they're game for the mission?"

Conor leveled a bright look at solemn Beolagh. " 'Tis no time to be turning coward, Beolagh. I say we do it."

Beolagh bit on his lip and thumbed his dark beard a moment. "What is the worst that could happen? End up like Lombard, trapped like a firefly?" Beolagh shrugged. "At least I'll know how the worms feel on the end of a fishing hook."

Conor tilted his head and nodded. "Indeed, you have it."

"Let's go find Carissa and see about that fishing pole," Gualtero said.

They crept back down the stairs and into the back corridor, stealing through the shadows back into the Queen's private corridor.

Time had a way of dragging while they waited. Viola, Sullivan, Evin, and Phineas Brock amused themselves for hours at a time exploring the wavering beach below the cliffs. For lack of anything better to do either, Acton, Russell, and Warwick followed them and returned laden with seashells and interesting rocks, which they spread out upon the ground around their campsite to examine and admire.

Even the breeze was warm that day. Their horses grazed to their hearts' content and then stood about swishing their tails or rolling in the tall grass. De Vere practiced fencing out in the high grass for a couple of hours and then stretched out, pulled his hat over his face and napped. Calderon sat in the shade of his wagon, hat low over his eyes and drowsed. Suedama, Trapnel, and Gripwell had gone down to the beach as well with their long poles in hopes of catching something to add to their dinner. Quinzano read philosophy in the shade of the wagon and kept an eye out for travelers.

Unable to hold them back any longer, Scudamore had accompanied Montargis, Hawtrey, Parslow, Kelyng, and Biagio to Nuneau Village a good stretch of the legs away. Scudamore carried a list of things they needed, but none of them walked in any great haste. The day was too warm and too nice for rushing about.

Far within the family wing's recesses, deep in a closet, Carissa and Olwen found the fishing pole belonging to their late father and turned it over to Gualtero and Anna Marpessa.

Armed with it, Gualtero and his two small allies headed back to the secret gallery. His parting words were simple: "Stay here. If I don't come back in two hours, you'll know we failed."

As soon as he and the two Leprecauns had left, Olwen turned to her sisters. "So what do we do now?"

Anna Marpessa clapped her hands together once. "Come. It's a fine day. Let's go bask on the balcony with our hobbies and enjoy the scenery, and most importantly, LOOK INNOCENT."

Between the three of them, they came up with a reasonably sound plan. Gualtero would swing Conor and Beolagh out on the fishing line toward the lantern that imprisoned Lombard. While Beolagh either liberated Lombard or attached the hook to the lantern – whichever was deemed more practical, Conor would attach a separate line and swing over to the chandelier above La Questa's resting place. From there he would lower himself within range of the bottle, somehow liberate the bottle and then carry it up into the chandelier. The plan was much too complicated and therefore risky for Gualtero's liking, but it was the best they could come up with.

La Questa had lain back on the cushions and dropped off into a nap. Since their last visit, she had opened the throne hall doors to have the full benefit of the balmy breezes as well.

"Well, at least that gives us an alternate escape route if everything goes wrong," Gualtero commented under his breath. He opened the grate and threw out the line. Missed. Gritting his teeth, he reeled the line back in and threw it out again. The line passed over the top of the lantern. Its hook hung down from the other side. La Questa still slept. He reeled in the line until the hook caught on the top of the lantern and then he reeled in the line until it was taut. "All right, I'll hold it steady. Don't fall off."

Conor and Beolagh clambered up onto the fishing pole and edged out onto the line. Braced against the pillar, Gualtero kept the line firm. Despite the imminent peril both Leprecauns faced, they scooted along the fishing line with the ease of trained acrobats. There wasn't a trace of hesitation in their determined strides. Astonished, Gualtero shook his head.

In two minutes, they had reached Lombard's glowing prison, springing off the fishing line onto its lid. Crouching down, Conor and Beolagh eyed La Questa a moment. She still slept. Conor prepared his line for the descent.

Beolagh peered through the tinted glass and then rapped softly.

Through the yellow tinted glass, he saw a small man peering up.

"Hello?" said Lombard, frowning, squinting.

Beolagh removed his cap. "'Tis I, Beolagh. We've come to get you out."

Lombard looked down through his glass floor. "Don't even try. She won't hesitate to put you in here too."

"Reinforcements are coming, but first we get you out."

Lombard opened his mouth to protest, but gaped as he watched Conor descend on the end of a very long line. He watched the Leprecaun head straight for La Questa and clapped his hands over his eyes.

Beolagh clambered about the top of the lantern until he spotted the latch that held it closed, but he couldn't reach it. Sitting back a moment, he pondered the challenge and then remembered his belt. In a blink he had whipped his sturdy belt from about his waist and leaning out over the edge, swung the silver belt buckle to and fro until it caught the latch. Then with all his might, he pulled.

The latch budged.

Gualtero stood amazed at the ease with which Conor rappelled down to the deep cushions surrounding La Questa. No heavier than a sparrow, he alighted and surveyed the challenge ahead. The iridescent bottle hung from a golden chain about the Jinniyah's soft, graceful neck. 'Easy enough', he thought. He'd just pry open one of the links. He took out his pocketknife and crept across the cushions toward the bottle.

La Questa's eyes opened.

Up went the latch. The lantern popped open.

Brows arched, La Questa sat staring at two bunnies sitting amid her cushions. One was a light brown bunny and the other was black. Ears laid back, noses twitching, they huddled, ready to flee at the slightest movement from her.

Then she saw her lantern swinging slightly overhead, darkened. She eyed the bunnies again. "Why do I have the feeling that you have something to do with his escape?" she murmured.

Neither bunny dared move.

Once he had his freedom, Lombard had leapt out onto the cushions and ran for the open doorway. Beolagh had tumbled off the lantern onto the cushions and snuggled up fast beside Conor when the Jinniyah's eyes opened. They saw the tiny figure of a man scampering around the corner. A quick glance upward saw the grate shut again and the fishing line drifting across the ceiling like a broken spider web.

Lombard scampered until he found cover beneath a table in the Queen's wing. He heard footsteps and then several voices rushing in.

"What happened?" Anna Marpessa said, hushed and urgent.

Lombard peered out from behind the long tablecloth's fringe. The Marpessa sisters stood clustered about a tall dark-haired man – Prince Gualtero. The Prince was peeking out a moment longer.

Gualtero closed and locked the door. "For what good **that** does," he muttered as he began to pace.

"What happened?" Anna Marpessa repeated.

"Did you get him free?" Carissa said.

"I don't know. I think so, but I didn't see him," Gualtero said.

"Something went wrong," Anna Marpessa said. "Where are your two friends?"

Gualtero sighed. "I have a bad feeling that La Questa has two new pet rabbits."

Anna Marpessa exchanged dire looks with her sisters. "Let us hope she does not try to make stew out of them."

Lombard stretched his arm out, ready to call out, but his nose began to itch. He heaved. He huffed. He huffed and then…"Achoo!" And then… "Ow!"

Gualtero and the Marpessas jumped and turned to see Lombard crouching beneath the table, rubbing his head, back to his old size again.

"Oh my!" Carissa rushed over to him and helped him out from beneath the table.

"Where did you come from?" Gualtero said.

Lombard stood up and let Carissa drape his arm over her shoulder, while he rubbed his head. He pointed toward the corridor.

"You ran all the way?" Anna Marpessa said.

Lombard nodded and met Carissa's earnest glance for a long moment. He pulled his glance away. "So what do we do now?"

"We still don't have the wings," Gualtero said, "and now she has Conor and Beolagh."

"Two new playthings." Lombard shook his head. "Did she see you?"

"I don't think so."

"Good, then she won't come looking for you, but she will come looking for me."

"We'll hide you," Carissa said. "I've created a new hiding place. Come with me."

Lombard let her drag him through an antechamber door. "You heard the lady. Best come along, Gualtero, unless you want to end up in that jar just like a lightning bug."

Gualtero sighed and followed them through the antechamber door.

Anna Marpessa closed the panel behind them and turned with Olwen to head back out into the corridor.

Opening the door, the sisters came face to face with La Questa, a squirming bunny rabbit under each arm.

La Questa's expression was pleasant, but her gaze pinned them to the spot. "'You like my new pets?"

Olwen reached out and patted the brown bunny. "They're so cute. Where did you get them?"

"I don't know. I woke up and there they were." La Questa watched both sisters closely.

"They must have come in from the garden before you took us away." Anna Marpessa reached out and scratched the black bunny's ears. "Poor things, they must be starved."

"Where is Lombard?"

"He isn't in your custody?" Anna Marpessa said, exchanging looks with Olwen.

La Questa tilted her head and smiled tightly. "You know he isn't. Where has he gone to?"

"That I couldn't say," Anna Marpessa said. "If he got free somehow, then I expect he's hidden himself rather well from all of us, because if we saw him and you came to interrogate us, as he knows you would do, we would have to betray him to preserve ourselves. For a bandit, he has shown a surprisingly expansive sense of honor as well as one of self-preservation."

La Questa's narrow smile widened slightly. She nodded. "I will find him, but in the meantime, I shall take my little pets for a stroll." Inclining her head, the Jinniyah strolled off, whispering to the trembling bunnies.

Anna Marpessa closed the door and grasped Olwen's hand until her heart stopped pounding so hard. "May we see an end to this soon."

15

From a deep sleep, she felt a gentle prod and rolling over onto her back opened her eyes.

A pair of oval yellow eyes peered down out of the night.

She stared. "Hello?"

"You must be Viola Marpessa?" said a deep, rumbling voice.

Viola sat up on her elbows and wiped the sleep from her eyes. "I must be and you are…"

"Arvid, King of the Wolf Trolls." The monarch extended a furry paw-hand down to her. "Pleased to meet you."

Viola shook his hand and felt herself pulled to her feet. "The pleasure is mutual."

Arvid surveyed the sleeping campsite, Faeries everywhere on their bedrolls sleeping off an active day. He spied the lone elf Sullivan Trooper lying a short distance away with his blanket pulled up to his chin and a little further over a long gray man stretched out beneath an inadequately long blanket with his dingy red cap over his face. A sound from the wagon seat drew his attention to a little red-haired man springing up in surprise and gawking at him.

"Ah, another of the little people," Arvid said.

"Just because I'm small - " Evin said.

"I expect you know Conor and Beolagh?" Arvid said.

"I did."

Arvid grinned, his sharp white teeth catching the campfire light. "Well, they are well, or were when I saw them last."

"When did you last see them?" Viola said.

"When they stepped through the Portal Mirror with Prince Gualtero Bainbridge. I expect they are with your sisters now, seeing if they can do anything."

"Or imprisoned as well most likely," Viola said.

"That is likely too. I have the mirror. What shall I do with it?"

"May I see it?"

Arvid led Viola, and Evin as well, over to the horse that carried the large mirror. His men untied and unwrapped it. They angled it just so to let the firelight strike it.

In a sumptuous dazzling eyeful, Viola gazed upon it. "Impressive."

"To say the least," Evin added.

Arvid nodded at his men and they covered up the mirror again. "What happens now?"

"We wait for the cloud pirates to fly into range." Viola looked up into the night sky. Sure enough, coming from the northwest she spied a massive cloudbank in the distance. The breeze gusted. She and Arvid caught the aroma of rain.

"Could they be riding the crest of those thunderheads?" Arvid said.

"There's only one way to find out. I'll go up and have a look," Viola said.

"No, not you. Send up one of these able lads to scout around." Arvid motioned at the sleeping Faerie men.

"Quinzano will know who to send." Viola tiptoed through the encampment and knelt down beside a burly man of many seasons.

Quinzano awoke with a start, but relaxed the moment he recognized Viola. When she explained the situation, he jumped up, snatched up a skillet and began whacking it. "Wake up and get ready to move."

All about the bandits jumped, flinched, and otherwise were startled awake.

"Careless brutes, the lot of you. We're getting lazy. Suppose the local sheriff had crept up on us. Montargis, Kelyng, Parslow, the three of you go off into that cloudbank and scout for the pirate ship. The rest of you break camp and stand ready."

"Are you coming with us?" Viola said.

Arvid considered the challenge and nodded. "Perhaps we can be of use, serve as a diversion if you like."

Viola watched the bandits scramble. Off to the side, Montargis, Kelyng, and Parslow stood taking final orders from Quinzano and then took flight into the electric darkness.

"That's one thing we'll have for certain – plenty of diversion," she said.

Jalil Futaih, Aziz, Jubran, and Yumni returned with clouds of deep dark frustration upon their brows. The throne hall doors slammed hard behind them as they gathered about La Questa once more.

Olwen fled from her hiding spot back to her sisters. "The other four Ifrits just came back." She closed the study door tight behind her and leaned against it.

"How did they look?" Carissa said.

"Very unhappy."

The three sisters exchanged looks.

Anna Marpessa glanced at the ventilation grate. "Did you hear that?"

"Yes," Gualtero replied lowly.

"We're in trouble," Lombard said.

"Everyone stay calm," Anna Marpessa said. "They tend to stay shut in for hours. We'll have until evening at the earliest before they come looking for us."

"Perhaps you should join us in the ventilation shafts?" Gualtero said.

"Perhaps you should," Lombard said.

"I shall bear it in mind, believe me, but in the meantime we three must act calm and be seen as innocent and idle." Anna Marpessa stressed sternly to her sisters, "Do not stray far from these ventilation shafts or from any side door passage that can bear you away from harm."

Her sisters agreed all too readily and the three of them set about their day's usual idle distractions as though nothing was wrong. Anna Marpessa kept frequent watch from her balcony as yet another landmass receded into the horizon and their course shifted slightly northeast across a deep gleaming sapphire ocean. She sighed and shook her head ever so slightly as she turned the pages of her novel, unaware of how Gualtero watched over her from behind another ventilation grid, his eyes framed by gilded iron lotuses.

Montargis and Parslow returned.

"There is indeed a ship sailing upon the encroaching storm. Kelyng remained behind to keep an eye on it," Montargis said.

"So now what do we do?" Parslow added, between heaving breaths.

Viola exchanged looks with her increasingly numerous allies. "Me, and Phineas Brock and Sullivan on Meadowlark will go up and bargain for our passage. The rest of you wait here."

Scudamore and Quinzano exchanged looks.

Quinzano said, "Let Scudamore, Suedama, and Montargis fly up with you for your protection."

"The more the merrier." Viola flashed him a smile. In that instant her wings solidified and flexed behind her.

Phineas Brock slung his sack of gold from Meadowlark's saddle pommel and climbed into the saddle. "Coming, Trooper?"

"Coming." Sullivan climbed up behind him and took a firm grip of the Unseelie Redcap Bogle's belt.

Meadowlark spread his wings and galloped for the cliff.

"Whoa!" Sullivan shouted as the roan pinto plummeted from sight.

Arcing upward, Meadowlark zoomed, veering westward.

"Ready, gents?" Viola said.

"We're ready," Scudamore said.

"Then let's be off!" Viola sprung into the air, spread her wings and fluttered them until she caught a current. Then she soared.

Close behind, Scudamore, Suedama, and Montargis flanked her. They fell in alongside Meadowlark and his passengers.

Dawn was yet two hours away, but it might as well have been broad daylight as far as Paco Dreng was concerned. The sun couldn't rise soon enough to suit him that night as he paced the deck of his cursed ship among the rumbling, swelling clouds. Half of his crew - Mogens, Bardolph, Halstead, Rendor, and his First Mate Wasim - slept below deck. The other half - Sherard, Fyren, Zerbino, and Errando - kept their ship steady on course and watched Paco Dreng pace and eye the night pressing close around their lamps' stubborn light. Every now and then there was a gust and all the lamps guttered perilously.

If Paco Dreng didn't know any better, he would have thought there was a presence in the clouds that night watching them, waiting for its moment to slap their ship about like a cat would a ball of yarn. They were well south of dragon territory, and dragons weren't shy. They would have made their presence known at once, swooped around his ship, scorched his sails, and batted them about with their long sinuous tails. Actually he would have preferred dragons to the sort of spectres that sometimes emerged from the clouds, wailing like banshees, walking his deck while he and his men barricaded themselves below deck armed with auspicious medals and anything else they thought could ward off harmful spirits.

The pirate captain's uneasiness proved infectious. His four men walked about with their hair standing on end, looking constantly behind themselves and repressed shudders.

To say that he was not expecting the visitors who landed with all the subtlety of a rogue bolt of lightning on his deck would have been strictly an understatement. Sherard leapt from the poop deck to escape being surrounded by them and stumbled to the prow to join up with Paco Dreng and the rest. For several heart-pounding moments, Paco Dreng and his men huddled together gathering their wits again.

"Hello?" called a young woman.

Paco Dreng and his men froze.

From below deck, Wasim emerged. "What was that racket?" He marched out onto the deck and scarcely spotted Paco Dreng and the rest when...

"Hello there," said the young woman again.

Wasim turned, his demands falling soundless from his lips.

A butterfly-winged young woman peered down at him. Flanking her stood a similarly winged roan pinto. A tall fawn-haired young man with pointy ears clambered off that horse's back. A tall gray man with piercing eyes and a sternly lined face remained firmly seated in the pinto's saddle, while four winged men, wearing clothing not much unlike ploughmen's attire, circled the deck.

"Greetings," said Wasim.

The other four crewmen began to emerge, but he held up his hand.

They stopped in the passageway.

"Are you the captain of this miraculous ship?" she said.

"No." Wasim jerked his thumb over his shoulder. "He is."

"Ah!" Viola trotted down the steps past Wasim. Extending her hand, she called out. "Hello, my name is Viola Marpessa."

Paco Dreng exchanged looks with Wasim and his men and then shook her hand. "Paco Dreng. What are you doing on my ship?"

"I've come to ask you for some help."

"Help?" Paco Dreng couldn't quite believe his ears.

"We would like to hire your ship to bear us west."

"Hire us?"

"We brought gold," she said.

"Gold you say," Paco Dreng said, exchanging looks with Wasim.

Foolishness ensued. It ended when Viola's would be kidnappers found themselves inexplicably and unceremoniously pitched overboard and left hanging by their ankles into the bottomless night. She and her friends allowed them to swing a little in the churning winds.

Paco Dreng and Wasim looked up and saw the young winged woman leaning on her elbows and peering down at them.

"You realize that we don't actually need you as much as we need your ship," she said. "We wanted to be nice and offer you fair payment in exchange for you and your able crew ferrying us to our rendezvous. It's up to you. I'll bring you all back up on board, but only if you all promise to behave yourselves and take us where we must go."

"What about the gold?" Paco Dreng called.

"You'll get it after you have completed the mission to our satisfaction," Phineas Brock called down. He had already placed the pouch of gold in an out of the way place and set his magic blue cap upon it, rendering it invisible again.

Paco Dreng wouldn't submit without some token resistance. "What sort of mission is that you're on? I won't have you risking our lives on some fool's errand."

"We are going to help rescue the Faerie Queen of Nuneau and her two sisters." Viola turned to Phineas Brock and Sullivan, muttering, "More they do not need to know just yet."

They nodded.

"So will you help us?" Sullivan shouted down to them. "Or do we have to have our sorceress friend here put you somewhere where you won't get underfoot?"

Paco Dreng bit his lip and folded his arms across his chest.

"Best accept and make the most of it, besides Halstead's getting a nosebleed," Wasim said.

"All right. Deal," Paco Dreng called up.

In an instant the ropes heaved and the pirates landed on their own deck like so many squirming fish. The strange young woman and her peculiar companions stood before the poop deck watching them. The pirates untied their ankles and staggered to their feet.

"So what do you want us to do first?" Paco Dreng said.

"Continue southwest until I say otherwise," Viola said. "Scudamore, if you would please, keep an eye out for our comrades. Montargis, would you go ahead and tell them that we are coming for them now. Ask King Arvid and his men to form up close."

"Yes, Princess." Montargis saluted her and leapt overboard.

Wasim arched his brows. "Princess."

"By relation, yes," said Viola.

"A sorceress **and** a princess," Paco Dreng muttered as he turned to supervise their crew, "the world keeps getting stranger and stranger."

Quinzano stood with the rest watching the clouds for their first glimpse of the pirate ship. The instant he saw its prow caught in a lightening bolt's sudden light, he turned to the others. "Stand ready."

A blue orb glided forth from the ship. By the time it had reached them the shining bubble had expanded. It engulfed them all in a blink and carried them skyward against the wind. They braced themselves. The bubble veered straight for the ship, bore down upon its deck and popped against the masts.

Breathless and wide-eyed, they all stood upon the deck, except for the wagon, Calderon, and his horses. In fact all of their mounts were missing, but when Calderon climbed up on deck, he informed them that his wagon and all their mounts were in the hold.

Paco Dreng, Wasim, and the rest gawked at the Wolf Trolls standing amid the Faerie men. For the time being, the glowing-eyed creatures seemed placid.

"Where to now?" Paco Dreng asked of the Faerie Princess standing beside him at the pilot's wheel.

Viola pulled her smiling gaze away from De Vere. "Turnabout and follow the blue orb."

"What blue orb?"

Viola smiled and cupped her hands together. She blew into them and opening her hands revealed a shining blue sphere. "This blue orb." She addressed it, "Lead us to my sisters."

The orb glided forth, heading west.

Paco Dreng and his men veered course and followed it like the evening star.

After the Ifrits had vented their frustrations, they sat before La Questa mute, with their heads bent low resting on their palms, cross-legged, and looking for all the world like dejected children trapped indoors by a downpour. She sat back amid her cushions, stroking her two bunnies, their little bodies coiled tight, ears laid back, noses twitching, and their eyes a little wild.

"So we are not even in the world of our origin," La Questa said at last. "I am correct?"

Jalil looked up and nodded. He continued pulling on a loose thread in his radiantly colorful silken trousers.

"You'll unravel that if you aren't careful," Yumni muttered.

Jalil shrugged.

Jubran fell back upon the rug and stared at the ceiling.

Aziz glanced again at the two little bunnies, cocked his head to the side and frowned. "Where did you come by those?"

"I woke up from my nap and here they were," La Questa said. "Do you like my pet bunnies?"

Aziz squeezed his eyes shut and opened them again. "Those are NOT bunnies."

La Questa eyed them. "What are they then?"

"Oddly enough, very little men. One is blond and the other is a rather sturdy looking black-haired fellow."

The others Ifrits stared, but all they saw were two trembling bunnies. But then Aziz was the only one who could tell truth from falsehood.

La Questa picked up the black one and gave it a long look, but it remained a bunny. "Reveal your true selves to me."

Nothing. Both bunnies twitched their little noses.

"Fine. Jalil, fill that brazier with flames and bring it before me," La Questa said.

Jalil jumped to his feet and lifted the brazier in his powerful arms as though it weighed little more than a plate. Kneeling before La Questa, he blew upon the brazier once and flames shot high and blazed steadily.

La Questa handed the black bunny to Jubran and the brown bunny to Yumni. "Hold them tight. Now give them a good look at the brazier, but be careful not to singe them – yet."

Both bunnies squirmed and kicked, but couldn't break free.

"Now, reveal yourselves to me or we roast you," La Questa said.

Still the bunnies squirmed and squealed.

"Very well." La Questa nodded.

Yumni and Jubran dangled the bunnies just low enough for the flames to touch their fluffy tails.

Immediately, they saw two quaint little men.

"All right! Enough!" shouted the blond one.

"Don't cook us," shouted the black-haired one.

La Questa nodded. Yumni and Jubran withdrew the two Leprecauns from the heat.

"What manner of men are you?" La Questa said.

Conor and Beolagh exchanged looks.

"We belong to the Seelie nation of Leprecauns," Conor said.

"Why were you in my chambers?" La Questa said.

"We were lost," Beolagh said. "We beg your pardon."

Aziz tilted his head to the side. "Then why the disguises?"

"If you were as small as us, wouldn't you disguise yourself too?" Conor said.

Aziz nodded. The logic was sound.

La Questa glanced up at her empty lamp. "You had something to do with his escape, didn't you?"

"Whose escape?" Beolagh said.

Aziz folded his arms over his broad blue chest. His scrutiny had the glare of the sun to it. Both Leprecauns fought not to cringe beneath it.

"You know very well of whom La Questa speaks of?" Aziz said.

Conor folded his arms across his chest and said nothing further.

Beolagh copied his example.

La Questa sighed.

Both Leprecauns felt the heat from the brazier on their heels.

Kicking, Conor growled, "Very well, what do you want to know?"

The heat fell away again.

"Did you have anything to do with Lombard's escape?" she said.

"I set him loose," Beolagh said, chin held high.

"Where did he go?"

"That I cannot say, but I expect he ran as far as his tiny legs would carry him and is well hidden by now. Palaces of this size favor little folk like us."

"Anna Marpessa sent you?" La Questa said.

"No, she did not," Conor said. "We volunteered for this mission." He had one eye on the blue Ifrit. He watched the Ifrit nod to La Questa.

"Just you two?" she said.

Both little men squirmed and looked anywhere but at her.

"If you insist on trying my patience," La Questa said, "I shall cook one of you and then hear the truth from the other, and if I am not happy with what I hear, I shall cook him too. Now, speak."

Conor and Beolagh hung their heads.

"Gualtero Bainbridge was with us," Conor said.

La Questa's eyes widened. "How did he get here?"

"By magic." Conor kept one eye on Aziz's deepening frown.

"Was that true?" La Questa said.

"A shallow truth," Aziz said.

"What sort of magic brought him here?" she said.

"A Diamond Mirror," Beolagh said.

"Does he have it with him?" she said.

"No, we left it behind," Conor said.

"You cannot travel through it and bring it with you simultaneously," Beolagh added quickly.

"I see," La Questa said. "Find a birdcage. I do not want these two underfoot."

The sounds of wind roaring through their corridors startled Anna Marpessa and her sisters. Olwen jumped and dropped her teacup. Its fragments scattered. The tea spattered. In the doorway to the conservatory stood La Questa and her four Ifrit companions. Carissa and Anna Marpessa managed not to betray their surprise. The former continued eating her buttermilk biscuit while the latter poured them both a cup of tea.

"What happened to your bunnies?" Anna Marpessa set the teapot down and proceeded to mix in her usual amounts of milk and brown sugar.

La Questa held up the birdcage and smiled strangely. "I traded them for these curious little men."

Olwen cleaned up her mess and in vain, attempted to wipe the tea stains from her pinafore. "I shall have to scrub this now." She removed the pinafore and stepped from the room. "I shall be back as soon as I have a fresh pinafore on."

The Ifrits eyed the young Faerie maiden as she slipped past them into the corridor.

"Jubran, do watch her and see that she comes back immediately," La Questa said.

Jubran inclined his green head and whirled after her.

"Where are Lombard and Gualtero?" La Questa said.

Anna Marpessa didn't hesitate. "Hiding. I know that's what I'd be doing in their place."

Aziz folded his arms across his chest and eyed the Faerie Queen and her sister more closely.

La Questa set the birdcage on their tea table. "You wouldn't happen to know where they are hiding, would you?"

Carissa bit into another jam-smeared buttermilk biscuit.

"Somewhere around the palace I expect," Anna Marpessa said. "Lombard has no wings so he can't fly off."

"The Queen is being evasive," Aziz said.

"Of course I am!" Anna Marpessa slammed her cup down. "Five jinn show up demanding to know where two of your friends are so they can do only heavens know what to them and you think I'm going to simply give them up?"

La Questa smiled. "Where are they?"

Anna Marpessa took a long sip from her cup instead.

Jalil Futaih saw Carissa glance furtively toward the ventilation grill, a supple little glance almost perfectly disguised as she brushed a lock of her rich hair back over her shoulder. It was enough for him.

"I think I know where to begin hunting," Jalil crowed.

Carissa froze, the color draining from her face.

Looming upward with confidence, Jalil inflated into a cloud of fiery orange smoke and whipped down into the ventilation shaft, disappearing without a trace except for the echo of his laughter.

Aziz noted both Faerie ladies' reaction. "Jalil guessed right. They are in the ventilation shaft."

La Questa sat to the table and smiled. "And now we wait."

They froze.

"Did you hear that?" Gualtero whispered.

"Someone is in the shaft," Lombard said. "We've got to get out of here." They resumed scrambling on all fours.

"Where do we hide now?" Lombard said. "They'll turn this place inside out and upside down and give it a good shake until they find us. Where CAN we hide?"

They reached a central point where their shaft met up with three others. Laughter rumbled down a shaft.

"Where is that coming from?" Lombard said.

Both men looked about.

"I can't tell," Gualtero said.

"Which way?"

Three shafts awaited them. One of them held a menacing Ifrit who would soon be upon them if they didn't move fast.

A gust of cool air flowed over them from the shaft to their left. "I have an idea." Gualtero punched Lombard in the arm.

"Ow!"

"Follow me."

Gualtero sped down the left shaft. Lombard scrambled after him. They rounded a bend and saw pale light at the end of the vent. Gualtero scrambled down it and stopped abruptly. Lombard bumped into him.

"Sh!"

"What's wrong?" Lombard hissed.

"Nothing yet. Wait a second." Gualtero peered out through the vent grate at a marble balcony and beyond it at endless blue sky.

A blast of hot air surrounded them from behind. Lombard covered his head and then looked back, amazed that they weren't yet in the Ifrit's clutches.

"Hurry, Gualtero."

"Wait here." Gualtero lifted the grate and climbed out soundlessly. In mere seconds he came back and motioned to Lombard.

Lombard climbed out onto the balcony and Gualtero quickly tied a curtain cord around him.

"What did you have in mind?" Lombard puzzled at Gualtero's speed.

"What you said gave me an idea," Gualtero said. "They may look everywhere within the castle, but I'm willing to wager that they won't think to look under it. I can fly. You can't so I'll carry you below and there we'll hide until we can figure out what to do next."

They heard a growl of frustration somewhere deep within the ventilation system.

Gualtero looped the other end of the cord around his waist and knotted it through his belt. Both men climbed atop the balustrade and peered down at the sea far below.

"Take a deep breath." Gualtero dived.

Lombard plummeted with him, his eyes squeezed shut. The wind roared around him and buffeted him. He felt gravity's terrible pull and looked down at that not quite so endless drop below. Hands shaking, he grasped the cord and hung on tight. Gleaming white walls whirled past his sight and then deep blue shadows. Lombard looked up and saw the granite foundations of Nuneau castle, jagged and full of ravines. Gualtero flew closer to them and began darting about in search of a hiding place. Lombard had to use his hands and feet to keep from banging into the granite crags.

"Careful!" Lombard uncovered his head after a near hit.

"There isn't time for that," Gualtero retorted. "We have to hide."

Gualtero poked his head up a shaft and then folding up his wings, clambered up into it. Lombard swung below, looking around and down, way down, and regretted for maybe only the second time in his life that his mother had not bequeathed faerie wings to him in the womb. A sharp tug caught his attention. A second one followed it.

Gualtero peered down from the crevice. "Help me, will you?"

Lombard began climbing the cord until he could reach the hand Gualtero thrust out at him. Then he clambered into the crevice and found himself inside a small cave.

"Perfect, wouldn't you think?" Gualtero said as Lombard looked about.

"Perfect enough."

Gualtero picked up several large stones and handed them to Lombard. "Lay these across the opening, but leave enough space for air to get through. We'll give them an hour to wear themselves out and then I'll take a prowl."

Lombard nodded as he laid the stones across the opening.

"Best come away from there so we can't be seen at all," Gualtero added.

Lombard crawled to the far recesses of the cave and curled up in an alcove. Gualtero climbed into one across from him and higher up. In the near darkness, Gualtero squinted at his pocket watch, made note of the time and settled down to wait.

16

"Do you see it?" Viola asked.

Paco Dreng lowered his spyglass, examined it, rubbed the lenses at both ends, adjusted it and peered through it again. "I can't believe what I am seeing, but there is no denying that I am seeing 'something'."

"Which is?" Phineas Brock said.

"A castle beyond these clouds." Paco Dreng lowered the spyglass and rubbed his eyes.

Wasim took the spyglass and took a long look. "And here I thought we were the oddest thing the clouds possessed."

King Arvid lowered his spyglass. "Now what do we do?"

"Considering what you said was in there, sneak up on it," Paco Dreng said.

"Fine," said King Arvid, "but how?"

Paco Dreng quailed beneath the Wolf Troll's bright, relentless stare. "Well, judging by the way that these clouds are drifting, we will intercept them in about an hour. Hopefully, the castle will become tangled in these clouds long enough for you to rescue your friends."

Wasim shrugged. "Wait for the clouds to surround the castle and then board it. Just like you would a ship."

"And hope we aren't seen before then," Sullivan said.

Paco Dreng looked at the clouds looming higher about them. "Unless those Ifrits you mentioned are fond of being zapped by lightning, I expect that they'll be huddled within by the time we arrive."

A shadow fell across them. Even as they watched, the clouds gathered strength, mustering reinforcements from the remaining scattered clouds. Without a word from Paco Dreng, his men scattered to their posts as a gust roared out of the cloud valleys and rocked the ship.

"Whatever you do," King Arvid shouted above the rumbling surrounding them, "keep this ship out of sight of that." He jerked his thumb at the distant castle.

White light rippled across the surging walls around them. Then a deafening crack.

Phineas Brock pushed Viola toward the poop deck. "Best to get under shelter. It would be unforgivable if you were struck."

Viola would move no further than the entryway, so there Phineas Brock, Sullivan, Evin, King Arvid, De Vere, and Quinzano lingered, while the rest retreated further back into the ship to wait. They watched Paco Dreng and his men steer their ship as ably as they had when it had once sailed Thetis Megara's beautiful ocean waves.

"Was that thunder?" La Questa said.

"'Sounded like it," Conor grumbled from inside the cage.

Beolagh pulled his cap over his eyes and settled back to resume his nap. "Batten down the hatches."

Olwen and Carissa drifted toward the open window and peered out.

"Looks like we're in for a thunderstorm," Carissa called over her shoulder.

La Questa locked gazes across the table with Anna Marpessa. "Lombard and the Prince are going to get wet."

Anna Marpessa turned the page of her gardening book.

The corridors filled with roaring wind.

"Ah, they've returned." La Questa smiled.

A spectral frown flitted across the Faerie Queen's brow.

Olwen and Carissa watched out the window.

"A most awe-inspiring skyscape, you must admit," Carissa said.

Olwen looked at the looming towers of moisture and air and nodded. Then she stared and blinked and stared again. There it was and then it wasn't. "Did you see that?"

Carissa looked over at her. "See what?"

Olwen leaned close. "A ship."

Carissa's glance shot back toward the gathering storm. "Where?" she said under her breath.

"Off to the right," Olwen whispered. "It crossed that vale there between the thunderheads." Olwen took Carissa's hand and held it hard.

Carissa squeezed her sister's hand. "If the situation turns nasty, I want you to hide fast."

Olwen nodded.

The four Ifrits streamed into the chamber, empty-handed.

"I cannot believe this." La Questa rose. "You did not find them?"

"They hid very well, Zumurrud," said Aziz.

"Evidently." La Questa bit her lip and turned. Her glance fell upon Anna Marpessa.

Anna Marpessa froze. Her heart pounded. She took a deep breath and lowered the book. "If you mean to dangle us before them as a means of motivation to get them to turn themselves in, it won't work."

"Why shouldn't it work?" Jalil said.

"You have to know where they are holed up before you can attempt to bargain with them in such a manner. If you attempt such a maneuver now, you would just be shouting in the wind."

"There is logic in that but you and your sisters remain my best means of persuasion."

Beolagh lifted his cap and exchanged looks with Conor.

Carissa released Olwen's hand. "If I say run, run."

"I hope you're ready," Wasim said. "Paco Dreng said that we'll be upon them in five minutes at the least." He glanced out at his shipmates braving the storm. Lightning flashed blinding white over them and then deep blue darkness returned just as the sky rumbled around them.

King Arvid looked back at the waiting Wolf Trolls and bandits. "We are ready."

The Wolf Trolls and the Bandits stood armed with ropes and grappling hooks slung over their shoulders.

Down in the hold, Phineas Brock and Sullivan finished securing the Portal Mirror to Meadowlark's back. Then they tied ropes to themselves and secured those to Meadowlark's saddle.

"Take care not to bash us against the walls, Meadowlark," Phineas Brock said.

"You just be ready when they open up the hold," Meadowlark said. The Faerie horse prepared his wings and looked up.

Enough time had elapsed and suddenly the light coming through the crevice grew almost too dim to see. Cool moist air whistled through the cracks. Thunder tremored about them.

Lombard and Gualtero uncovered the hole.

"I'll have a look around." Gualtero handed the cord's end to Lombard, gave him a brief grin and plunged out into the air.

The air beyond filled with white light and then thunder exploded.

"I hope he doesn't get fried to a crisp out there," Lombard muttered.

Anna Marpessa slammed her book down on the table and stood up. "What is it that you want? You kidnap me and my sisters, deprive my people of their rightful monarch, and now you threaten us and for what? If I'm to suffer and die, I should like to know why."

La Questa faltered. "It does not concern you."

"I beg to differ. When you kidnapped us, it became our concern. What is it truly that you want so very badly?"

"To return home."

"And that's all?"

"That is all that it has ever been about," La Questa said coolly, "not that I didn't have plans for the duplicitous one who banished us…"

Anna Marpessa rubbed her forehead. "Why in the name of all that is sacred did you drag us into this? It didn't have to be like this. Tormenting us isn't going to help you get home. You could have come to my court as a visitor and stayed on as a guest and we would have done everything possible to help you find your way home. I would have consulted with the sages and sorcerers on Shadow Mountain."

La Questa shrugged. "It never occurred to me."

"What?" Anna Marpessa shouted.

La Questa flinched and touched her right ear.

The four Ifrits flanking her watched the confrontation, closely.

"You have been most forbearing with us during these difficult times," Yumni said.

"Balderdash!" Anna Marpessa retorted. "Give me that." She yanked the small iridescent bottle from about the Jinniyah's neck, snapping its delicate handle. "I have had enough of this." She smashed it upon the floor.

The bottle exploded and shimmering light rose up in a cloud and settled about the three sisters. When it subsided, translucent wings shimmered again upon the Marpessas' backs.

"No." La Questa furrowed her brow and closed her eyes briefly.

In an instant, the three sisters stood within the birdcage with Beolagh and Conor.

La Questa picked up the cage and walked out, followed by her Ifrit companions.

Gualtero poked his head through the crevice. "Come on. Help has arrived."

Lombard handed him the curtain cord and when Gualtero had it looped and knotted about his middle, climbed out and let go.

Gualtero flew out from beneath the castle. The sky opened up. In a flash of lightning Lombard saw a ship cutting a swift course through a blackening sky straight for the castle.

"Reinforcements?" Lombard shouted. "I see a skull and crossbones."

Gualtero grinned down. "They're on our side. You'll see." He veered upward toward one of the many balconies.

Lombard watched the ship. "Hurry, Gualtero, I think it's going to collide with us."

Held aloft by his determined fluttering, Gualtero climbed hand and foot up the side of the castle. As soon as he could, Lombard began clambering up behind him. The wind gusted, trying to push them off.

Gualtero tumbled over the balustrade onto a balcony and rolling onto his back, gripped the cord and braced his feet against the balustrade. Lombard climbed up and fell over the balustrade.

The pirate ship slammed into the wall below. Gualtero and Lombard felt the whole castle shudder.

"WHAT WAS THAT?" came a voice from within.

"Quick!" Gualtero and Lombard scurried to the right and hid behind a fat pillar.

"You rum-sodden oafs! We were supposed to come alongside, not plow into it!" There followed an unholy litany of oaths and threats that made Gualtero and Lombard exchange wide-eyed looks.

"Are you sure they came here to help?" Lombard said.

Gualtero grimaced and shrugged.

A shadow flitted briefly above them. They looked and saw a Faerie horse disappear over the rooftop, trailing a large oval object behind it. Lightning filled the sky.

"What was that?" Lombard leaned out to catch another glimpse, but the mirage had vanished with the lightning.

A grappling hook flew into the air and came down on the marble floor in front of them. As it withdrew, it scraped the floor and then caught on the corner balustrade. A second one followed it and found a secure hold close beside the first one.

"We're being boarded," Gualtero said.

La Questa wavered in the grand corridor. The birdcage swung as she turned. Beolagh, Conor, and the Marpessas clung to the gilded bars. "Something is amiss. See what is the matter."

The four Ifrits dissolved into smoke and rushed past her toward the four main balconies and peered down for a moment. Karim Jubran dived over the side, vanishing from sight.

Wind gusted into the palace. The dense curtains blew high. Thunder rolled overhead. Its reverberations filled the grand corridor and in its wake came a chorus of voices, most inarticulate in their startled terror.

"What in blazes is that?!"

"Get away from my ship!"

"Now!"

Yumni turned back. "Invaders!"

La Questa raised the birdcage and peered inside. "Friends of yours?"

None of her prisoners dared say a word.

"No matter," La Questa said. She lowered the cage and met Yumni's glance. "Deal with them."

Jubran swooped round and round the marooned ship. Paco Dreng, Wasim, and the rest of the crew threw anything they could lay hands on at the green Ifrit. But Jubran saw what was happening.

"Jalil! Aziz! Yumni! Brothers, come at once. There are soldiers here," Jubran shouted.

La Questa hesitated. "Soldiers." Then her brow furrowed. "Stop them."

Scuttling low to the floor, Gualtero and Lombard entered the Grand Corridor and hid off to the side. La Questa had not seen them, but Anna Marpessa and Conor had.

"Where do these monsters come from? The clouds?" shouted Halstead.

"Leave my ship alone!" Paco Dreng shouted.

The Ifrits veered toward the dark figures climbing the ropes. Their magic failed to touch them. They exchanged alarmed looks.

"This fares us ill," Aziz said.

Jalil expanded to twice his size. "Then force must do." He rushed upon the invaders.

Russell looked over his shoulder and yelped.

"Climb faster," De Vere shouted. He reached the balcony first and drew his sword. The green Ifrit swooped again and De Vere sliced at its cloudy tail.

Aziz laughed and reached for Acton. Acton gripped the rope tight and shut his eyes.

"Leave him alone," De Vere shouted. He put one leg over the balustrade.

Aziz laid only one black talon on the Faerie lad when the space surrounding Acton filled with blinding blue-white light and a crack like thunder. De Vere stumbled back, his arm over his face. Acton yelped and fell. Gripwell caught him and held him tight until he took hold of the rope again. The shock sent the blue Ifrit rolling out toward the clouds. Aziz's brethren faltered. Blinking against the phenomenon, they watched Aziz tumble and roll and finally get his bearings back. He hovered in the distance. No matter how much Jalil and Jubran urged him, he held back from the fray.

"There is magic at work here," Yumni said. "A sorcerer perhaps hides among them."

"Then we must find this magician," said Jalil, "and rout him."

Aziz swooped far around the ship and veered into the palace through a window. "La Questa."

She turned and looked up. "Aziz."

Aziz showed her his singed finger. "There is a powerful magic shielding the invaders."

"Find its source and capture it."

Aziz bowed and withdrew again through the window.

La Questa held up the birdcage and glared. "As long as I possess you, they must bend to my will." With that she whirled into the throne hall. The great gilded doors slammed shut behind her.

King Arvid was the first to reach the top and clamber over the balustrade onto the balcony. The palace within seemed much too dark and much too quiet. He drew his sword and adjusted his crowned helmet. "I know I saw Gualtero come up this way. Where did he go?"

At the sound of his rumbling voice, Gualtero poked his tousled brown head out of the shadows. "Arvid!" he hissed. "This way!" He waved the Wolf Troll King forward.

King Arvid stomped into the palace and was pulled aside into an alcove.

"You mustn't let those jinni see you," Lombard said.

"They can gawk all they want. They can't stop me." Arvid stepped out into the open and waved on his men. "Come this way." Arvid turned back around and gave Gualtero and Lombard a tight sharp-toothed grin. "It has become all too apparent why Viola Marpessa was sent to Shadow Mountain to grow up. The little lady has a true gift. We are all of us under her special protection."

Gualtero and Lombard crept out into the open.

"Where is she?" Gualtero said.

"I wish I knew." Arvid gazed down the grand corridor toward the throne hall doors at the far end. "We will need her."

De Vere entered from the balcony a little further down. Flanking him ventured Lombard's men.

"Lombard!" Acton rushed to him.

Lombard enveloped him in a big brother's hug.

"Here he is – in the lap of luxury no less," Scudamore said.

Lombard winced under the powerful blow of his comrade's hand on his shoulder. "I'll take a bedroll under the stars anytime over this – believe me." He winced again as each of his men pounded him and tousled his blond hair.

De Vere peered down at the ship. The four Ifrits clambered all over the pirate ship. They ripped open the hold and plunged within.

Calderon leaned over beside him. "The horses. My wagon."

Horses whinnying and neighing filled the air.

"They wouldn't hurt the horses, would they?" Calderon said.

De Vere's expression darkened. "Let's hope not." He took a deep breath, consigned his splendid charger to its fate, and turned about. "What are our orders?"

"Find La Questa and free our friends," Lombard said.

"Wait up!" Paco Dreng climbed onto the balcony. "We don't dare stay behind, not while those infernal beings are tearing my ship apart."

His men followed him in great eagerness, casting worried looks back at their ship.

"Stay close. Be alert and do what I tell you," King Arvid said.

"Yes, Sire," Paco Dreng said as his men gathered behind him.

"Then follow me." King Arvid exchanged nods with Gualtero and Lombard.

Gualtero and Lombard took the lead, treading softly and looking every which way.

Evin peered out into the narrow hallway. "It does not appear that anyone saw us trespass."

"Good," Phineas Brock said.

"I can't undo this knot," Sullivan said.

"Cut it then," Phineas Brock said.

Grumbling, Sullivan took out his long knife and worked on the cords binding the Portal Mirror to Meadowlark and then those encasing the object in its cloth. The cloth fell away and the Portal Mirror gleamed with a soft iridescence in the stormy blue shadows. Lightning ricocheted across the sky outside and briefly the mirror sparkled and shone.

Meadowlark laid his ears back as the entire castle reverberated from the thunder.

"There," Sullivan said. "Now what?"

Phineas Brock wiped it off with his handkerchief. "Bear it downstairs and find Viola. You take that side. I'll lift this side. Meadowlark, you and Evin walk ahead of us."

"And if you see any trouble, run," Sullivan said.

Phineas Brock gave him a severe look. "Just be sure to give us a whistle first."

Evin shoved the door open. "Right. Let's be off then and make heroes of ourselves." He bounded down the corridor.

Meadowlark strolled after, his ears pricked. His hooves resounded off the wooden floor.

"A little louder if you please, the Ifrits can't hear you," Evin said.

Meadowlark stopped and looked down at him. "How would you like to be a smudge on the wallpaper?"

"Point taken," Evin said and resumed his pace. He stopped at the top of a staircase, propped his hands on his hips and waited.

Meadowlark stopped close beside him and peered over the balustrade.

Shuffling, Phineas Brock and Sullivan sidled up to Evin and wiped their brows.

"This thing is heavier than it looks," Sullivan said.

Phineas Brock peered down the stairwell. "This could be interesting."

"Oh?" Sullivan looked down too. "Oh."

"What do you suppose happened to the stairs?" Meadowlark said.

"Why take the stairs and leave the balustrade?" Evin said.

The balustrade wound its lonely way down to the marble floor below.

Sullivan looked over at Phineas Brock. "Detour?"

Phineas Brock muttered incoherently.

They picked up the mirror and shuffled down a side corridor.

Viola stood in a comfortable and decidedly elegant sitting room. On a sunny day it would have been filled with wonderful light, but amid the turbulent clouds, darkness flowed with each gust of air. Embroidery lay abandoned on a round table along with a book, three gilt-edged porcelain cups still containing tea, and a teapot. Viola picked up the teapot. It was cold to the touch and its contents swished only lightly as she set it down. Under other circumstances she would have created light, but she dared do nothing that would betray her presence to the Ifrits yet. The carpeting absorbed her footsteps as she headed for the door.

A small thumping sound to her left stopped her. Viola peered off to the side. The sound persisted, like something small urgently flailing about inside a confined space. An elegant desk stood against the opposite wall. She headed for it. The sound grew more frantic. Its lid stood locked though, but it took only a thump of her index finger and the utterance of a small word – 'open', and the lid unlocked. She raised the lid and saw dancing about within it her Omnipedia. Smiling she snatched it up.

The Omnipedia's cover flew open to the first page. *'Glad to see ya!'*

Viola smiled. "I'm glad to see you too."

It turned a page. *'If you're here to rescue everyone, you had best make haste. It is all chaos on the main floor and your other friends are trapped on the next floor up. Apparently, the stairs have vanished.'*

"'Best get a move on, hadn't we?" Viola said.

The Omnipedia shut its cover and she tucked it deep inside the pouch she had slung about her shoulder. She gave the pouch a reassuring pat and slipped out into the corridor.

It wasn't hard to figure out where to go. Viola could hear the fracas all the way back into the Queen's private chambers. Running around the corner, a light erupted ahead and she covered her eyes.

"Catch a hold of them!" a woman cried.

"Their confounded magic prevents us," retorted a male voice.

"Do not waste your time with their allies. Capture the Prince and Lombard," she snapped. "They are unprotected."

"Run, Lombard," shouted Quinzano.

"No, this way," shouted Gualtero.

"Block them," de Vere shouted.

"How? They're made of air and smoke," Paco Dreng yelled.

"Just reach out and touch them. It seems to startle them," Scudamore shouted.

Viola peered round the corner column, looking down. A woman with dark bluish skin and dense coils of black hair garbed in rich flowing peacock colors stood in the doorway to the throne hall with a gleaming birdcage hanging from her right hand. Within that cage she saw several little bodies moving about, but she couldn't quite see who they were.

A strange chase erupted below. Springing and leaping, Lombard and Gualtero ducked amid the columns. Hard behind them swooped four large figures, their colorful bodies blurred with smoke. Scrambling after them and cutting around ahead of them, darted bandits and pirates, with their hands outstretched to give the Ifrits a little shock courtesy of Viola's spell. King Arvid marched through the chaos directly toward the throne hall. His men flanked him, their swords drawn and gleaming in the frequent lightning flaring around the open balconies. Another blinding crack of lightning filled the main corridor from without. The castle shook with thunder.

Paco Dreng, Wasim, and his men formed a brief wall between Jalil and Aziz and Lombard, but when they swooped around behind, Lombard darted back out into the open before they could snatch him up. The bandits rushed again to get between Lombard and the fiery orange and airy blue Ifrits.

Quinzano and Scudamore directed Lombard's men this way and that to intercept the green and golden yellow Ifrits before they could get close enough to Gualtero to catch him. The two Ifrits swirled together in swift council and then separated again. The green one charged directly toward the bandits, his arms open wide. They weren't expecting that. One corner of the main hall filled with stark light as Jubran filled his arms with bandits and received a nasty expected shock.

Gualtero scarcely hesitated as he covered his face with his sleeve when he felt himself swept up. He looked up into Yumni's golden frown and scowled right back. Stunned, Jubran fell away from the bandits and then curled past them, retreating to La Questa's side as Yumni arrived with his captive.

Amid another terrible flash and pirates falling over backwards at the shock, Aziz and Jalil shot out of their midst, bearing Lombard between them. They alighted beside La Questa and exchanged satisfied nods with Yumni and Jubran on her other side.

La Questa smiled.

King Arvid stopped mere steps away from her, his men arrayed on both sides of him. His glowing eyes took in the five individuals staring out at him through the birdcage's bars. "Greetings, Your Majesty, I apologize for not coming to pay my respects at a time when you are at your ease."

"It is good that you came at all," Anna Marpessa replied without a trace of fear.

"Anna?" Gualtero peered down at her. He reached for the cage, but Yumni pulled him back two steps.

King Arvid leveled his gaze on La Questa. "I am King Arvid from the Northlands. Who might you be, Interloper?"

La Questa smiled at the firm grip the Wolf Troll King had on his powerful sword. "La Questa, Empress of the Ifrits. My brethren Jalil Futaih, Aziz Faruq, Karim Jubran, and Yumni Mubashir."

The four Ifrits stood a good head taller than their Empress and none of them seemed inclined to say so much as a word of formal greeting as they kept a firm grip on Lombard and Gualtero.

"What brings you and your *army* here?" La Questa said.

King Arvid looked at the breathless pirates and bandits gathering alongside his bodyguard. "We've come to liberate the Faerie Queen and her friends."

La Questa held up the birdcage and peered within at her prisoners. "You cannot pry them from my grasp."

"Nonetheless, you must relinquish them," King Arvid said.

"I will not simply relinquish them," she said.

Aziz frowned and looked at the balustrades belonging to the upper gallery. "A horse?" he muttered.

Viola leaned back into the shadows before Aziz spied her. She looked back down the gallery and saw Evin and Meadowlark approaching. Behind them lumbered Phineas Brock and Sullivan with the mirror wobbling between them.

De Vere backed up several steps toward the side staircase. If he had to, he would throw himself in the Ifrit's path.

Viola waved her hands at Evin and Meadowlark and shook her head wildly.

Meadowlark stopped and lifted his head, his ears pricked.

Evin darted forward. "Princess!"

Viola laid her finger over her lips and shook her head.

"Someone is up there," Aziz muttered to Jalil.

"Hold the Bandit King. I shall go for a look," Jalil said.

De Vere could not get near the staircase. Out of desperation, he hurled his sword across the space between him and the stairwell. It had been nestled firm in his hand when Viola invoked the protective spell earlier aboard Paco Dreng's ship. It cut through Jalil's smoky tail and anchored him to the oak paneling, driving in almost up to the hilt. Jalil stopped so suddenly that it winded him. He could not get free. If he touched the hilt, it shocked him. If he struggled, the sword seemed to drive just a little deeper into the wall.

"You dare…" La Questa's electric gaze shot toward De Vere.

King Arvid laid the tip of his sword against her collarbone. "If you so much as bat an eyelid against the lad, I'll drive this home."

La Questa withdrew half a step, studied the Wolf Troll King a moment, and gave a sidelong glance toward her birdcage. "Give me that brave wretch and the sorcerer who made you untouchable and I shall give you all of my captives."

Sullivan and Phineas Brock edged round Meadowlark. Evin and Viola waved them on. Meadowlark scarcely moved his ears.

"No deal," Quinzano said.

La Questa lifted her left hand before her, palm upwards. In it rested a large bejeweled locket. She smiled at it. A light flashed from her eyes and into the locket.

Lombard and Gualtero were gone.

La Questa held up the locket and let them see the newborn living lights within it. "Give me the sorcerer then or these heroes will suffer for it."

"We cannot do that," King Arvid said.

"Why not be gracious and merciful and free our friends?" Scudamore said.

"Indeed, it does not have to be this way," King Arvid said.

"You will not give me your powerful protector?" Her smile dimmed, leaving behind a hard expression.

They stood mute and immovable before her.

"Very well." La Questa threw the locket toward a balcony.

"No!" Acton flung himself after it.

The locket hit the marble floor and slid across it and right off the edge.

Acton flung himself against the balcony's balustrades. The locket had vanished amid the storm clouds on its swift descent toward the ocean far, far below. "No," he choked.

Evin gawked past the balustrades. "Did you see that? I cannot believe she did that! What a terrible thing to do!" His voice carried far in the stunned silence below. He clapped his hand across his mouth.

Viola saw all eyes turn their way. La Questa's brows arched.

"Hurry," Viola hissed.

Sullivan and Phineas Brock lurched forward. The Portal Mirror slipped from their grasp and hit the floor at a slide. Sullivan fell on his face. Phineas Brock stumbled after it, but it was as though a tide had caught the mirror and bore it away.

The mirror slid, bumping and jouncing against the marble balustrades all the way down. Hitting the bottom, it slid until it reached the exact center of the chamber and there it stopped.

"What is that?" La Questa said.

"I shall look into it." Jubran rose above the assembly and rushed toward the mirror.

A white and roan blur whipped past Viola. With a resounding thud, Meadowlark landed above the mirror, his four hooves splayed outside the edges of the mirror's perfect frame. He laid his ears back and bared his teeth at the green Ifrit, his wings and hooves ready to combat Jubran if need be.

Jubran swelled up to his full height and glared down at the Faerie horse. He pulled back his hand and swiped down at Meadowlark. Abruptly, a petite young Faerie woman landed between him and the horse, held up her hand, saying simply, but firmly, "Back."

The force of her command sent Jubran rolling back against the corner wall.

"It's their Sorceress," Jubran called out.

Viola motioned toward the staircase. Sullivan, Phineas Brock, and Evin darted out and between the three of them, lifted the mirror.

King Arvid smiled at La Questa and turned back to join Viola. His men flanked him, swords still drawn and their eyes on the Ifrits.

The pirates and the bandits withdrew, forming lines on both sides of the mirror.

"I will deal with her." La Questa glided forward. The birdcage swung in her grasp.

Viola examined the mirror as she polished it with Phineas Brock's fine handkerchief. It gleamed anew. Returning the cloth to her friend, she turned, clasped her hands behind her back, and waited for La Questa, her head tilted slightly as she eyed the Jinniyah. Briefly she eyed the people caught in the cage, two Leprecauns and three elegant Faerie ladies who peered out at her.

Aziz, Jalil, Jubran, and Yumni gathered behind La Questa, waiting for her command to pummel the rescuers.

"That was a terrible thing you did to the Prince and the Bandit King," Viola said evenly.

"I do not see you shedding any tears," La Questa said.

"Thetis Megara will recover them once they fall into her domain."

La Questa held up the cage and smiled at her prisoners. "Have you come for these?"

"Of course I have come to help my sisters," Viola said.

La Questa and the Ifrits looked anew at her.

"Sisters?" said Yumni.

Viola arched her brows and nodded once. "I understand that you are willing to barter for their freedom."

La Questa looked her up and down and nodded once. "Is that mirror worth their freedom?"

Viola glanced across their faces. "Actually, the question is – what can you guarantee us in order to make use of the mirror?"

"I do not follow," Aziz said.

Viola motioned toward the mirror Phineas Brock and Sullivan held up. "This is a Portal Mirror that we borrowed just so we could bring an end to this crisis in a manner satisfactory to all concerned."

"A Portal mirror?" Jalil said. "It permits travel?"

"Anywhere you wish to go," Evin said.

"Home," said Jubran.

"Let us have it and I shall give you this." La Questa held up the cage.

"We cannot give it to you," Viola said.

"Then we shall take it," Jalil said.

"Even if you took it, you could not keep it," Viola said.

"Explain," Yumni said.

"For one, it belongs to the Milady Solaine de Morin, who lives in the sky. To her it must return. Secondly, while it will let beings pass through it, it is impossible for them to take it with them," Viola said.

"So in other words, you had best make sure you know where you want to go," King Arvid said, "because there is no coming back."

La Questa took on a strange, sad expression. "It will take us home?"

"Envision your destination, ask the mirror to bear your thence, and then all you have to do is step into the mirror," King Arvid said.

La Questa stepped forward. Pushing the cage into Viola's hands, she touched the mirror frame with gentle hands. At last she pulled her eyes from its gleaming surface and met Viola's gaze. "I am sorry for all the harm I have inflicted. We have searched everywhere for our homeland and had begun to despair that we would find it again."

Viola nodded.

La Questa looked over her shoulder and smiled. "Let us return to where we belong."

King Arvid motioned. "Step back, everyone, or you might get pulled in behind them."

"How can we be sure that this is not a trap?" said Jalil.

Viola sighed. "You'll just have to trust me."

"I will not step into that mirror and be trapped there forever as we were trapped in Badenoch," Jubran said.

Aziz looked a long time at Viola and then spoke. "She believes that it will deliver us home."

"It brought the Prince Gualtero here right enough," King Arvid said. "Therefore, it should bear you home in good speed."

"Yes, I see." La Questa closed her eyes. "Show me my homeland."

The Portal Mirror's surface shimmered and softened. Within its depths formed a vista overflowing with warm sunlight. Purple-tinged blue mountains rose in the distance and in the foreground surged a green valley and the sloping mount that stood guard beside a wide river. Lastly, a village and a castle of whitewashed stone appeared upon the mount and on all sides going down to the valley floor. Then they saw the people moving about as they always did on their daily routines.

Viola peered 'round at it. "Is that the place?"

La Questa nodded, her eyes glistening.

"How do we know it is not a mirage?" Yumni said.

"I shall pass through it first," La Questa said, "and you shall watch me pass. If this image remains constant, you shall see me flying above our great Prince's castle. There I shall wait for you, my brothers." La Questa turned and regarded the other Ifrits.

They exchanged looks and then nodded.

La Questa took a step back from the mirror. "Bear me home please."

Dissolving into a swirling mass of smoke, she passed into the mirror. It shimmered in her wake. The four Ifrits pressed forward to see - and see her they did. La Questa swooped wide over the castle and alighted in solid form atop the central turret. She waved at the sky.

As though scooped up by a fist made of wind, the other four Ifrits rushed through the mirror. The vision disappeared, rippling in their wake and those that remained saw only themselves looking back.

"Good riddance," Phineas Brock said.

"And yet the Queen and her two sisters remain trapped in their reduced forms," said King Arvid.

"Whoops! I was supposed to get them to set things to rights before I sent them home." Viola peered in at her sisters and the two Leprecauns. "This is going to take some research."

17

Anna Marpessa, Carissa, and Olwen remained the size of dolls. Gualtero Bainbridge and Lombard de Montfaucon were somewhere in the depths of the western ocean. And no one knew quite how to steer a floating castle. Under the circumstances, Viola sent for help.

Sullivan mounted up on Meadowlark and set off swiftly across the continent toward Shadow Mountain in the east. While they waited for a response from Master Sorcerer Macy, the others relaxed as best they could. Paco Dreng and his men worked putting their ship back to order, while Lombard's men worked with King Arvid's soldiers to transfer their mounts and the gypsy wagon to the castle's main floor. The grand central corridor quickly resembled a stable and took on the atmosphere of a country tavern.

Although Viola had assured Paco Dreng and Wasim that the people of Shadow Mountain would do them no harm, they were impatient to set off again. After their one bad experience with Queen Thetis Megara, which doomed them to sail the ocean of winds, they wanted nothing more to do with the 'potent peoples' as Wasim termed them. As soon as their ship was fit and free of its living cargo, Paco Dreng and his men gladly set sail, content for once with only Anna Marpessa's simple words of gratitude and Phineas Brock's bag of gold coins. They headed westward – far away from the land of Faeries, magic scholars, and Wolf Trolls.

The storm broke. Rain blew in through the windows, so there was a scramble to close them all. Then they all settled about tending to their animals, and amusing themselves in a reasonable manner. The bandits gathered in groups and played cards on the carpets. Acton sat gazing out the windows, too anxious to do anything, but fret about Lombard. De Vere brought a table out of the parlor and Arvid's men brought out several chairs. Phineas Brock spread a cloth over the fine table and Viola sat to it with her nose buried in her Omnipedia. Anna Marpessa and her sisters fluttered up to the table and sat upon a fat dictionary that Arvid supplied them for a bench.

Viola watched her sisters settle down upon it and shook her head. "This is not how I visualized our reunion."

"Indeed, I would have arranged for a public celebration to announce your return," Anna Marpessa said, exchanging weary smiles with Carissa and Olwen.

"Are you certain that Lombard and Gualtero will be fine?" Carissa said.

"The fish in the deep like shiny things and they love showing their Queen their new trinkets," Viola said. "I expect some dolphin or sea turtle is bearing our heroes to Thetis Megara as we speak. She will recognize it as something out of the ordinary. We just have to make certain that she knows we're looking for it."

"Perhaps we should drop a message in a bottle then," Carissa said.

"Master Sorcerer Macy will see to it that she is informed," Viola said. She turned a page in her Omnipedia and sighed. "So far, I don't think any of these cures will work."

A page flipped on its own. *'Surely one of them will.'*

Viola turned the page back. "If not, perhaps Macy or someone else will know what to do."

Beolagh, Conor, and Evin had been sitting on the steps a little further up conferring. They broke off their conversation with nods.

Evin cleared his throat. "Is anyone else feeling a mite peckish just now?"

King Arvid exchanged looks with Phineas Brock seated in the chair across from him and then they looked to Viola.

"I'm famished," Viola said.

"I could use some refreshments," Anna Marpessa said.

"Me too," said Olwen.

King Arvid stood up. "Well then, where is your kitchen? Or do you have one?"

Anna Marpessa pointed toward the side corridor behind Viola. "Follow that all the way to the end and you will find the family kitchen and a pantry." She met Viola's glance and shrugged. "We have banquets only once a week, so it seems a waste to keep people toiling around the clock in the large kitchens just to feed us three, so there is a second smaller kitchen. I expect my advisors and my commanders have been spending much of their time in the greater kitchens having coffee and sandwiches while they try to figure out what to do."

"Let us hope they don't give themselves ulcers worrying," Viola said.

King Arvid rounded up volunteers from among his men and the bandits. "Let's go see if we can't rustle up a decent feast."

They shuffled down the corridor, admiring the art and sculpture along the way.

Conor called back. "We shall find some dainty thimbles for you ladies to drink from."

"We would appreciate it," Anna Marpessa called after the Leprecauns.

De Vere ventured up to the table, bowed to the miniature Queen and her two sisters and pulled up a chair beside Viola's.

Viola exchanged looks with him and sighed. "Quite a challenge."

De Vere glanced again at her sisters. "It certainly looks like it."

Viola turned another page and resumed skimming. De Vere read over her shoulder.

Anna exchanged looks with her sisters. Then she leaned close to Carissa. "It looks like you aren't the only one with a new beau."

Carissa nodded. "And a handsome rogue he is too."

Within half an hour King Arvid and his volunteers returned with trays laden with food. The assault on the trays was orderly and soon thereafter the hall was full of contented feasting.

Viola tapped another spell with her finger. "Save this one for me too," she commanded the book as she closed it with a sigh and took a bite of a grilled cheese sandwich. Chin in hand, she chewed and with wearied eyes regarded her three tiny sisters.

The three Leprecauns had figured out how to set up a picnic of sorts in the center of the table for themselves and the Faerie ladies. Polite to the last, they served Anna Marpessa and her sisters before they settled down beside them to eat too.

King Arvid sat last to the table and spread a napkin over his lap before he reached for a sandwich and the everlasting pot of coffee. "Any luck?"

De Vere handed him the bottomless sugar bowl. Phineas Brock handed King Arvid the cream.

Viola looked into his glowing eyes. "If anything, there are too many options and considering that we have no idea which one will be most effective, we may have to try them all." She met Anna's glance and arched her brows. "However, setting the castle back down where it belongs should be relatively easy so long as the crosswinds aren't too difficult."

Scudamore and Quinzano exchanged looks.

Quinzano lowered his cup. "If you need any help, simply ask."

"Thank you, I will I'm afraid," Viola said.

"Oh dear," murmured Anna Marpessa.

Immediately after their meal, they cleared everything away. Viola removed her sisters to the kitchen and set them upon the table there. She opened her Omnipedia and proceeded to attempt one spell after another. De Vere and Acton cleaned up after each attempt while the Marpessas made rudimentary attempts to dry off and resume some semblance of dignity. Head in her hands, brow furrowed, Viola rattled off another list of ingredients and Arvid's men and the bandits searched the castle and their belongings for the eclectic range of herbs and objects.

Failure.

Viola laid her head on her arms. "Does anyone have any headache powder?"

King Arvid handed the Marpessas more clean handkerchiefs so they could clean up as best they could.

Viola lifted her head and rested her chin on her palm. "There must be something I overlooked."

The horses neighed and whinnied in the grand hall and the castle jolted.

"What was that?" Scudamore said.

"That would be our dragons pulling the castle directly to Nuneau."

"Saire!" Viola jumped up and ran into the old sorcerer's arms.

Saire gave his ward a lingering hug and stroked her distressed hair out of her face. "I hear you've had quite an adventure since I entrusted you to Prince Gualtero." He surveyed the eclectic collection of individuals arrayed in the kitchen.

King Arvid smiled a sharp-toothed grin and inclined his head.

Saire inclined his head in return. Then he tipped his flying cap to Anna Marpessa and her sisters and fought back a smile. "You look as though you've been bathing in tomato soup, Your Majesty."

Anna Marpessa smiled readily. "That was part of the last attempt." Then she turned grave. "Has anyone found my Prince and the Bandit King?"

Saire smiled and reached into his waistcoat pocket. Out came the amulet. "They were returned to us safe and sound." He gazed into its depths for a moment and then hurled it at the kitchen hearth. "Out with you!"

The amulet shattered and amid the hearth ash landed Gualtero and Lombard in dazed heaps.

"Couldn't there have been a less violent way of accomplishing that?" Gualtero said.

Lombard groaned and sat up. "Stop the spinning."

Acton rushed to his side and hauled him onto his feet.

Lombard grinned at him and tousled his hair. "Hello, little brother."

"Hello, Lombard."

Scudamore, Quinzano, and the rest thronged around him, slapping him on the shoulders so hard that his knees would have given out had not Acton been bracing him.

Phineas Brock gave Gualtero a hand and steadied him until he could lean upon the kitchen table.

"Some ice should take care of that knot on your head," Saire said.

"Lovely," Gualtero said. Then he saw his stained, tiny bride gazing up at him from the table and tilted his head. "What happened to you?"

"I've been trying everything to restore her to normal size again," Viola said.

"Everything?" Saire said.

Viola picked up the Omnipedia and showed him the spells.

Saire took the book from her and leafed through the pages. "I see." He closed the book and set it down. "Of course! It's so simple." He rummaged through the cabinets. "Ah, here it is." Smiling simply, the old sorcerer shuffled to the table and handed a pepper mill to Viola. "Go to it, child."

Viola ground out some fresh pepper directly over her sisters.

Gasping and heaving violently, first Anna and then her two sisters let go violent sneezes and exploded into their full sizes once more. Rolling and stumbling, they fell off the table, sneezing terribly.

"Give them some damp towels to press to their faces," Saire said. "Ladies, rub your tongues hard along the roofs of your mouths. That'll help stop the sneezing."

De Vere pumped water onto three dishcloths and handed them out. Gualtero put an arm about Anna Marpessa's shoulders and pressed one of the cloths to her face. Lombard did the same for Carissa. King Arvid took Olwen into a fatherly embrace and pressed the wet towel to her nose.

"That's it?" Phineas Brock said. "Pepper?"

"Not exactly," Saire said. "Any of those spells should have worked. All that was missing was a catalyst to spark the transformation, make the ingredients work as it were."

"That's how I sprung back into my full size!" said Lombard. "I sneezed too."

"I wish I'd known that," said Viola.

Saire regarded the assembly and noticed how one particularly dashing dark-haired young Faerie chap's gaze lingered on Viola and the quiet smile he took on. He glanced down at his former ward and saw the warm expression spread across her face as she locked eyes with him.

Anna Marpessa sniffled into the towel and smiled at Gualtero.

"You look a mess," he said.

"I'll survive," she replied.

"Where's Sullivan?" Gualtero said.

"He's out on Lindo's back helping to steer the castle back where it belongs," Saire said. "Come and see."

White tail idly swishing, Meadowlark stood on a balcony gazing about at the three dragons straining in their harnesses, wings beating the wind in unison relentlessly eastward.

To the far left, Viola recognized Hubert, Alison the Terrible's dark bluish gray dragon, and Thatcher, Alison's apprentice, a young dark-haired woman about Viola's age riding in Hubert's saddle. To the far right flew pale Lindo, with Sullivan sitting firmly in Saire's saddle. In the center flew Andreev Eliathan, Macy's magnificent black dragon, the largest and noblest of the beasts of Shadow Mountain. His fine saddle was vacant.

"Where is the Master Sorcerer?" King Arvid said.

"Macy waits for us at Nuneau. Alison the Terrible is with him. They are preparing the Queen's subjects for her return. We shall need their help to mend this castle too," Saire said.

"Oh dear." Anna Marpessa glanced down at her stained, ruined habiliments. "I think we had best get cleaned up. It would not do for our people to see us in this manner." She pulled free of Gualtero's embrace.

"Do you want me to help you?" he said.

"Are you my husband?" she said, a teasing smile bright upon her lips.

"Not yet."

"Then you may not. When you are indeed my Consort, then you may scrub me to your heart's content. Come, Carissa. Olwen."

Viola headed inside after them. "I'd best make myself useful. Besides, we have a lot of catching up to do."

Saire nodded. "There goes a most promising family."

"Indeed," Gualtero said.

Saire narrowed his focus on Lombard. Lombard straightened his collar and smoothed his moustache. "Bandit King, eh?" Saire said.

"Not anymore. I've retired," Lombard said.

"Good for you. Princess Carissa wants a man keen to settle down."

"I'm her man then," Lombard said. "The only adventures I want now are the ones I can find in my own back forty."

Saire patted Lombard on the shoulder. Then he regarded De Vere and saw the thoughtful look the young man pulled away from the doorway and turned toward the southern horizon. "And what about you, whippersnapper?"

De Vere hung his head briefly and then nodded. "There are things I must accomplish. Places I must see."

"You are young yet." Saire nodded. "There is ample time."

"Let us hope so," De Vere said.

Anyone witnessing Queen Anna Marpessa's triumphant return would have thought she had been off on a mere pleasure voyage instead of been kidnapped. Shining and beautiful, Anna Marpessa stood upon her public balcony and smiled at the throngs gathered in the castle courtyard. Sentries and courtiers stumbled up the marble steps, arms laden with bundles of flowers, which her servants rushed to place in every room of the restored castle.

The Faerie folk would talk about that day for years, recounting how the castle appeared like a vision on the soft golden horizon and then floated into Nuneau city by the power of dragon wings; and how with great concentration Master Sorcerer Macy and Sorcerer Alison the Terrible surrounded the castle with a powerful, shining electric cloud and sealed it again to its original foundations. Then the Queen came out upon the public balcony with ALL of her sisters and received her people's joyous welcome.

Inevitably, Nuneau exploded with celebrations well into the night. The Queen had made several announcements before the sun began to set. First, a permanent treaty of alliance had been drawn up between the Faerie Folk and the Wolf Troll people. That delighted the merchants and guilds folk to no end. In the morning, their Queen would marry her Prince and make him King Consort of Nuneau, bringing the tense relations between his father's island confederation and her realm to an end.

Princess Carissa intended to marry Lombard de Montfaucon at a private assembly afterwards, as soon as the new King Consort publicly ennobled him. Master Sorcerer Macy agreed to officiate at both nuptials. The afternoon air filled for an hour with dragon wings as his colleagues arrived from Shadow Mountain to attend the next day's festivities. While their masters and mistresses settled in guest chambers throughout Nuneau Castle, their dragons settled down along the beaches to frolic in the waves and sleep among the cliffs.

That evening, Queen Thetis Megara arrived with her retinue aboard her gleaming mother of pearl vessel.

Nuneau shone far into the night.

Viola left her sisters Anna and Carissa in their dressing chambers suffering the feverish attentions of their dressmakers. Olwen was dancing in the ballroom with King Arvid and his officers among the many guests present. The Wolf Troll King had invited the young Princess to visit his mountain kingdom and meet his only daughter and heiress Sivia so that her sisters might have time alone with their consorts. Viola had agreed to go along too. It would be an opportunity to explore portions of her homeland with Olwen, who had never left Nuneau – willingly – before.

Out of gratitude for his assistance, Anna Marpessa agreed to build a grand museum for Phineas Brock's extraordinary collection. That very hour he sat conferring with the Queen's best architects in her study.

Lombard and Gualtero endured the small army of tailors who had come to sew their wedding uniforms.

Scudamore and Quinzano were down in the city visiting tailors so that they too would have fine new suits to wear to their leader's wedding the next day. As happy as they were to see their leader and friend so happily situated, the feeling among them was bittersweet. The Queen's gratitude had extended to them as well. Each possessed a fine annuity that would see them through the rest of their lives in great comfort. Hawtrey shed genuine tears when he realized that he could resume his former life as a gentleman and could not be persuaded to touch even a spoonful of wine from that day on. They would sit among the guests the next day to see their friend knighted and then married to the Princess that had captured his heart. Then they would disband for good and all. Acton stayed behind with Lombard to be fitted for his own suit. He alone would stay behind in Nuneau, but he planned to accompany Olwen and Viola to King Arvid's kingdom in the north.

Macy and his colleagues divided into two parties. While Macy and Saire enjoyed the ball and feasted and visited with Sullivan Trooper and Queen Thetis Megara who was the honorary hostess of the ball, Valeria the Grand took her former apprentice Thatcher and led a minor expedition into Nuneau to enjoy the city.

A trifle overwhelmed by people and noise, Viola strolled from place to place, observing the celebrations and activity with a smile. Finally she found herself out in the Queen's private garden. Meadowlark was there, being tended to by the Queen's own stable hands.

"Good evening, Viola," Meadowlark said.

Viola watched the stable hands brush his white mane and tale and comb his flanks with tender care. "Good evening to you too, Meadowlark," she said. "Are you pampered enough yet?"

Meadowlark grinned. "Not yet, but it's getting there. They're promising to polish my hooves next. Why aren't you within with all the rest?"

"I needed a little peace and quiet."

"Aren't you getting fitted for a fancy gown too?"

"Valeria gave me something lovely to wear. Will you come with us to visit King Arvid's home?"

"Phineas Brock needs me with him, but I shall see you when you return. They plan to start building his Museum of Marvels this autumn. We will be transferring his treasures to the Queen's dungeons all summer."

Meadowlark's ears pricked and swiveled to the side.

Viola followed his glance and saw De Vere strolling on the far end of the garden. She stroked Meadowlark's nose. "I'll see you tomorrow."

"See you then, Princess." Then Meadowlark closed his eyes. "That feels good. Brush a little lower though. There, that's the spot."

Viola strolled on an intercept course and met up with De Vere at a fountain. He faltered and then smiled.

"It's a lovely evening, isn't it?" she said.

"It is a rare fine one," he said.

"Why aren't you down in town getting fitted with the rest?"

"I have something to wear."

Viola captured a firefly in her hands and then released it again into the night air, admiring its determined little flight. "You can really see the stars tonight."

"Indeed." De Vere looked up and then around at the carpet of glistening lights in the night.

"I hear they have an excellent observatory in Nuneau that is open only on nights like this." Viola grinned at De Vere. "Do you want to go and look at the stars up close?"

"Actually, I would."

They set off down the garden path toward the city gates at the far end, where Nuneau bustled.

The Great Public Hall stood happily crammed almost to the rafters with wedding guests as first Master Sorcerer Macy married Gualtero to radiant Anna, and then crowned Gualtero King of Nuneau beside his wife. King Gualtero then summoned Lombard forward and made him a Duke of the Northern provinces, a Prince of the realm and a Knight in service to the Queen. His men cheered as he turned and held his new noble sword aloft.

When Princess Carissa appeared that afternoon, her lustrous hair flowed down her back to break again the hearts of her former lovers. As she stood beside Lombard, Macy performed the marriage ceremony.

Viola witnessed all of this beside Olwen, 'Sir' Sullivan Trooper, 'Sir' Phineas Brock, Squire Acton, and King Arvid. She had attracted as many stares as Princess Carissa's dashing blond rogue of a suitor, but she kept watching for De Vere. If he was there, he stood somewhere out of sight.

At last De Vere appeared, clad in his gleaming ceremonial black armor, he rode into the hall on his proud destrier. He dismounted with grace and vigor and kneeled before King Gualtero and Queen Anna. Without further ado, they knighted him. He rose with a shining face to accept various gifts: from Macy and Alison a powerful sword and a shield made upon Shadow Mountain; a spear and lance from Valeria the Grand and Saire the Ancient; a tabard from Queen Anna Marpessa emblazoned with her coat of arms; an elaborately decorated scabbard from Carissa; sturdy boots from King Arvid; an Elven bow and a quiver full of arrows handcrafted by Sullivan; an embroidered sash from Princess Olwen; and a lucky medallion from Sir Phineas Brock.

As the last of these gifts were bestowed upon him, Anna Marpessa said, "Queen Thetis Megara shall bear you south on her very own vessel to the Land of Many Kingdoms. Represent us with honor and goodness, Sir De Vere."

"I will to my dying day," De Vere said, inclining his head.

"What will you give him, Viola?" Olwen whispered as she resumed her place beside her.

"My eternal friendship," Viola murmured, as De Vere looked her way and inclined his head subtly. Discreetly, he touched a small silver pendant with a star made of sapphires at its center. She touched her own pendant, the companion of his. "It will preserve him when all else fails," she said to Olwen.

Bowing again, De Vere turned and led his destrier out. He did not linger, but headed down the Queen's dock to where the Sea Queen's special vessel awaited him. Its sails unfurled the moment he and his horse boarded it. De Vere had told himself he would not look back, but he did and there standing on the dock was Viola, smiling brightly in her gown and robes of lavender and dove gray.

"Remember your promise," he called.

Viola folded her arms over her breast. "I said I would visit you every winter no matter where you stay and I will - so make sure you've got a warm place to stay."

"How about an igloo?"

"That I'd like to see – you in an igloo."

"Forget I mentioned it."

Viola regarded the ship. "Bear him safe to his new life."

The ship loosed its moorings and glided out to sea. They waved at each other until the enchanted ship disappeared into the southern horizon.

"'New friend, Viola?" Saire said. His hands burrowed up his sleeves for warmth against the sea air's chill.

Viola turned and joined him. "A new and very worthy friend. I hope he doesn't get hurt down there."

"He is strong and brave and has a very noble spirit. I think he will do fine."

Viola strolled with old Saire up the dock back into the castle. "After all this excitement, a quiet normal little life seems, well, a little boring."

"Oh, I don't think you'll have to worry about boredom for years to come."

THE END...for now.

www.ingramcontent.com/pod-product-compliance
Lightning Source LLC
Chambersburg PA
CBHW031113260626
47172CB00001B/346